Novels by the author

The Morgan's Knot Serial Fantasy

Morgan's Knot
Island of the Children
Ice Island
Islands of Concrete and Steel
Islands of the Mind
Islands in the Sky
Islands of Dark Miracles

(for mature audiences)
Dealer
Nellis Gray
SunnyBreeze
Mac Murphy

Visit: www.rickstiller.com for more of his books, photographs, and music and www.morgansknot.com for the latest on the Morgan's Knot series.

Islands of Wisdom

Morgan's Knot – A Serial Fantasy

Episode VIII

By

Eric Thomas Stiller, Jr.

Thanks to Christopher Weeks for the Moon & the Stars

House of the Four Seasons Publishing

ISBN - 978-1-7326505-3-4

Visit www.morgansknot.com

For the child in each of us

Islands of Wisdom

Morgan's Knot – A Serial Fantasy
Episode VIII

Former President Bartlett accepted his new role without hesitation, although convincing the Secret Service of the need for a change in their security procedures involved far more thumb-twisting than persuading the Israelis and the Palestinians to sit down at the same table or convincing both Houses of Congress and the members of two opposing political parties to agree to pass any measure that might benefit all mankind.

With all the other commitments and requirements of an ex-president, he could only dedicate three days a week to his new position but the rewards far outweighed the imposition and he cherished the time he spent in this endeavor. Spinning his chair, he turned to bask in rippling rays of golden sunlight cascading down through the blue waters of the northern Atlantic. An endless school of silver tuna, shimmering daggers, glinted close to the glass and, in the distance beyond the third dome, he could see divers moving massive curved beams into place for the newest bubble being constructed for this city beneath the sea.

Although most of the world would never know of his new title, he was as proud of it as he had been when he took the oath of office as President of the United States, Chancellor of the International School for *Seers* and Keepers. Given his druthers, the title might have included wizardry or magic, for he still viewed the Powers of the Crystals and the things these people could do as magical, but he was pleased and honored that he had been asked to help organize the institution.

His years in the Economics Department at Harvard provided a model for the structure of the school but offered nothing to define the scope of concepts and information that were required to reach the level of Master *Seer* or a first-class Keeper of the Powers. Those who achieved that lofty status had invested their lives in the quest and, now, they were trying to break it down into actual courses that followed a definitive path, compressing decades of experience into a five-year program.

After the battle over the North Pole, *seers* and Keepers from all corners of the globe descended on Morgan's Knot, taking up every spare bed on the island, congregating around the observatory, arguing over the obvious and ominous technical advances of the Dark Forces and the lack of a unified effort by the Forces of the Light to merge their collective knowledge to counter the next confrontation that was sure to come.

There were too many ideas and opinions to reach a consensus or to develop a plan of action. After two contentious weeks without progress, Adrian and Alius brought the former president to mediate, under the guise of providing a short tour of Morgan's Knot and the wonders of the Powers. Bartlett was still unsure about how they managed to transform time, so no one at the house on the Cape knew that he was missing, something to do with that little blond girl, Kelly, who repeatedly asked to sit on his lap and kept fiddling with an old pocket watch.

While everyone else crowded into Ponte's parlor, kitchen, and hallways, spilling out onto the lawn and the path beyond, five *seers* and five Keepers sat at the dining room table for three days, before an accord was reached. Bartlett grasped the concepts in short order and pushed the negotiations forward with absolute focus on the question, "What is the best course of action to give us the greatest opportunity to impede or defeat the Dark Forces and develop the wonders of the Powers to benefit all mankind?"

He never wavered, listening patiently, as endless opinions were proposed, discussed, and noted. In the end, they decided on a foundation of coordination and education. Sky, Master Chi, Mary, and Simian accepted the task of building a curriculum to immerse young apprentices and expand the knowledge and powers of every *seer*, while Dadeus, Sir Isaacs, and Master Jung assumed a similar challenge to develop laboratories to facilitate the education of aspiring Keepers. Ponte and Nanchez chose to act as coordinators in gathering the technologies and techniques from every Keeper on the planet.

The ancestry of every *seer* would be traced back through centuries to see whether there might be others who, like Adrian, never discovered the source or purpose for their special talents. Jofre, George, and John volunteered to oversee the construction of a cluster of new domes that would become the center of knowledge. In addition, everyone agreed to expand Adrian's campaign to educate those who lived in the real world, especially the children, for, in the end, the responsibility for the future would become their burden to bear.

Systems were being constructed to connect every Keeper with instantaneous communications and the sum knowledge would be brought together in an atmosphere modeled after the ancient library of Alexandria, where the world's recorded wisdom, from Greece, Rome, Persia, Egypt, and empires across the globe, was collected, translated into all the major languages, and made available to the finest minds of their time.

It was a bold concept that demanded a unified effort and absolute commitment from everyone involved but it was the only path that offered a chance to defend the Powers and life, as we know it, against incessant assaults by the Dark Forces.

The former president faced down countless enemies and sent young men and women into battle to preserve freedom and democracy but, as Sir Jonathon informed him almost five years before, this adversary was the real force behind the puppets, who carried out those barbaric campaigns.

The old spy's husky Scottish accent still lingered in Bartlett's memory of that late-night conversation in the Oval Office, "These are the people who live in the darkness, who'll not be satisfied to control one country or even a major empire. These demons want to control the entire world and rebuild it on a model shaped by the Devil himself. We have no defense against their powers or their weapons and there is only one group on the planet that has any chance of stopping them."

"And who might they be?" inquired the president, who might have been even more skeptical had the authority not been Sir Jonathon.

"The Forces of the Light." He paused, "I don't know enough yet, because they exist in a world that we don't see. I know that's confusing but it's my understanding that they've always moved within society, without anyone really noticing that they were any different than the rest of us. Just as the Dark Forces live in a shadow world, I'm convinced that there are places on the Earth, where societies of these people live and work to defend everything that you and I believe in. I just have no idea of where to look. There certainly isn't any evidence in the archives of the intelligence community."

He sipped his Scotch, "There have been myths and legends for thousands of years about these two forces facing off against one another in gargantuan battles that were recorded as fable, because the realities were far beyond our capacity to accept them as truth. From what I've deduced, there are places in history where man made giant leaps in technology, architecture, social organization, and belief systems, transforming seemingly insignificant clans into empires. I would offer Egypt, the tribes of Central and South America, China, Greece, Rome, and, Atlantis, if you care to indulge in myth as history, as a few examples. On the other side are those dark periods, where humanity seemed bent on consuming itself…Germany, Cambodia, Kosovo, Africa, more than a few episodes in Central and South America…for that matter, our ancestors who administered the Dark Ages and the white settlers who pillaged the New World."

"So, you're saying that those periods that reached either extreme were somehow the result of the struggle between these two phantom forces?"

"That's exactly what I'm saying!" thundered his aging roommate. "It's there for the finding in the history books and it continues to this day."

The president sat back in his chair and took a sip of his drink, "You know that I've always been an ardent student of history but…what you're saying is outside the boundaries and constraints that our version of academia has created for itself. I'm not sure that I want to believe you but it solves so many mysteries…"

"The point is that we need to learn much more about these conflicting forces and find a way to do what we can to support the Forces of Light."

"I agree," said President Bartlett quietly, musing on the insight. "The future of mankind might well depend on it. If you're willing, I'd like you to undertake this investigation…personally."

The old spy's eyes crinkled into a sly grin, a shrewd smile that brought them to the brink of being expelled from the university more than once, back in the day, and sipped his whiskey before he replied, "I've been thinking about retirement anyway. Give me what I need and you've bought yourself a new secret government agency. The opposition would have a field day with this one!"

The two men shook hands. Sir Jonathon stood almost a head taller than the president but shared equal admiration and respect.

~

Zepallo was suspended inside a gray bubble in the incubator beneath an artfully constructed artificial coral reef in the Caribbean Sea. Special circuits equalized his internal energies in a process that would take weeks, if not months to complete.

The wave of power that rolled off the spire above the ice castle at the north pole caught the Dark Lord, in that instant before he vaulted into the safety of the vectors. His habit of exposing himself to the enormous intensity of the Black Crystals was legendary. Unfortunately, the pulse born of the energies of all the Black Gems overloaded the fragile tangle of nerves within his body. The Doctor could not be sure whether there would be permanent damage, should he be lucky enough, strong enough to survive.

Beta and Gamma were both in critical condition, although with the advances the medical team was making, it was entirely possible they would recover. The clones were being cared for in the infirmary and he would check on them shortly.

Outside the sphere, in the purified ocean water of the incubator and alongside the gray bubble containing his Master's body floated smaller, iridescent green balloons nurturing the surviving embryos in various stages of development, from the damaged center in the Savu Sea, south of Indonesia. The new lab was not fully functional but he was pushing the technicians to finish preparations as quickly as possible, so they could begin production with the DNA samples that had been replicated and delivered to thirteen of their installations around the world for safekeeping. Of the seventy-five infants, he had only been able to save thirty-three but they were healthy and thriving in their new home.

Memories of that day still made him queasy. His escape depended on quick thinking and good fortune. He was not a man of action, not one to lead the troops, rather he prided himself on using his mind to overcome impossible tasks and untangle the riddles and mysteries of life.

Moments after a wave of positive energy crippled their defenses, pods of whales crashed through the facility, smashing into the domes, one after another, until cracks appeared and the ocean rushed in. Their effort had been synchronized with the power surging through the circuits and the coordination of the attack indicated planning and execution worthy of the finest military minds in conjunction with rational beasts.

The Doctor gathered as many of the embryos as he could manage, moved several other physicians, nurses, and the babies into a mini-sub that was docked in an interface near the nursery and slipped into the vast vacuity of open water.

The facility in the Savu Sea was the only one damaged, although it was not destroyed, and demolition and repairs were already underway. Renovations were nearing completion in New York and the Caucuses, three new compounds were under construction, and this new incubation center was already in use.

The campaign had failed and, in the days since the battle, several distinct groups were maneuvering for political position. Each maintaining a diplomatic cloak of invisibility, should Zepallo survive and reclaim his throne. They had witnessed his retribution and none relished the idea of provoking his wrath.

One thing was assured, the Doctor's expertise was needed now more than ever. His knowledge provided security and, in this time of flux, he found that comforting. No matter who assumed power, the technology for the production of clones would be an integral part of the future.

~

Alius found Adrian meditating, floating a foot above the floor in the observatory. Sunlight skimmed through a slim slit in the curved doors housing the telescope, slicing through dust hanging in the still air, tracing a silhouette of the young *seer* in a slender golden arc on the worn planking of the floor. With his arms outstretched and his legs crossed beneath him, the shadow resembled a cross within a crescent, a symbol known through thousands of years as the emblem of the Forces of Light.

Adrian opened his eyes and slowly descended to the floor, "I sensed you coming…"

"I've been worried about you," whispered Alius quietly.

"I was thinking about Orana and trying to find her energy…" his voice trailed off, distracted, as if something new had crept into his mind.

"And what did you find?"

"I feel her in exactly the same way I felt her before she died. It's as if she's in her cave in the plane of the animals."

"Maybe we should go and find out," sighed Alius. "We haven't had a day off, since long before the battle and, I don't know about you, but I was scared that we wouldn't succeed…that, maybe we wouldn't survive…"

Adrian stood and wrapped his arms around the little blond *seer*, "You saved me and, as long as we're together…we'll protect each other."

"That's what worries me. Raffe and Sky were injured. We lost lots of other *seers* and warriors, including Orana, and she might be the greatest loss of all." She paused, looking up at the magnificent telescope, "When you and I fought on the mountain, the Powers seemed huge and the world that we were fighting over was confined to this island. Now it's become something else…there's no innocence about it, no sense of wonder. It's about survival and we're in the middle of an arms race between opposing sides - each using science, technology, and wealth to claw ahead of the other. Isn't this exactly the same thing that happened between the United States and the Soviet Union or the nations of Europe before the World Wars?"

"Yes, it is," smiled Adrian, "but it's also been repeated many times throughout history. With each new discovery, each new weapon, one side or the other gained leverage and battles were won or lost. I understand the Keepers point of view but I want to be very sure that the *seers* learn to use the Powers, not just the technology. They need to learn to think, to feel, to move boldly when the time is right, and when to wait."

"They also need to believe in The Balance with their spiritual cores. We must defend it…" Alius' eyes filled with tears, "Can we go to the animals? Please?"

"Alright," said Adrian quietly, taking her hand and moving into the vectors.

The streaming colors were vibrant and there was no hint of the grating of the dark energies, as they passed into the plane of the animals and landed in the golden meadow.

Unis and the herd of unicorns were not in the pasture and, other than a warm wind rustling the grasses and trembling through the leaves in the trees, there was only silence.

Alius whispered, "Not a creature was stirring…"

"This is strange," replied Adrian. "This world is always filled with the sounds of life."

"Maybe we should go to the cave," suggested Alius.

They levitated above the trees, up the side of the mountain, and landed on the path at the entrance to the cavern. Adrian smelled the smoke of a pinion fire wafting from the entrance, "That's the smoke from her fire!"

He took Alius' hand and led her into the darkness. After several turns they could see the glow of the flames and Adrian started walking faster but Alius grabbed his shoulder, "Wait! Look just in front of you!"

It took only a fraction of a second for his eyes to shift focus from the end of the tunnel to two inches in front of his nose. His breath moved an intricately woven silken web that stretched across the width and height of the passage. A surprisingly loud voice called from just above his head, "It would take years to devour something your size!"

Adrian looked up to find a rainbow-hued spider leaning to inspect him. Its feet glowed electric green, its hairy legs an ocean blue, the body was as yellow as the sun in the morning, and the eyes glowed with the intensity of two red beams in the darkness. "Why have you spun your web to close off Orana's cave?"

The glowing spider scampered across the web to face the boy, "To preserve her memory! Why?"

"Perhaps we should start over," said Adrian quietly.

Holding on to the web with its two hind feet, the spider leaned out to within an inch of Adrian's eyes, four of its legs clawed at the air between them. "Why would we want to do that?"

"Because…I'm Adrian, a student of Orana's. We were there when she died."

The spider leaned left and right, inspecting his eyes. "I believe that you are telling the truth, but why have you come here?"

"Because I…felt her…her energy, as if nothing had changed, as if she was still alive."

"What is it that you want?" asked the tiny predator, scurrying across the web to bundle up a moth who made an unfortunate turn in search of the flickering flames.

"I guess I just need to sit by her fire and learn to believe that she's really gone."

"That shouldn't be any problem."

"But how do we pass into her chamber without destroying your beautiful web?"

"Oh, come now…that should be easy for a *seer*!"

Alius giggled and took his hand, moving into the vectors and back again on the other side of the barrier. Adrian turned around to find the spider waving with its front legs and laughing raucously, "You are a *seer*!"

"I have a question. Where are all of the other animals?"

"Ah, you noticed, very good. They're having a meeting on the plain," said the spider, who stopped waving and stood very erect.

"What are they taking about?"

"They're discussing whether there is anything that the animals can do to stop man from destroying the Earth."

"What do you mean?"

"The melting ice at the North Pole flooded thousands of square miles of coastland, destroying the habitat of all sorts of creatures. It will be years before things get back to normal. Accommodations need to be found for them elsewhere and there's already a great migration. It's all so…unsettling."

"So, when Zepallo thawed the polar ice, it affected the plane of the animals?"

"Obviously!"

"Are you saying that the weather is the same in both planes?"

"Of course, it is! The physical world is exactly the same…the ocean currents, the weather patterns, and the global warming. That's what they're talking about, how to stop the pollution that will destroy us all."

"I never thought about that," said Alius.

"Me neither," replied Adrian, "but it does make perfect sense."

They turned into the chamber to find a large, fresh fire burning in the pit. There were no coals and the flaming logs had yet to form ash. Songbirds provided melodies that echoed through the cavern and a long slender shaft of gilded sunlight filtered down through the smoke to the spot where Orana always sat, her hair fanned out around her, her aura shimmering, a small knowing smile on her lips.

The two *seers* sat down on a blanket next to the fire and the silver tea service appeared before them on the flat rock. There were two cups, a tiny pot of honey, and the tea in the pitcher was hot. Alius poured the amber liquid into the cups, added a few drops of honey, and handed one to Adrian.

The flavor exploded inside his mouth, a rush of sweet and bitter traced the hot liquid as it coursed down his throat into his stomach. He had forgotten about Orana's tea. Slowly, the sensations and memories of her lessons crept through his body and overwhelmed his mind. He gazed with total focus at the emblem on the wall, was aware of the rippling sound of running water, the mesmerizing song of the birds, the sweet scent of the pinion smoke, and the determined thud of his heart beating in his chest. Allowing his senses to reach out, he knew that, other than the rainbow spider and Alius, of course, there was no other living creature nearby, except… the energy of Orana. The sensation was strong and, at first, he assumed that it was just being in her space but there was more to it than that. Some part of her was still here.

Adrian felt her eyes burning into his soul, her energy reaching out to embrace him, just as she had before his lessons started. He flashed through the white world and watched himself grow from an infant to a very old man, he flew through the jungle, out over the blue-green ocean, crashing down through its surface to the cold depths of the world where life began.

"What just happened," asked Alius, as he gasped for breath.

"I just went through a very fast version of the lessons that Orana provided for me. I can feel her. She's here…somewhere."

"I'm almost as sensitive as you are but I don't feel anything, other than a very strange numbness from this tea."

Adrian touched her hand gently, closed his eyes, and concentrated. His body lifted above the blanket and an electric blue aura radiated around him. The sunbeam moved across the fire and wrapped around the glowing egg surrounding the young *seer* like a snake constricting its prey, but gently…ever so gently, its light so intense that Alius shielded her eyes and turned away.

The cave filled with thousands of hummingbirds, the buzz of their wings droned behind the sharp echo of their chirping, as they swooped around the fire pit. A lustrous vision of Orana appeared in their fluttering wings, her white hair flowing around her like a flaming shawl, her eyes gentle but strong, her lips curled into a curious smile, "What is it that you seek?"

Adrian spoke but felt as if he was hearing his own words from far away, "I felt you…I guess I couldn't…or didn't want to believe that you were really dead."

The quivering apparition of the ancient woman smiled, "I am here."

"But…are you…?"

"I am living but certainly not in the sense of being alive. There are some advantages…"

"I don't understand," replied Adrian quietly.

"You saw my body die but did you see my spirit or my energy disappear? No, you were too busy seeing with your eyes instead of with your heart!"

"But…I saw you…"

"You saw what I intended for everyone to see. I am far more powerful, if they presume that I'm dead, that I can no longer affect the battle one way or another!"

The young *seer* was confused. "I'm afraid you'll have to explain this to me."

A third cup of tea appeared and the ghost *seer* sipped from the tiny teacup and returned it to the china saucer with a steady hand. "Alright, I'm surprised that you haven't figured this out for yourself. Just as there are many planes in the real world, there are many realities in the spiritual world. Our energy never ceases, it just moves from one reality to another, just as you can move from the real world to the vectors or the plane of the animals. There are several other planes that you need to learn about when you've time.

Anyway, back to the subject…it is to our advantage for the Dark Forces and our own comrades, for that matter, to assume that I died in that collision with the flying saucer. What a wonderful way to go! Spectacular, certainly spectacular!" She snickered but her eyes were deadly serious, "As far as anyone else is concerned, I'm dead, but to you, my young student, I will make myself, my knowledge, and my talents available, whenever you might need me. There is much to do and little time to do it in."

"What do you mean?"

"Well, now that you mention it, I do suppose that time is a bit different on this side of the looking-glass…let's leave it at this…you won the battle. You managed to stop that maniac and to kill Alpha, as well as many of their troops, but Zepallo and the two surviving clones will be back. You inflicted heavy damage to one facility but they're already back in production at another and they're building more around the world."

"The Keepers are organizing themselves and they've started a school for *seers* and Keepers on Morgan's Knot, where they want to bring together all of the knowledge and technology in one place. Sort of a research library."

"It's about time, although I do blame myself for isolating various groups from each other. I always thought that it provided an additional layer of security…perhaps I was wrong. We're only a half-century behind the enemy, the Keepers have a lot of catching up to do."

"We got President Bartlett to be Chancellor of the school, to help organize everything."

The ancient *seer* smiled, "There are many powerful people in the real world, who would be more than willing to offer any assistance they might, if they're asked in the right way."

"We've got an attorney in Washington who's helping us fight against Zepallo's holdings in the financial markets."

"That one is the devil. If he can't figure out a way to buy it with somebody else's money, he'll steal it. Either way, he won't be satisfied until the world is transformed into a very dark place. I grew up a child of the Dark Ages and spent the better part of a thousand years fighting to see that those mistakes are never repeated. Now it's your time to lead the battle."

Adrian withdrew, as the words resonated through his body and touched his soul, "I'm sure I'm not ready to take your place."

"You won't be taking my place. You'll be making your own. That's what your lessons were about, that's what your life has been about…learning to believe in yourself. As you will learn, there are many fine and talented *seers* in the world. You'll need their help but you will lead, you'll see the vision and the path and find the strength to follow it. I knew that from the first moment you entered this cave."

"But how…?"

"You've learned to listen and you're just beginning to learn to see. Seeing along the vectors is only a small part of the talent but that's why we're called *seers*. In time, you'll learn to see beyond the moment, into the future, as well as the past, through the planes and the various levels of reality. That vision is a heavy burden that you must carry with you like a sack of coal across your back but you already know that once you begin the journey, you can never turn back."

"How do I find you?"

"You already know the answer," smiled Orana. "You knew to come here, you felt it. Open your senses and I'll be there, always."

She closed her eyes and slowly disappeared, a wisp of smoke in a faint breeze, and Adrian settled back onto the blanket. Alius was in a deep peaceful sleep, lying on her side with her hands beneath her head. The young *seer* leaned over and kissed her forehead.

"What just happened?"

"I don't know. We were drinking tea and then you curled up for a little nap," said Adrian quietly. "I think we should be on our way."

He held her arm, as she struggled to her feet, brushed back her white hair, and rubbed her eyes. "I wonder what was in that tea? All I remember was a bright light and then you waking me."

"You didn't miss much," laughed Adrian.

"What did you do while I was asleep?"

"I meditated and learned that the Dark Forces were only bruised by our efforts. They're in full production again. Alpha is dead but the others survived."

Alius pressed her palms to her temples, "My head hurts. I don't think that I'm quite myself at the moment but I do think that we need to inform our friends."

~

The two *seers* found Unis and the other unicorns standing on the ledge overlooking the valley that meandered through the mountains to the horizon. A great din roared from an enormous congregation of animals covering the grassy plain, filling the rivers, hovering in the trees, and crowded on the rocks for as far as the eye could see.

The two *seers* stood next to Unis and bowed to the herd. Adrian turned and asked, "What are you discussing?"

The beautiful unicorn leaned close and whispered, "Many of our friends are worried that the destruction that man is causing to the environment is beginning to affect our way of life."

Alius said, "I don't blame them. We honestly did not know that the physical things that happen in our world also happen here."

"There's an old saying that a butterfly sneezing in South America causes hurricanes to be born in Africa. I'm afraid that we are all dependent on the same water, the same air, and the earth beneath our feet…it's all the same world."

"We've tried to make them understand and I think that some of the children see what we're trying to teach them. They rose up and stopped the fighting for a little while and they'll become the moving force in the next generation. It's the adults in power, they don't see or care about the damage that's being done by their campaign to consume the last bits of useful materials from the four corners of the Earth for maximum profit."

A warthog shouted, "If they destroy the world, we all die!"

"If it's us or them, I vote for us!" hollered a young screech owl standing on a low sweeping limb of an ancient oak.

Alius whispered, "What do they mean?"

Unis bowed her head, her gleaming horn pointing out at the herd, so her mouth was turned back towards the *seers*, "They're talking about invading your world and killing everyone they can find."

Alius gasped, "They can't be…?"

"Yes, they can. There are political forces within our community, just as there are in yours. If the wrong crowd gets enough support, anything is possible."

Adrian stepped to the edge of the precipice and raised his arms above his head. A thundering roar reverberated across the valley as the animals recognized the young *seers* they followed into battle more than once.

"You know me, as I know you! We've fought side by side against the Dark Forces and we've been victorious!" He lowered his voice, "I understand your fears and your frustrations with the changes that are occurring in the environment. There are many humans who are working to change the way the Earth is being treated and they are just as worried as you!"

The animals remained politely quiet, although there were a few comments and catcalls. "For the first time in history, all of the Keepers and all of the *seers* of the Forces of Light are gathering together to share their knowledge and coordinate their efforts to defeat the Dark Forces. We're constructing a facility that will house all of the information and techniques that have been gathered over the centuries. Students will come to the school from every point on the planet and they'll leave with a complete understanding of The Balance, joining together to fight for all that is true and right, and dedicated to making the world a nurturing home for everyone."

There were murmurs flowing through the crowd. Adrian raised his hands, "I know your power and I respect your position but I must ask you…no, I must beg you to give us a chance to begin this process. The Dark Forces would welcome an invasion and the disruption to our way of life. It would provide them with the perfect opportunity to take over and the end result would be darker than any of us might fear. There is another way, we must stand together!"

The young *seer* sensed a change in the energy coursing through the valley, it moved out across the hundreds of thousands of faces peering up at the ledge. A raucous chanting rolled through the animals, "Soon, soon, soon."

Gerald, a handsome lion who helped defend Morgan's Knot, stepped onto a rock directly beneath the ledge. "First, we all have great respect for you and we hope that you know that we will support you at any time in the defense of The Balance, but you also have to understand that all of us are concerned about the world around us. It's changing dramatically and not for the better."

"I understand exactly," said Adrian, "and I will do everything that I can to change the way things are being done in my world. We've found that the Dark Forces are involved with many of the industries that are spewing filth into the environment and we're moving to foil them wherever we can make an opportunity. You have to understand that this will take some time but I promise you that I will find a way to make people see the danger."

"That is all that we could ask of you," replied the stately lion. "It is your brethren that cause us concern. We'll give you until a year from this day. Come back to us on that day and we'll discuss the progress that has or has not been made. Is that fair?"

Adrian smiled, as he bowed to the huge menagerie, "I accept your most gracious offer. Thank you."

Gerald roared and the crowd began to disperse through a dense cloud of dust that rose up, painting the sky a crimson red that yielded, here and there, to slivers of gilded light spilling over the western mountains.

Chapter Two

Chancellor Bartlett fidgeted with the golden crystal, suspended from a chain hanging around his neck. Ester had presented it to him, after Professor Ponte and that giant, Nanchez, burst into his office one morning during his last visit, all smiles and pleased with themselves. "We've come up with a direct link between your office and your home on Cape Cod. You'll be able to pass back and forth whenever you wish," said Ponte.

"It's direct, so you won't have to worry about the Dark Forces," added Nanchez, smiling down at the former President like a proud man-child awaiting praise for his accomplishment form the headmaster.

Adrian and Alius appeared two days previously to escort him to the island, along with two bodyguards who had passed the scrutiny of not only the Secret Service but Sir Jonathon's computers. They were above reproach and more than willing, although explaining their unique duties proved rather awkward. At first, neither believed Bartlett or the only other person in the government who knew the true nature of the former President's 'travels,' the new Chief Executive, President Shannon.

After a lengthy discussion in the Oval Office, Bill and Bob were sworn to secrecy and would make themselves available, twenty-four hours a day, whenever Bartlett needed to attend to his duties on the island. Other agents covered his normal security requirements but the twins, as he called them, were always in attendance during his time on Morgan's Knot.

Sara drove them to the little shop in the village in the trolley where they were scanned for their diving suits. President Bartlett was tickled that he would be allowed to attend the classes and to join in the construction, although he allowed that he had never been particularly proficient with tools. The guards were hesitant to agree to allow their charge to attempt something so dangerous, so Sara arranged for them to take their diving instruction first and then to be present when the new Chancellor began his own.

Bill and Bob were due back from their third day of instruction momentarily. They were more than enthusiastic about the technologies that allowed them to be as free as fish in the water. After the first lesson, their doubts about the safety of The President faded and they appeared anxious to include him.

Adrian and Alius materialized on the carpet before his desk, "We're sorry to interrupt but we have some new information and we'd like to share it with you before we talk with the Keepers and the *seers*. We know that you'll be leaving soon, so we thought it best to begin with you."

"Well, my wardens haven't arrived back from their diving lessons just yet, so I'm pleased to see you. What have you to tell me?"

Alius started hesitantly, "We can't tell you how we found out these things…it's a matter of…honor."

Adrian was more forthright, ignoring the fact that he had not been completely honest with Alius, "We learned that the clones are back in production, that the whales only damaged the incubator, and that Zepallo and two of the clones survived the battle at the North Pole. In addition, the Dark Forces are constructing new facilities and renovating their old ones." He hesitated for a moment, "We might have won the battle but the war goes on."

Bartlett sat back in his chair, "Then we'll have to redouble our efforts to get this school and laboratory functioning as soon as possible. I know the Keepers and your fellow *seers* are working as fast as they can to create a curriculum for the classes, the network that will tie everyone together, and that they've started coordinating the insights and techniques of the first group of Keepers from all corners of the globe. Is there anything that we should be doing in the real world to assist in these efforts?"

Alius spoke very quietly, "I think President Shannon should be informed that the threat is still out there, perhaps not imminently but it will certainly arise again in some not-too-distant tomorrow."

"I'll take care of that," said the President. "I'm doing everything I can to help create a stable foundation for this new organization but I have to admit that I feel rather inadequate…as if there's something more that I should be doing."

"Mr. President…or Chancellor," smiled Adrian. "Just having you here to mediate, to guide, and to teach our leaders how to lead is more help than you will ever know. For thousands of years these people have lived and worked in secrecy, fighting when they had to and hiding when the battle died down. They've never been connected, never had the opportunity to join together as an organized force, and certainly never had a chance to merge their talents and their knowledge for the common good."

"You've learned a lot in a very short time," added Alius, "and the more you understand of the Powers, the more you'll be able to contribute."

"There is one more thing," added Adrian. "The animals are affected by the pollution that mankind is creating. They're not happy with us."

"That's something that I worked to cure while I was in office. I'm ashamed to say that I don't feel that I did enough."

"Then that's what you can do in the real world to help," smiled Alius.

"Alright, I've been informed. Now go and tell the people who can do some good, the Keepers and your fellow *seers*. I have some duties to attend to back in reality and I'll be seeing the president. We'll discuss the concerns of the animal world. As far as I know, we'll be returning on Tuesday."

Adrian and Alius started to leave, when the President said, "Are you sure that this vector tunnel that they've set up will really get us back and forth? I know that Bill and Bob have been briefed but…they're not *seers*."

Alius smiled, walked behind Bartlett's chair, reached around to take the golden crystal in her hand, and pressed the clasp with her index finger. The air before the desk swirled into a disk of spinning liquid silver and an oval opened, revealing the study in his home on Cape Cod.

"All you have to do is step through the gate and you'll be there," said Alius. "It's faster than traveling through the vectors and the plane of the animals!"

The former President smiled bashfully, "I should just believe in your powers but there's so much that I've yet to learn."

Adrian stepped in front of the desk and looked down at the former leader of the entire free world, "I've only known about all of this for a couple of years and I wouldn't have believed any of it before that. You've grasped large pieces but, as The Professor always says, 'There's always more to learn.'"

"I'll agree with that!" laughed Bartlett.

As he turned to leave, Adrian said, "I do have one question. We found some interesting photographs of Ambassador Robbins in my grandfather's computers. It seems that he was not as trustworthy as we might have hoped. What happened to him?"

"He was relieved of his duties and reassigned to a small cell in a rather cold prison in the far northern reaches of artic Canada. I don't think that we'll be seeing him anytime soon."

~

A groggy Colburn Tierney rolled over to the jangling phone and stared at the clock, it was three o'clock in the morning. He picked up the receiver and held it to his ear, mumbling, "Hello?"

"Coke, it's Adrian."

The attorney sat bolt upright, instantly awake, "It's good to hear from you. We haven't had a chance to talk since the hurricane."

"A lot's happened since then," replied the *seer.*

"Likewise."

"I think we should meet. Are you free tomorrow?"

"I only have one client, these days, and he keeps me very busy. I could fit you in at, say, two o'clock?"

"That would be fine. At your office?"

"Yes."

"See you then."

Coke hung up the receiver and rolled back on his pillows. His wife, Martina, opened her eyes and stared at his silhouette. "Why is it that your only client can only call in the middle of the night?"

Her husband laughed, "I think it might have something to do with his age. Didn't you stay up all night at every opportunity when you were his age?"

"Oh, yeah. We'd have sleepovers and we'd giggle and laugh and talk about boys. I'm sure my parents never got any sleep on those nights. What did he want?"

"To talk. Tomorrow."

"What about?"

"Well, if my suspicions are correct, the flooding that occurred all over the northern hemisphere was probably precipitated by the Dark Forces. The fact that it stopped, as suddenly as it started, makes me think that our young client had more than a little something to do with it."

Martina rolled on her back and stared at the ceiling. "I have to admit that I doubted you, when you first told me about Adrian and the Powers, about Morgan's Knot…I know that you haven't told me everything but I think I'm ready to see this place…to meet these people. You were right when you said that this was bigger than your job at the firm. I don't know whether it's the sheer power that these people are dealing with or that the rest of us aren't aware of what's really going on."

She rolled over and nestled against her husband's shoulder, "I'm proud that you made the right choice. You can make a difference."

~

Adrian materialized in Coke's office at precisely two o'clock. He was wearing his blue robes and the attorney was surprised that Alius was not with him. He rose to greet his young client with a hug, "I'm glad to see you. Come sit down."

They sat in two large chairs, positioned cattycorner in the windows, so each had a view across the city to the Potomac. "Tell me," said Coke. "The flooding? Was it the Dark Forces?"

"Yes," replied Adrian. "It took a legion of warriors to invade their ice castle at the North Pole and stop the process. We lost some very special people."

"I'm sorry."

"It's always been this way and it always will, until mankind accepts the responsibility for their own existence."

"You are very wise for your age."

"I've had good teachers. In fact, I'm hoping to have more opportunities to learn from the masters. We've formed a school for *seers* and Keepers from all over the world to share our knowledge with each other and to bring together technologies that have never been revealed before, sort of like a library, where great minds can come together to explore their ideas and look at problems in a new way."

"Sounds like the Library of Alexandria to me."

"President Bartlett made the same association. He's the Chancellor of the school."

The attorney gasped, "But how…?"

"Well, after the battle at the North Pole, Keepers from all over the world came to Morgan's Knot, demanding that the Forces of the Light join together to improve our technologies to keep up with the Dark Forces. Everyone had an opinion and they couldn't agree on anything…too many great minds in one place. The President had asked for an opportunity to visit Morgan's Knot, so Alius and I went to pick him up and showed him around the island."

"You didn't happen to mention that you needed his help as a mediator?"

Adrian smirked, "Well, no. We might have avoided mentioning it at the time."

"So, what happened?"

"Well, we went by the observatory and there were Keepers and *seers* wandering around the garden and the house, forming into groups to discuss and argue. It didn't take the President long to put things in order. He made five *seers* and five Keepers sit down at the dining room table and he wouldn't let any of us go until we reached an agreement on the course that we thought best. It took three days."

"You kidnapped the former President of the United States for three days and no one noticed?"

"Well, we had to ask our friend Kelly to alter time a little bit. She has a special watch, a turnabout, that allows you to move forward or backwards through time. I don't understand it, really, but it's come in handy and she's the only one who knows how to work it."

"That's incredible. You have Bartlett as the headmaster of your new school and no one knows about it?"

"Well, President Shannon does and so do Bill and Bob, the Secret Service agents. They come to the island with the President and they're all learning to dive."

"Oh, now you're making me jealous. I really want to learn how to dive like that. It looks like such freedom in the water."

"It is."

"My wife, Martina, heard our conversation last night and said that she'd like to meet the people who live on Morgan's Knot."

Adrian smiled, "That could be arranged. Actually, I'd like you to see the new school, when you have the time."

"How about this weekend?"

"We'll come and get you but it might be easier if we met here in your office. I know how to get here."

"I see your point. Just say when."

"How about Saturday morning? Now, what did you want to talk to me about?"

"I would guess that you haven't been keeping up with the financial pages?"

"No. That's why I have you!"

"Touché!" laughed Coke. "Okay, after we talked the last time, I had my staff go through the lists that your grandfather provided for us, and found that the Dark Forces have major holdings in World Oil, which is the largest oil company in the world." He paused, "You now have enough shares, with some help from sympathetic friends, that you technically control the company."

"What happened to Zepallo's representatives?"

"There are twenty-four seats on the board. They have eight. We have nine and enough support to direct the course that World Oil is going to take."

"And that's enough to control the company?"

"Yup."

"Wow. Did we spend all of our money?"

"No, actually you've more than doubled your money since we formed the foundation. With the income from the gems and gold that the Crystals produce, we have money to invest and I found something that I think that you might want to pursue."

"What's that?" asked the young *seer.*

"The simple story is that water is the key to all life on the planet, yet there are places in the world, South America in particular, where certain giant corporations are buying up the water rights to streams and rivers and trying to resell that water to the local population at a substantial profit. Everyone in the industrial world pays for consuming water, because it has to be piped from source to treatment to homes, but these guys are way beyond paying the overhead and making a reasonable return. They claim they're reinvesting in power plants and water purification, but information from the computer files and our investigation suggests they're investing those funds to buy more water rights in other places. They plan to monopolize water."

"That's incredible. How could that happen? Water comes from the clouds. How can a company own the rain? The water? It belongs to everyone."

"That's right," said the attorney, as he stared into Adrian's blue eyes.

"So, let's put them out of business."

"I was hoping that you'd say that!"

"It's the right thing to do."

"You know that I love working with you."

"Well, I…we appreciate all your help and I hope that you are being compensated for all that you're doing to help us."

"I'm proud to be a small part of something much larger, much more important than just being a lawyer who enjoyed his job but maybe for the wrong reasons," admitted the lawyer, as he stroked his gray moustache.

"I had an interesting conversation with one of my mentors recently. She said that there are lots of normal people who would be happy to contribute to the cause in any way they could, if they were asked in the right way."

"That's true. Your foundation employs hundreds of people…lawyers, accountants, investigators, computer specialists, engineers, all sorts of people. Each of them was hand-picked, told the real purpose for our enterprise, and each volunteered without hesitation. As word was quietly spread to those we hope we can trust, other groups offered expertise, capital, and alliances. Our clout in the financial world is becoming legendary."

Adrian sat back and stared out over the city. Every country in the world paid attention to the pulse of Washington. Decisions made here affected people all over the planet in one way or another. "We're starting to have enough capital to block some of the financial moves of the Dark Forces. Do we have enough to begin doing things that are…I don't know, more positive too?"

"Sure. Like what?"

"Well, I don't know…feeding the hungry, providing drugs to cure sick people who can't afford to pay for them, finding caring homes for children who've lost their parents, protecting the wilderness, the lakes, and the oceans for the animals, cleaning up the environment…things like that."

"Well, our oil company has suddenly had a change of heart and is only drilling in places where it will not endanger the habitat or the wildlife. Where they have drilled and run pipelines, renovation projects are underway to restore the land to its original state and to provide more places where the animals can cross the pipelines without restriction. In addition, we now have a subsidiary that is exploring alternative sources of energy like the sun, wind, geothermal heat vents, even algae. So, we're beginning to do some positive things."

"What about the rest of it?"

"I'll run through the lists and see whether there might be opportunities to do both at once."

"Great."

Chapter Three

Lyra grasped her father's hand, as they marched up the steps and into the cool shade of the enormous building. Huge columns thrust the roof into a deep blue sky above a wide veranda, ornately paved with intricate tiles that reflected the golden rays of the setting sun.

They turned to gaze out over the harbor to the lighthouse towering above the city, it was said that its beacon was visible to ships to the horizon. Certainly, Cleopatra's seat of power was the center of trade in the Mediterranean but it was also the depository for knowledge from every corner of the planet and those ships supplied information that fed an insatiable thirst.

Alexander the Great, of Macedonia, and his General, Ptolemy, established the port as the capital of Egypt when they conquered the country in 323 B.C. Government representatives intercepted every visitor to the city and confiscated any texts that they might be carrying, copied them, keeping the originals, and returning the copies to the owner. The first library was established as a place where scholars could gather to research ideas and discuss concepts with the great thinkers of the world.

The single library had grown to include many buildings, museums, exhibition halls, theaters, and classrooms that could accommodate three thousand students at a time. A scholar could read original manuscripts of the works of Plato or Socrates, study the mechanics of time, astronomy, mathematics, philosophy and religion, analyze working models of the Archimedean screw, the first pump capable of moving water uphill continuously, and those who had the gift could earn their way through the system to learn from the masters themselves.

Lyra's father said that it was a glorious moment in the history of the world, where the best minds from Greece, Persia, Rome, and Egypt gathered together to make giant leaps in understanding the world, which included not only the physical planet but the many different views of the spiritual cosmos as well. The library held seven hundred thousand scrolls and most of the texts had been translated into several languages. "In this moment, Alexandria and the library form the center of the universe of knowledge."

Raman knelt down beside her, "I must speak with some very important people and I trust that you will be patient until I'm finished."

"May I see the clock?"

"Ah, yes. It is just inside," replied her father, as he stood and led her through a giant gallery surrounding the main library. In the center, stood a small tower that displayed the time of day, a calendar, and the positions of the sun, moon, the five known planets, and the stars in the heavens.

Lyra ran to the edge of the shallow pool surrounding the mechanism, "How does it know?"

Her father looked down at her with a gentle smile, "How does it know what?"

"The time, the day, the month, and where the stars are…all by itself?"

"To be honest, it doesn't. Many great thinkers have studied the movements in the heavens, the passing of time, and noted how often these things repeated themselves. Then one great man devised this system to display the information. I know that's confusing but now that the barriers that prohibited women from studying at the university have been dismantled, there is no reason why you should not become a scholar yourself."

He had fallen madly in love with his daughter the first time that he held her in his arms, after her birth, and stared into those incredible blue eyes…her mother's eyes. She had inherited her father's olive complexion and thick black hair that fell past her shoulders but her beauty hinted at his wife's ancestry from the northern fringes of the Roman Empire.

"What makes it go?"

"Water."

"Really, just water?"

"Well, water that moves through the machine at a very steady pace. It never speeds up and it never slows down, so the movements are constant. I'm told that it has not needed a correction since it was first placed here."

Lyra looked confused.

"Say you filled an urn with water and poked a small hole in the bottom. What would happen?"

"The water would run out."

"Correct. Now, if we filled the bucket to the very top and paid careful attention to how long it took to empty, then the next time that we filled it, we could be fairly sure that it would take exactly the same amount of time to empty again."

"Yes, I understand."

"Well, this is the same idea. The water flows through it at a precise rate, moving gears that turn the dials to provide information that we can understand."

"Then the clock knows how fast time is passing or the stars are moving…?"

"I think you've got it!" smiled her proud father. "Come along, I see Thesius approaching and I must not keep him waiting."

The old philosopher walked slowly, his white robes brushing the ground around his sandaled feet, as he shuffled across the tiled floor. His head was completely bald and he stooped, as if he carried the weight of his knowledge on his back, but his black eyes sparkled like those of a small child who is about to share an amazing secret. "I am pleased that you could come, won't you follow me to a more intimate spot that I have reserved for our meeting?"

They passed through a large room, its walls lined with diamond shaped bins that held the scrolls of interest to the scholars who were studying time. Lyra noticed that the scrolls were organized by the color of the single ribbon binding them, perhaps indicating the subject of each collection. A balcony wrapped around the circumference of the chamber, providing addition storage and space for study beneath torches or near slits in the walls that allowed bands of light to trace across the floor.

An elderly man sat on a bench surrounded by several students sitting on mats at his feet. She couldn't understand the language that he was reading from a manuscript in his hands, but the students were focused on his every word. A little farther along the gallery, an entry on their right opened into a round theater, with seats climbing the far wall. A tall woman was speaking to several hundred people in Greek, her words carried to her audience, yet were muffled at the entrance behind her.

At the end of a long corridor, they entered a small study. The inner surfaces were covered in blue tiles that matched the color of the sky just before sunrise, smaller bins of scrolls bound in deep green ribbons were inlaid in the walls, and several large pillows were arranged around a stone table that rose from the floor with a small hole at the center that emitted a slender yellow flame. A flask of cool water, simple cups, and a platter of buns and goat cheese filled a golden tray next to a slender vase holding three large white flowers that Lyra had never seen before. She leaned over the table and inhaled their deep rich scent, allowing her father and Thesius to take their seats facing each other.

"I am pleased that you could come so quickly, there is much to discuss."

"You know that I'm at your service and in your debt."

"As you know," said the scholar, "we're at the pinnacle of knowledge in our time. Never before have all the great thinkers in the known world contributed to a single collection nor has there ever been a place where those same people could congregate, interact, and share their knowledge with their counterparts from other nations, other empires. This is an island of understanding, a place in time and history where the promise of mankind glimmers and gleams for a few short moments before flickering out in the darkness that always returns. These walls form the ramparts in defense of the only place on the planet where the workings of the mind are of more value than a man's heritage!"

"We are fortunate to live in these times."

"What does the explorer find when he reaches the very pinnacle of a mountain?"

"That there is no further possibility of ascent, instead, there is only descent."

The old man was quiet for a moment, as he looked into the eyes of his confidant financial mentor, "There are many levels of understanding...in our world. There are the great mysteries that those around us are trying to solve but, beyond that, there is another world, another level that we must shelter."

"I'm afraid that I do not understand what you are trying to say."

Again, the scholar hesitated, "There are secrets that must be protected against any eventuality. Certainly, they could be hidden or destroyed...but they are the secrets that form the balance between man as savage and man as civilized, intellectual human."

"Who else knows these...secrets," inquired Raman.

"There is a small group who have passed this knowledge from one generation to the next, from one place to another, but in this age, we are all too well known to chance transporting these documents to safekeeping."

"And you are asking me to...provide this service for you?"

"You are a trader, a man who travels to markets in lands across the seas. No one would find it unusual for you to be moving from one destination to another."

"That's true, but why would you allow someone outside your inner circle to know about these things?"

"Because, in the end, this knowledge will save the human race. Used in the right way, it may provide a defense against those who would see our world digress into chaos, as it was centuries ago. Countless times throughout history, they've cast a dark shadow across the hope and promise of the best that we might achieve and they will rise again. We're doing the same thing with the scrolls in the library, making multiple copies of every document and sending them in small batches to trusted thinkers all across the world. If there is a disaster, at least some of this knowledge will survive."

"If I am to be asked to provide the service that you require, then I will have to understand at least the basics of the information that I am carrying."

The old man smiled, "That will be arranged over the next few weeks. You should bring young Lyra, I'm sure that she would find the subject interesting."

Raman turned and looked at his daughter, who was staring at the three white flowers, although she heard every word that had been spoken and she wanted more than anything to be included in her father's instruction, the young beauty gave no indication that she had been paying attention to their conversation.

He turned back to the old scholar, "We are ready to learn."

~

On the third day, Lyra hugged her father and followed her guide, Sheira, through a long dark hallway to a garden hidden behind high walls. Tall trees shaded rows of flowering shrubs bordering a pool with a waterfall cascading from a small island in the center. The two girls stood at the edge of the pond, watching the reflections ripple and splash. A large yellow butterfly flitted through the flowers, landing on Lyra's shoulder. She reached a finger, touching its front legs, and the beautiful creature climbed onto her hand.

Sheira leaned close to share the wonder, "Do you believe the things that I've been telling you?"

Lyra blushed, "It's all so…I don't know, unbelievable and, yet, I know that it's all true. I feel it in my heart. Does that make any sense?"

"Yes, it does. Some of us have grown up with this knowledge, it's just always been a part of our reality, but it's harder for someone who's grown up in the real world." She drew Lyra's hand closer, to inspect the iridescent colors on the butterfly's wings. "I think this living wonder is a sign…a sign that you have a special power."

"I don't think there's anything special about me. I'm just beginning to believe that these things make sense."

"Let's learn a new trick," laughed the tall girl, who removed her sandals and stepped to the edge of the little pool. She stepped onto the water and walked casually across the surface to the tiny island, where she turned and looked at her young student, "Come on, you can do it too."

Lyra's mouth was hanging open, "But you just…you just walked on the water!"

"I know, it's easy. Just see where you want to go and don't pay any attention to the water. It's just like walking on the ground."

The young girl removed her sandals and stuck her toe in the water. She hesitantly put one foot out and lowered it into the water. She sank up to her knee.

Sheira laughed, "You're thinking about the water! Think about standing here, beside me. Look at me and concentrate. Now walk to me!"

Lyra backed out and took a step and then another, each leading closer to her young mentor, until her concentration finally lapsed and she reached to grasp Sheira's outstretched hand. The *seer* screamed "I knew you could do it!"

The young beauty looked down at her feet, which were standing quite firmly on the surface of the water. "Is it a trick?"

"No, that was real. You have a talent that few in the world possess and I hope that you'll allow us to help you learn to use it to defend our ancient principles."

"I would be honored."

~

A month later, three of Raman's stout trading ships prepared to sail with the morning tide. He and Lyra followed Thesius and Sheira into a small anteroom where two men in saffron robes waited. Thesius made the introductions, "I'd like you to meet Ganimum and Agus, who have the items that are to be transported."

Everyone sat down around a small table, onto which the two men placed four large books. They were not like the scrolls in the library, these had covers of gold and silver that glowed in the soft light creeping into the room through a long narrow crevice in the wall.

Thesius placed his hands on the books, "These are exact replicas of the original works that have been handed down from one generation to the next for millennia. We believe that they were first produced on Atlantis and we've found a process that duplicates their technology but, even for our expert Keepers, it's a tedious and time-consuming endeavor. Individual parts are constructed by separate teams and only a few people understand the final process that allows them to be so…unique."

Lyra reached out to touch the golden cover of the book nearest her, "Why are they of different colors?"

"We don't know," sighed the old scholar, "but there were two originals, unique from each other, yet equal in every other way. We suspect that it might have something to do with the opposite forces produced by the Black and Golden Crystals. Your captain has been supplied maps that will guide you to Gaul and then to a small port on the northern side of Hadrian's Wall, where your ships will be met by our representatives. Young Miss Lyra will know whether they are genuine."

Lyra touched the golden and black crystals hanging from a slender chain around her neck. Their contacts would be wearing similar adornments. She lifted the cover of the golden book and stared at the characters marching across the inner pages.

Sheira spoke quietly, "They do not offer information, you must ask and they will respond."

"Will we succeed on this journey?"

The figures rushed around to form the word 'yes.'

~

Lyra locked herself away in her father's cabin at the stern of the mighty ship, puzzling over the gold and silver books entrusted to their care. She asked questions, endless questions, and found that the figures on the pages would respond to inquiries about the Powers and about the state of the Earth. They seemed indifferent to personal queries but emitted different energies, the Golden Book was warm, the Silver Book cold and fierce.

The books displayed maps with glowing jewels indicating where the positive and negative Crystals were located on a peninsula on the northwestern coast of Gaul. Curious about how she might have inherited these powers, she learned that there were pairs of Crystals in many places in the world but she was keenly interested in a pair located beyond the Roman holdings to the northeast of Gaul. Her mother told her stories about her ancestry, the people who lived in the snow country and she vowed, someday, to visit that place and to find the bond to her heritage.

Over the next sixteen years, Lyra grew to be a powerful merchant woman, who never doubted that her destiny had been determined on that first voyage. She carried copies of the Books to allies across the known world, forming a web of contacts that would culminate in the birth of the Forces of the Light.

When the unique identity of her homeland finally disappeared, their history and traditions wiped away by invaders who imposed their own customs and beliefs on her people, she disappeared into the snow country and lived on to guide our forces through the centuries. "I inherited my place from her, just as you will from me."

Adrian sat up in his bed. The window was open and, like pale ghosts, the curtains swayed in the moonlight. He almost felt that he was watching Lyra's white robes disappearing into the night, just as she left Alexandria on a final voyage and never returned. Orana's story filled his mind, the detail, the faces and, for the first time, he grasped the lineage that forced him to follow this path but, in spite of his training and his talents, he felt very alone with the responsibilities that his mentor was leaving to him.

Chapter Four

Beta and Gamma occupied a ward opposite the incubator, their bodies immobilized for months in a coma while they healed, but now both were conscious, responding to stimuli, and ravenously hungry. The staff offered a thin broth and dry toast, which did not satisfy either of them. An hour later, they consumed eggs, bacon, fruit, raw cereals, and almost a gallon of juice. Two hours after that, they demanded another meal and their energy level seemed to be rising in direct proportion to their caloric intake. The Doctor was astonished at their progress and walked across the corridor to check on the Dark Lord, who was still suspended in a gray cocoon in the incubator.

The *messengers* in the control sphere indicated that the balance of energies in his body was nearing normal or at least normal for this specimen. The Doctor could see movement inside the sheer fabric that restricted Zepallo and he knew that it was time to transfer him to the hospital, where he could be examined. The factions, maneuvering so cautiously, would be despondent.

~

Three days later, the Dark Lord regained consciousness. He stared around the room at the white walls, the white ceiling, and the white sheets on his bed, all dimly lit by the dark *orbs* in the ceiling. "Oh, I do find these facilities depressing," he groaned, as he pushed himself up into his pillows.

The two attendants turned from the monitoring station across the room and hurried to their patient. The tall blond woman whispered into a *messenger* on her wrist, while the muscular man pulled a small light from his pocket and aimed it into Zepallo's left eye. The patient brushed the man aside, "I can see perfectly well. Where is The Doctor?"

The airlock hissed as The Doctor rushed into the room, his white smock billowing behind him, "How are you feeling?"

"I feel horrible but I guess that's to be expected after being stunned by a megadose of dark energy and then being trapped in that oversized water-balloon! What day is it? How long have you kept me sedated?"

"It's been more than four months since the battle. There was some doubt as to whether you would survive this latest injury."

"I'm sure there are many who might have cheered," sneered Zepallo. "Who's in charge?"

"Regis and Cadeau have been directing operations in your absence from the facility in North Korea."

"That does not surprise me. Each would pick a place where they knew they were safe from our enemies and from those within who would take my place. What damage did we suffer?"

"The incubator in Indonesia was partially destroyed by pods of whales. Our defenses were incapacitated by a wave of positive energy that swept across the globe from south to north. I would assume that it was the same surge that destroyed the project at the pole."

"What of the clones?" fumed the Dark Master.

"Alpha was lost but Beta and Gamma seem to be recovering. I saved thirty-three of the infants and they're in good health. I also rescued several hundred embryos that are thriving in the incubator here."

"Where is here?"

"We're in the new sphere in the Caribbean. Most of our systems are functioning at capacity and the labs are almost ready for production. The damaged domes are already being repaired and I am told that they will be completely renovated within a year."

"A year!?!"

"The damage was considerable, although it was not a total loss."

Zepallo started to sit up and sank back into his pillows.

The Doctor took his right wrist and stared at his watch. "You have just regained consciousness. I would suggest that you allow us to help you regain your strength. Things are under control for the moment. Use this time to heal."

The Dark Lord snorted and closed his eyes.

~

The old Master, Ptolemy, died in the command sub that was destroyed during the invasion of Morgan's Knot but he left a very talented and ambitious son, Marcus, who was meeting with Regis and Cadeau in the bowels of the cavern beneath the mountain in North Korea. Throughout the transition of power, the young heir showed great deference to Zepallo and supported the new leader with fawning enthusiasm. His superiors recognized his abilities and assumed that he possessed the latent talents to become a master but, for the moment, he was too young and, in spite of his heritage, lacked the political liaisons that might allow him to ascend to the throne he so coveted.

"I understand that our Dark Lord has survived?" inquired the young Master. His dark eyes burned beneath a furrowed brow, straight white hair touched his massive shoulders, and slender ruby lips curled into an evil smile that could easily have been confused with relief or frustration.

"That's true, we've just received word from The Doctor," replied Cadeau.

"He's regained consciousness," added Regis, "and it won't be long before he'll return to his rightful place."

"After the fiasco at the North Pole, I must assume that some of our colleagues might have wished for a different outcome," sighed Marcus.

"We've heard rumors to that effect."

"What will happen to those brave souls, now that things are returning to 'normal'?"

"I would not want to be in their shoes," whispered Regis.

"With all the progress that's been made, it almost seems that things are moving under their own momentum, in spite of the setbacks," commented Marcus.

"It does seem that way but we all know that none of this could have happened without a guiding hand," observed Cadeau.

"What we need is a strong but steady hand. One that will not allow distractions or a need for revenge to get in the way of our true destiny," said Marcus, waving his hand at a giant screen that displayed the lairs of the Dark Forces. "When these facilities are all complete, there will be no power on Earth capable of standing against us. It is only a matter of time and patience. We have no need to rule the world when we can simply direct the rulers."

"That's true," replied Regis cautiously.

"There's only one person who stands in the way of our ultimate, bloodless victory," said Marcus.

Regis and Cadeau glanced at each other, afraid to respond. Finally, Cadeau spoke, "The time for that may well have passed."

"Perhaps!" thundered the young *seer*, as he bowed formally and vanished.

~

Late Friday afternoon, Professor Ponte sat at a console in a laboratory under construction in the third dome. The long straggly hair growing reluctantly around the reaches of his shiny bald head had turned from gray to white over the past few years and it fell in curls around the collar of the long coat that he had taken to wearing with a bright yellow polka-dot bow tie. His attire was somewhat different than the robes that everyone wore while they were working in the domes. Perhaps, secretly, it was in keeping with his desire to support the image of the rumpled, eccentric scientist working in his little workshop in the wee hours of the dawn. Over the past few months everything had changed in the world of The Powers and so must he but he did not share that consideration with anyone.

Long hidden allies and comrades joined together for the first time in history. Certainly, each had known others but just their initial contact as a group expanded everyone's knowledge, opened doors of understanding and possibility, and most of all…yes, most of all, it signaled the beginning of a new age for the Forces of Light.

Adrian was certainly, as everyone secretly referred to him, 'the one' and Orana had shared that insight with each of her 'students' before her demise, for many of the *seers* and Keepers who were participating in the school and the laboratory also studied with her. They would show him the reverence and respect he deserved and there would be no political maneuvering, for there was no purpose in that enterprise. Everyone, to a man and a woman, understood that the threat posed by the Dark Forces, with their sudden and lethal advances, was far more important than any personal ambitions.

The old man sat back in his chair, rested his tiny glasses on top of his head, and gazed out through the transparent sphere that surrounded this room. Workers were fabricating the spaces for research and development, communications, and the library that would house all of the knowledge that was scattered about the planet, secreted inside the minds of the *seers* and Keepers of their world. Information passed down from one generation to the next, each adding their little bit of insight or unique curiosity, before handing it off to the next in a lineage snaking back through the centuries. A rich relentless history stitched itself together like pieces of a puzzle magically falling into place to form a portrait of a tree, its leafy branches wrapped around the globe, the vectors cradling the balance, beautiful flowers representing the Positive Crystals scattered across the Earth, and a thick gnarled old trunk rooted in the very soil that spawned their culture.

Perhaps not surprisingly, considering that he and Nanchez collaborated to conquer the disparities between the Powers of the Black and Golden Crystals and their intersecting vectors…no, not surprising at all that they understood more about the global web of vectors than any of their peers. Dadeus proved his understanding during the battle at the pole but the others never had a reason to work with the energy system as a whole before this challenge.

What pleased him most was that each of the other Keepers, whether through their own strange curiosities or secrets handed down from their elders, had some thing, some part that no one else had considered or explored. Sir Isaac and these blasted portals of his…they were not particularly complicated but certainly proved convenient in making oft repeated journeys, whether short or long, and avoiding the possibility of interception by the Dark Forces. Genius, pure genius! Madame Danali's incredible understanding of the interaction of The

Powers with the Earth itself and Master Jung's grasp of countless mysterious planes was equally amazing and there were so many others.

Understanding, then combining and implementing, all of these concepts would take time and time was a luxury in short supply. Each new aggression by Zepallo and his comrades was escalating, expanding, reaching out to probe every bastion for weakness or vulnerability. The Keepers of the Dark Forces had conquered the riddles of cloning, a capacity that could potentially provide an endless legion of identical and expendable fighters. The fact that they seemed to be cloning Zepallo himself added the additional peril that they would inherit his powers and his persona…everything that made him not only formidable but truly evil.

At the opposite end of the spectrum was President Bartlett. Ponte was relieved when Adrian and Alius brought the former President to mediate the gathering of Keepers and *seers* who descended upon the island and colonized his house. In fact, after the three days and nights of negotiations, the Professor had only respect and admiration for the man. He grasped the complexities and subtle nuances of The Powers and the dedication of those who served them, yet he would not be moved from his own convictions. Everyone at the table had been treated as an equal with a courteous but firm demeanor, their thoughts and ideas considered with dignified attention, and disagreements transformed themselves, in his hands, into solutions. There was no one better suited to guide this enterprise or to act as their liaison with the real world.

He found it amusing that Adrian and Alius had not bothered to mention this task to their guest before he arrived. They were so very sophisticated in so many ways and yet, at times, the child in each revealed itself, if ever so briefly.

A motion behind him broke his train of thought and he turned to find Adrian standing in the passageway. "Come in, my boy, come in," gestured the old man.

Adrian walked over and placed a hand gently on the Professor's shoulder. His jaw dropped open, as he gazed around at the progress of construction in the dome. In the center an enormous circular table was being constructed. "What's that?"

"What does it look like?"

"A round table," replied the young *seer.*

"Exactly! I'm afraid that I've taken a bit of license from ancient fables but, after our session in the dining room at the observatory, I decided that the council should present itself as a democratic organization, where every thought, every idea, and every opinion is valued. When it's finished, it will comfortable seat fifty...with addition of wings that will rise from the floor, one hundred.

"This is incredible!"

"It's only the beginning. We're already interlacing bits and pieces of different ideas and technology. The construction is moving along and we'll have six domes soon enough, in addition to the school."

"I need to make some time to help out. I haven't had a chance to dive in a while."

"You've had enough to deal with over the past months."

"There just doesn't seem to be enough time...or maybe enough time left."

The Professor looked up at the young *seer* and sighed, "I've been thinking the same thing, lad. We don't know what's happening on the other side but, from what you've told me, they're racing to complete a chain of facilities that will ring the planet. There's no way to know what they're planning next, let alone their capacity."

"I believe that Zepallo is back in charge, that Beta and Gamma survived, and that they're producing more clones," replied Adrian.

"The only good thing, about that...devil, is that he is a known quantity. Obviously, there are others behind him."

"There's something strange about having him as my opponent. At times, I can almost see inside his mind, hear his words, and understand what he's feeling. Like the battle over the ridge, I knew that he couldn't win. I knew it in my heart and I could see it in his eyes...his aura changed colors..." said Adrian quietly. "I understand that he believes in himself and his goal, so completely, that he could not allow anyone else in his command to move out of range, where he could not control every detail of every situation."

"A true dictator…a megalomaniac, perhaps even the devil himself."

Adrian sat down in the chair opposite the desk with a view, through the expanse of glass behind the Professor, of the last rays of the sun streaming through dark water. "That's the real threat…the clones, I mean. They could produce thousands of copies and each would be as evil and deadly as he is. All we can do is organize ourselves, share information, and teach each other everything we know to be right and true…and then offer the people of the world a chance to believe in themselves."

"I have to admit that I find myself torn between the wonders that are already beginning to evolve in the laboratories and a feeling of…responsibility to The Balance. Maybe it's just a hesitation, a wish to slow things down just a little bit so we might maintain control and focus."

"As I always say to myself…there is no other choice."

Ponte nodded slowly, amused that he had pondered the same thoughts only minutes before, "I hear that your attorney is coming for a visit?"

"Yes, I'm supposed to escort him and his wife tomorrow."

"He's going to prove a useful ally."

"I believe he's becoming one of us."

"Then we should make it convenient for him. Why don't you come back to the observatory with me? Sir Isaac is working with Alius and Sammy on the portals. I'm sure that they could program one to allow safe passage."

"That would be great," smiled Adrian. "Then we wouldn't have to bring them through the vectors."

"Exactly!" laughed the old man, his glasses jiggling on top of his bald head. "My biggest complaint about the portals is that I wasn't smart enough to invent them myself! I've set them up to move from the observatory all around the island, which saves time and energy."

Adrian laughed, "I miss your little red trolley!"

~

Colburn Tierney and his wife, Martina, sat in the two chairs looking out across the city, sipping coffee from sleek ocean-blue mugs, bearing the logo 'H_2O', that suddenly appeared in all the coffee services throughout the company. It was Saturday morning and there was no one else in the office, yet they both spoke quietly.

"Did you set a time?" asked Martina.

"No, he'll be here soon enough," laughed the attorney, taking her hand.

"I guess I'm just a little bit anxious about all of this. I know in my heart that all you've told me is real but…there's something other-worldly about it. Does that make any sense?"

"Yes, it does," he smiled and turned to a swishing sound, as Adrian and Alius materializing on the blue carpet in front of the lawyer's desk. Coke rose to hug the young *seers* and then introduced his spouse, "Adrian and Alius, I'd like you to meet my wife, Martina."

Alius curtsied and Adrian reached to shake her hand, "We're pleased to meet you and I know that you'll enjoy your visit to the island."

"I've been looking forward to this opportunity," she smiled up at her husband. "Coke has told me so much about you."

Alius reached into the pocket of her robes and withdrew two golden crystals on slender chains and said, "The Keepers have come up with a new trick to move you back and forth to Morgan's Knot. They designed it for President Bartlett and programmed these to act as a gate from here."

The adults took the chains and fastened them around their necks. "How does this work?" asked Coke.

"Well, these allow us to travel directly, rather than going through the vectors and the planes," replied Alius as she took his crystal and pushed on the clasp that held the stone. The air swirled and warped into a spinning film of liquid silver. An oval aperture spread within the shimmering metal to reveal the floor of the second dome.

"All you have to do is step through the gateway and you'll be there. When it's time to return, you'll end up right back here in your office," smiled Adrian.

"That's incredible!" laughed the attorney, hugging his wife.

"It's not quite as romantic as the plane of the animals," said Martina.

"No, it isn't," said Alius, "but this way we don't have to worry about interference from the Dark Forces."

"I see your point."

Adrian gestured with his hand, "Shall we go?"

Alius took Martina's hand and stepped through the gate, followed by Coke and Adrian. The portal closed behind them with a tiny pop. Martina spun around in place, taking in the sunlight filtering through the water above the enormous bubble. As in the first dome, the landside of the sphere was lined with offices and classrooms, while the sea was visible across the entire expanse of glass on the opposite curve. A long ramp led down to an interface and the mechanical workings of the structure, while airlocks joined each of the domes to the others.

"It's everything that you described and so much more..." whispered Martina.

Alius smiled, "This is the second dome. When they complete the latest one, we'll have four and, eventually, seven. This sphere houses the offices and meeting rooms for all of the Keepers, the *seers*, and the staff, which is headed by Chancellor Bartlett. The first dome was constructed to relieve overcrowding at the old school and as the first interface with the ocean. The third is nearing completion and it will house the laboratories, a large meeting space, communications, and a library to bring together all of the knowledge, the secrets, and our history that's been hidden in bits and pieces across the world since time began."

Martina's jaw dropped, "I have a lot to learn about all of this..."

Adrian laughed, "I didn't know anything about The Powers or *seers* or Keepers or even The Balance before I arrived on the island and that was a little more than two years ago."

"But you're the...The *seer*."

Adrian blushed, "I did not choose to be a *seer* but I am a *seer* because I inherited these gifts through my mother. By accepting that responsibility, I'm left with only one path to follow. I've learned a lot but there are many others who know far more than I do. Perhaps I've been lucky."

"You're too modest," smiled the attorney's wife. "I know that my husband has dedicated his career to helping you and I was wondering whether there might be anything that I could contribute?"

Alius asked, "Are you a profession woman?"

"I own a public relations company."

The two *seers* started laughing before sputtering, "We don't mean to offend you and we certainly don't think that your profession is humorous. We've been trying to figure out how to make the people of the world understand what the future might hold."

Alius interrupted, "Adrian spoke before the United Nations…twice…and the children understood the message. I'm afraid the adults didn't quite get it."

"We need to find a way to convince them that, together, we have to save the world by stopping pollution, providing refuge and habitat for the animals, feeding the hungry, helping the sick, and ending the killing. We can't do all of that through the Powers. President Bartlett is using his influence but we need someone to help us find the medium for the message."

"I could help you with that!"

They peeked into the third dome and toured the school before guiding their guests down to the interface. Coke smiled, "I sure would love to learn to dive like the people we met the last time I was here!"

Adrian smiled, "As a matter of fact, my mother is waiting outside to take you to her seamstress shop to scan you for your diving suits."

"Are you kidding? Both of us?"

"Yes, both of you. Come on," said Adrian as he led them up through the main hall to the tunnel leading to the bluff above the beach. Sara was waiting with the trolley.

Chapter Five

Dadeus and Raffe emerged from the elevator in the observatory just as Ponte stepped through a portal. "Ah, I'm glad that we found you," said Dadeus. "We're trying to set up a triangulation program for the vectors and I must return to the Island of the Children to coordinate our technicians. Raffe has been kind enough to offer to escort me."

"Haven't they set up a portal for you yet?" asked the Professor.

"No, they haven't had time and they've enough to do for the moment. We'll be fine and, once the circuits are set, we'll return immediately."

"I guess I've become spoiled using these conveniences. Sometimes the old ways are still the best ways."

Raffe laughed, "Don't worry, I'll get him there and back in one piece."

"I have no doubt, laddie, just watch out for the Dark Forces. We know they're watching the movements on our vectors in the same way we're watching theirs."

Raffe grasped Dadeus' forearm and closed his eyes. A moment later they moved into the vectors. The blazing colors streamed past and the low hum seemed smooth. There was no immediate threat of interception.

Within minutes they landed on the plaza that was now surrounded by formal buildings fronted with towering white columns. Hibiscus and bougainvillea bloomed profusely in the green spaces between the structures beneath arching palms that shaded pathways paved in broad smoothly polished squares of white stone. The two columns before the firepit still dominated the center of the square, a reminder of life before the children and the animals drove the pirates away and the two worlds finally merged. The path to the pyramid had been cleared, revealing a paved causeway, constructed by the ancestors who fled to this island so many generations before.

Dadeus straightened his robes and stroked his beard, "This shouldn't take too long. Do you want to join me or do you have other things to attend to?"

Raffe blushed, "I should at least visit my parents. I haven't seen them in almost a month and I was hoping to go up to see the growing fields. It's been a while since I had time to walk the ridgeline. Mary told me that they're maturing nicely."

"That they are. Check in with me in a couple of hours and I'll know more," said the old Keeper, as he sauntered away.

Raffe trotted across the square and up the stairs to the library, where his mother worked. Morag stood with her back to the door, arranging her latest acquisitions on a round stone table, as her son entered and snuck up behind her, wrapping his arms around her waist. "Surprise!"

She turned in his arms and gave him a big hug and a kiss on each cheek, "I've missed you, you rascal. When did you get back?"

"A few minutes ago. I just brought Dadeus from Morgan's Knot to work on some circuits. You won't believe how fast things are moving and changing. *Seers* and Keepers from all over the world are moving in and out, adding their bits and pieces, and they've got three domes dry and another four underway."

"It sounds as if they're keeping you busy."

"I'm helping to set up the school and working with the computers. Who would have thought that a kid who grew up on an island of children in the middle of nowhere would learn to use the finest machines in the world?"

"I've always believed in you," smiled his mother.

Raffe hugged her and asked, "Where's Dad today?"

"Oh, he and several of the other men have taken one of the trawlers to the mainland to pick up another load of stone. They're still building," she said, as she waved her hand toward the plaza. "It will never be finished."

"You're probably right about that," laughed Raffe. "What time do you get a break?"

"Oh, in an hour or so, you know Emily is always late."

"Good, I'll come by and we can have some time together over a meal."

"That would be lovely. I take it that you're going back to Morgan's Knot?"

"Yes, as soon as Dadeus is finished with his people."

"I miss having you near but I know that you have things that you must do…"

Raffe kissed her on the forehead and headed for the door, "I'll be back before your break."

He strolled through the plaza, past a group of children playing with two young lion cubs and a small brown bear. An elephant was pushing a round stone disk towards the new construction at the far end of the plaza and two giraffes were pulling dead palm fronds from the trees beside the council's offices. He turned into the path leading up through the jungle to the waterfall and noticed that the usual symphony of bird songs, the rumble of animal sounds in the forest, and the skittering of the young chasing each other through the underbrush were missing.

Flowers covered the banks of the pool beneath the gushing falls like an iridescent blanket and he was reminded of the years he spent on the surface with the other children, without knowing that his parents lived in the underworld. That recurring twinge of resentment gave way to a vision of the first time he shared this place with Adrian and his friends. Tic sat on that rock across the pond and Brandy paddled about like a motorboat with too much weight in the stern. He wondered why he had not seen his friend Blackbeard, the monkey, who always presented himself when Raffe arrived back on the Island of the Children, as if he knew that the *seer* was coming.

He was roused from his thoughts by the swish of someone moving out of the vectors. A tall figure, dressed in dark robes, materialized above the water and turned to face him. Raffe reached for his sword and extended the blade.

A young man pushed back the cowl of his robes to reveal strong features chiseled into a pale complexion, dark eyes, and a very straight nose above thin red lips. His long white hair fluttered in a gentle breeze as he raised one hand, with the palm extended to Raffe, "There will be no need for that. I come only to talk."

"What could we possibly have to talk about?"

"Perhaps we have a mutual enemy," whispered a deep voice.

Raffe gripped the handle of his sword with both hands, "and who might that be?"

"We both know the answer to your question."

The young *seer* was unsure of his foe and the message he was hearing. "Why would you want to stand against Zepallo…?"

"Because he's failed so many times, wasted so many lives, and made a mockery of the traditions that have held our civilization together for millennia."

"You want to take his place!"

"Of course, I do! But I'm a more reasonable man, a talented *seer* with a clear vision of our future, and one who can lead rather than dictate…and I'm a student our history. I believe that you call the equilibrium between man and nature 'the balance' but there has always been a balance between the Light and the Dark. It is as it was always intended to be…until now."

"I've learned something of our history and I understand that the battle has always been to the death but I have to believe that, eventually, there will be an ultimate victory for one side or the other. I intend to make sure that it's our side."

"Why should we fight each other? There are ample spoils for each of us."

"We have no interest in taking anything from the rest of the world. Rather, we intend to see every human, every living creature free to choose their own path to security and fulfillment."

"That will never happen. There are too many who are greedy for riches or power. Very few will be satisfied with an equal share of anything. Don't you see, we hold the violence of the real world in check. It's the equilibrium of strength between our two sides that has kept mankind from destroying itself. Certainly, the struggle must continue and we'll strive to achieve victory just as you will but, in the process, we control those who would destroy the world. That's our destiny, our responsibility. It's been this way since before recorded time and I intend to see that it continues."

"I guess we'll have to see how this plays out," replied Raffe.

"We digress, my young friend," smiled to Dark *seer.* "I can see that your arms are tiring from holding that sword. Please, I mean you no harm."

"What is that you want?" hissed Raffe. His hands were beginning to tremble with the weight of his weapon.

"I would like to set a trap for my leader and there is only one person in the world who has any chance of defeating him."

"We would not gamble with Adrian's life on the chance that he might be able to kill Zepallo."

"I think there might be a way that you could claim a great victory and I could assume the throne that is rightfully mine, after which there would be a long period of peaceful competition between our two sides."

"Why should I believe you?"

"You shouldn't but I hope that you'll consider my proposal and that you would be kind enough to pass it along to your friends. That's all I ask."

"I'll certainly tell my friends of our meeting, so they might be prepared if you reveal yourself to them."

"I can promise that I'll only present myself to you…and then, only in private moments like this."

"By the way, who are you?"

"My name is Marcus. I was in the cavern in New York when your friends came to rescue you from that mad spectacle at the United Nations. My father was The Elder of the Dark Forces, before he died in the battle on Morgan's Knot. He was horrified by the publicity and the attention that it drew to the secret powers. As far as he was concerned, Zepallo was a highly talented egomaniac possessed by a singular demon and intent on becoming king of all mankind. He will waste no opportunity to impose that vision on the real world or waste the lives of our finest warriors in a display of self-glorification."

"I see," replied Raffe. "So, you think you deserve to take his place?"

"I do because I inherited my father's sense of history, restraint, and purpose. There will be no need for these insane campaigns when I'm in control. We'll have far more than we might ever need and there is no point in trying to control the entire population of the world. It's an inconvenience that we can do without."

"I'm afraid I don't believe you."

"I can't go into details." The ruby lips curled into something resembling a friendly smile, although the dark eyes still burned with passionate intensity. "Just consider what I've proposed and I'll find you again, when it's convenient for both of us. A few days, perhaps?"

Marcus bowed, touched his fingertips to his forehead, and vanished. Raffe began to hear the sounds of the jungle beyond the rush of water spilling into the pool. He withdrew his blade and returned his sword to the pocket of his robes.

~

Adrian and Alius were huddled on the couch before the struggling remnants of a fire in the hearth in the parlor of the observatory. Professor Ponte leaned forward, as he listened to Raffe recount his conversation with Marcus. He wore that same long coat and a bright pink bow tie that seemed strangely in keeping with this inner sanctum that held bits and pieces of his ideas and creations, walls of books, piles of notes, and a collection of amusements that would delight a child of any age.

"I wanted to talk with you first, before we shared this with the others."

"I'm glad you did," replied Ponte. "For the moment, I think we should keep this to ourselves."

"But we have the greatest minds in the world here on the island," exclaimed Alius.

"I know but to share this information would set in motion a cascade that could only result in a confrontation with the Dark Forces and we're not ready."

"They'd want to protect me…" whispered Adrian.

"That is correct," replied the old man. "Our friends view you as the champion who will take Orana's place...the person who has the vision, the passion, and the ability to guide us through this time. Certainly, everyone understands that you're young and have a lot to learn but every person connected to our cause would gladly give their lives to protect you and, consequentially, the future of The Light."

Adrian opened his mouth in a rush to respond and then closed it. He could hear Orana's voice inside his mind and he knew that he could not reveal her, even to his best and most trusted friends. Finally, he looked up and said, "I can't lead if I'm surrounded by protectors and I can't grow to be the person that I'm expected to be, if I'm confined by those very expectations."

Alius took his arm, "We all understand that. It's just that you've become a symbol of hope to a great many people...not only our people, but people who saw you speak at the United Nations, the kids who joined in the children's crusade, and the animals who are depending on you to save their way of life too."

Suddenly, he was standing in the bow of the Jasmine on their return trip from the Island of the Children with tears streaming down his cheeks and he felt lost in the expectations of all of the people who looked up to him. Perhaps it had been the moment when he realized the weight of the responsibility of being a *seer*. He could hear Morgan's voice, soft but firm, whispering, "You can't go back to being the person you were when you arrived on the Island and you can't stop being famous for the things that you've done. All you can do is be the best you can be. Everything else will fall into place."

Ponte stood up and paced back and forth, "We've just been given a peek into the dysfunctions of the Dark Forces. More than one group is vying for power, in spite of the fact that we're fairly sure that Zepallo survived and has recovered enough to reclaim his position. This young Marcus is audacious enough to solicit the help of sworn enemies to topple his leader. This one might be even more dangerous than the Dark Lord himself."

"Still, the long and short of it is that Marcus would like me to agree to a duel with Zepallo, which means that he does not have the nerve or the strength to accomplish the task himself. Either way, he wins. He has nothing to lose, if he's covered his tracks with his own people."

"That's true," said Raffe. "If you win, he becomes the Master. If you lose, he can wait for another opportunity. There's no sport in that."

Adrian laughed, "Besides, I'm not sure that I could defeat Zepallo right now. The last time we met in the Ice Castle, I felt his energies had increased dramatically and there was a calm intensity in his eyes…it was different than the other times we've fought. I was lucky."

Ponte turned to Raffe, "He said that he would contact you again. Let's see how far he's willing to go. He expects you to be hesitant, to fear a trap…but you can still be curious, probing, without agreeing to anything."

"The next meeting will only reinforce the points he made in your first contact," said Adrian. "If he feels there's even the slightest possibility of convincing you of the merits of his plan, then he'll appear a third time in hopes of an agreement."

"You're right," agreed Alius. "He's trying to forge a short-term, mutually beneficial treaty with his enemies, to take the throne from Zepallo. Why should we trust him?"

"Then that's the tact I'll take, pushing him on a guarantee of this covenant to the Forces of the Light. Why should we risk our leader and our future for his ambitions?"

"You're on the right track," smiled Ponte. "Let us know when you've made contact and, remember, not a word of this to anyone until we have a chance to talk again."

~

Adrian sailed through the darkness and landed near the garden. He stared up into the stars that filled the sky and recognized Orion chasing the Pleiades into the ridge behind the House of the Four Seasons. Saturn followed Mars across the mid-heaven and the light of a full moon rippled across the ocean to the east.

He climbed the steps to the kitchen door and found, in spite of the hour, Coke and Martina sitting with the family at the large oval table that occupied one side of the kitchen. Sara rose and walked over to hug her son, "We were wondering where you'd got to. Have you had dinner?"

"Yes, Ester made a stew for everyone at the observatory. I'm sorry I didn't let you know that I'd be late…time got lost somewhere…"

"Don't worry about it, come in and sit with us. We've just been talking with Coke and Martina about the battle at the pole. You tend to leave out details when you tell the story."

"He's just modest," laughed Elsie, offering a plate of cookies.

Adrian blushed, took a chocolate chip cookie and stuffed it into his mouth to avoid having to respond, before squeezing between Molly and Megan.

Molly piped up, "He survived it, isn't that enough?"

"Now Molly," said George with a smile. "There would be no heroes if someone didn't recount and enhance the tale."

"I'm interested in why the Argentineans, Iranians, and Algerians abandoned their embargo of shipments of oil?" asked Megan.

Coke smiled, "It comes down to their need for cash. We knew they were bluffing because oil is their primary source of income. When several other major producers moved to fill the void, they caved in and resumed the shipments."

"Did World Oil have anything to do with that?"

"Well, in a backhanded sort of way, perhaps," laughed the attorney.

"I'm glad that you're on our side," giggled Megan.

"I am too," replied Coke, "and I'm looking forward to working on the computers tomorrow. That's where I can help."

"There's a terrific book in all of this," said Martina. "Maybe someday one of us will get to write it."

"Oh, it's already being written," said John. "For the first time in our history, the bits and pieces from every corner of the globe are being brought together so we might begin to understand how all the strands fit together."

"Only one person knew that history personally," said Adrian quietly, "and she's dead."

Martina reached across the table to touch his hand, "Were you close?"

"She was my…teacher…or maybe, mentor."

"Tell me about her."

Adrian smiled a small sad smile, "She was a thousand years old and led the Forces of Light since she was a girl during of the Dark Ages. I was completely intimidated when I got the chance to study with her and imagined all sorts of horrid possibilities, but she guided me through my lessons with a steady vision of what I needed to learn."

"What did she look like?"

"Well, she was old!" laughed Adrian.

The Cuban woman laughed, "I know that, what else?"

The young *seer* reflected back to the first time that he had entered her cave, "She had long white hair that fanned out around her like a glowing shawl. Her eyes were gentle one moment and fierce the next, and, somehow, I knew that there was no way I could hide my deepest secrets and fears. I remember thinking that I wouldn't want to have to face this woman in battle, even at her age. Her aura was pink and reached out to wrap itself around me like a warm blanket and her lessons were not like anything I might have expected."

"How so?" inquired Coke.

"As she explained it to me, each person has strengths and weaknesses. The lessons are individually designed to promote those strengths and overcome the fears."

"What did you learn was your greatest asset?" asked Martina.

Without hesitation, Adrian replied, "My love for all of these people."

"And your greatest weakness?"

"My love for all of these people."

"That's a very adult way of looking at your place and purpose in the world."

"I know," said Adrian, "but it's true."

"You are a remarkable young man," said Martina.

"Thank you but I'm just a small part of something much larger."

"I still find it hard to believe that all of this really exists…has always existed…and no one in the real world seems to know anything about it."

"They're not ready to accept the truth," replied Adrian. "The children understand. The adults don't want to see."

"That's very observant."

"The children's crusade proved it," added Megan. "Children have to learn about hate and war and killing from adults."

Coke laughed, "Adrian's grandfather and I used to muse about the idea that if you sent the generals to fight the battles, instead of youngsters, there'd be no wars."

"Here, here!" cheered George.

Sara had been quietly observing the conversation, "We're no better. The children have fought the battles against the Dark Forces."

Adrian looked across the table at his mother's sad eyes, "This is a different situation."

"I understand that but it doesn't relieve the feeling that we are powerless to help or protect you."

"You're doing all you can and so is everyone else. We each have a part. My being a *seer* is purely the luck or curse of heredity, it just skipped your generation. You might have inherited the gift and I have no doubt that you'd do things exactly the way I have. With all that's happened over the past few months, we're beginning to join together all the little pieces of knowledge and understanding that will lead to new powers, new technologies, and new opportunities for promoting all that is right and true."

"We've talked about this many times and you know how I feel when you go off on one of your missions. I'm terrified until you are safely returned to this house."

The young *seer* stood, walked around the table, and wrapped his arms around his mother's shoulders. "And you know that you're the reason that I must do what I must do…"

~

Zepallo stood on the podium of the control pod at the center of the dome beneath the desolate mountains of North Korea, flanked by Beta and Gamma. Regis and Cadeau stood at attention, frozen in place, as the Dark Lord inspected the purple bubbles flitting around enormous screens wrapping the entire cavern with flickering, dancing images of maps, graphs, charts, endless streams of statistics, news and video feeds, including a satellite channel monitoring Morgan's Knot.

He turned to his lieutenants, "A status report!"

"Repairs to the incubator in Indonesia are ahead of schedule. Final construction is nearing completion in New York and the Caucasus, as well as the facility in the Caribbean. New domes are being excavated in the Sulaiman Mountains between Pakistan and Afghanistan, the Andes, and Zimbabwe," replied Regis.

His comrade added, "The vector interweaving project continues and we're nearing eighty-five percent completion."

"And what of the…political climate?"

The two men remained silent, their eyes cast down to the Dark Lord's boots.

"Come now, gentlemen, we all know that there are groups among us who would not hesitate to seize power at the first opportunity. I might have been…incapacitated but that experience did not make me deaf, dumb, or blind."

Regis muttered, "There have been rumors, M'Lord."

"There are always rumors. It is fact that I am looking for!"

"We have not been approached by anyone. Our allegiance goes without question and we'd be the last to know and the first to die in a coup-d'état," said Regis.

The Dark Lord mulled the comment, staring at the two men. "I see your point. It doesn't matter, I know who the conspirators are and they will be dealt with in short order. I want a meeting of all of our Keepers and *seers*, as well as my generals. Here! In three days!" His twisted features relaxed and his voice was quiet and calm, "In the meantime, replay the energies that flowed through the vector web during the great meltdown. I need something positive to sooth my anger."

Chapter Six

Adrian hovered a foot above a patch of electric green grass that stretched to the gardens behind the kitchen. Tic curled into a furry ball to nap in his shadow and Brandy stretched out on his back, paws in the air, as the late morning sun warmed the island and the great oak tree cast a dark shadow over the path near the vegetable patch.

The young *seer* had not made time to concentrate on the sounds of the universe for days and felt an overwhelming impulse to follow the vibrations to Orana to seek her council, her insight, and her wisdom.

The tones of the harmonies of life were interposed with jagged discords of the harsh grating of starvation, anguish, death and the displacement of war and, in the background, he was aware that the energies of the dark vectors were growing stronger. In his past efforts to understand the sounds, he had been aware of convulsions across the planet but, during this encounter, he could feel the massacres in central Africa, he recoiled at the concussion of a bomb going off in Jerusalem, he smelled the pollution from factories spewing their waste into the air and the streams that passed through the great forests of the world, and his stomach growled in sympathy with the millions of children who were going to bed frightened and hungry.

His body convulsed and he crashed to the ground, startling Tic, who jumped up, screeching, and ran frantically in circles. Adrian shook his head and, on Tic's third pass, grabbed him and plopped the old Tomcat in his lap. He took a deep breath and gazed around at the colors of summer, as a flutter of monarch butterflies clustered around Elsie's flowers at the border of the vegetable garden. He heard the cardinal in the oak tree calling to her mate with a sharp tic-tic-tic, the grasshopper buzzing, and a clatter in the kitchen. Brandy rolled over and stared up at him with sad golden eyes, "That was somewhat less graceful than usual. Are you alright?"

Adrian reached over scratched behind the red dog's soft right ear, "Usually, when I meditate, I can hear the sounds of the world.

When things are calm and peaceful, there's a gentle steady tone. When bad things are happening, the sounds are ragged and harsh but, today, I not only heard but felt things that were happening in the world as if they were happening to me."

"That sounds frightening!"

"It was…which is why I fell."

"I guess that's reason enough," panted the Irish Setter. "It's warm out here."

"There's water by the garden. You know where it is."

"I'll be back," said Brandy as he trotted off through the shadow of the oak tree.

Adrian stroked Tic, "Sorry about that."

"It's alright. I was having such a nice dream and then you tried to squash me!"

The young *seer* laughed, "You might have picked a better spot to lie."

"Touché! But your shadow offered a nice cool oasis in the grass."

Adrian's fingers stroked Tic's soft fur, as he settled back into his meditation, visualizing Orana's fire and reaching out to feel her aura. He could see a trace of color, like a wisp of pinion smoke dissipating in the slightest breeze leaving only a hint of fragrance to recall the apparition. He could hear her voice in the distance, as if whispering from the depths of a deep grotto, and he could sense her presence everywhere but nowhere, for there was no point of reference, no place where he might find her.

He opened his eyes in frustration to find Alius sitting quietly beside him in the sun.

"Anything interesting today?"

"I was listening to the vibrations…and there are clashes of violence, death, and war and the growing sound of the dark energies," said Adrian quietly, as he sprawled on the grass. "For the first time, I felt all those things instead of just hearing them. I felt the suffering and the pain…"

Alius reached over and took his hand, "There are some parts of this gift that…I don't know, balance out the magic. It's as if we have to stand between the wonders of The Powers and the cruelty of the real world. If you let it become personal, if you let it creep inside your soul, then you'll be of no value to those who need you most. Understand it, work to change it, but see the world as a whole. We're fighting for everyone."

Adrian smiled and leaned over to kiss her forehead. "I couldn't do any of this without you…especially you."

"There's something I want to know."

"What's that?"

"What happened when we were in Orana's cave? I fell asleep and there's a gap in there that I don't understand."

Adrian pursed his lips and was quiet for a moment, "There must have been something in the tea…"

"There's more to it than that. What were you doing while I was unconscious?"

"I was…meditating, meditating on the things that I learned from Orana…the things she said and the way she looked at life and history."

"What did you learn?"

"She made me feel that there is always hope where there is purpose and that we have a lot more to learn before we can truly understand."

"Understand what?"

"Well, for instance, one of the things that she said to me was that there are other planes that we haven't explored. Unfortunately, she didn't teach me how to reach those places but perhaps Master Jung might help or we could figure it out on our own. Just knowing there's more is reason enough to continue what we've been trying to do."

"Can you still feel her energy?"

"In her own way, she'll always be with us," smiled Adrian.

"I wish I could have studied under her," said Alius. "I've often wondered what my lessons would be about…probably a lot to do with being raised on the Dark side."

"I don't know about that...you've become a respected leader. Everyone listens when you speak because they know that you'll offer an insight or a piece of information that no one else has considered. Besides, you're usually right."

Alius giggled, "Don't tell anyone that it's not some special gift!"

"Is there an instruction manual for girls somewhere? It's as if you all know things that boys never think about."

"There's a certain magic to being a girl."

"I'll have to agree with that, although I can't explain why. Maybe that's why women were worshipped and held in high esteem by our ancient ancestors."

"As I've learned, that's the tradition on the island. Every woman is as equally valued as each man. Everyone contributes and that's what it's really all about."

"Well, we haven't had that problem since our first meeting on the mountain."

"We've come a long way since then," smiled the blond *seer*. "Besides the fact that you told the President several things that I didn't know about, there's just one more thing."

"What's that?"

"When you woke me up and we stood to leave the cave, I noticed that there were three cups on the tea service."

~

Zepallo inspected the renovations in the dome under the labyrinth of tunnels that snaked beneath New York City. The enormous chasm had been gutted and refitted with the latest technology. It would be ready for operations to begin within a month.

Accompanied by a small cadre of council members, Keepers and *Seers*, the Dark Lord moved on to the facility in the Caucasus mountains. The flood destroyed the circuitry and it had taken more than a year to get the systems functioning again. With the latest upgrades, this center could be ready a month after New York.

He turned to his comrades, "I'm pleased to see that our progress was not impeded during my absence."

Lord Petry bowed, "We continued as you would have expected."

Old Sigmond muttered, "You continued because you had no other choice!"

Zepallo turned to Marcus and stared into his eyes, "What do you think?"

Without hesitation, he replied, "Our future depends on a steady, continuous effort like bees building a hive or ants excavating a hill."

"That is very astute for someone so young."

"I believe I learned that from you, Sire."

The Dark Lord placed his hand upon the young *seer's* shoulder. "There is much more that you might learn from me," he said, as his grip tightened. "You would not consider someone else as your leader, would you?"

Marcus grimaced in pain, as the Master's pulses rippled through his body, "I am indebted to you for everything I have."

Zepallo released his grip and stared at the *seer*. There were no telltale hints of fear or deception betrayed in those steely young eyes and his energies were smooth. *This one is strong.* "I'll have you as my ally, my charge. To betray me is to begin a long tortuous journey to an excruciating death."

"I am your servant," replied Marcus, with a slight tilt of the head.

The group moved on to the new construction to the south of Kashmir and then to the council meeting in North Korea in a command saucer, similar to the one that remained buried in the ice at the Pole. The assembly was comprised of warriors who had fought their way through the ranks to become generals, the most talented *seers*, senior Keepers, and those who directed the day-to-day operations of the empire. There were perhaps two-dozen who actually participated in critical Council decisions but each of the members of this group had earned positions of power through intelligence, talent, or sheer ferociousness. Most were ambitious, greedy, and jealous, and none of them would hesitate to make a grab for power, should opportunity present itself.

The only control was fear, fear of ruthless retribution at the hands of the Dark Lord. Discipline and order must be maintained to achieve his ultimate goal and he could leave no doubt about who would lead the Dark Forces. To show any sign of weakness would invite anarchy and revolt.

Two hundred men sat in stadium seats surrounding a tiny podium in the center, the cowls of their dark robes shielding their faces in deep shadows. The *orbs* dimmed and Zepallo appeared in a pool of cold blue radiance in a pit of darkness. The audience rose to applaud.

"I understand that there has been some concern about my well-being," began the deep whisper. "As you can see, I have survived to lead my legions and fight another day!"

Again, the participants clapped and cheered with enthusiasm.

The Dark Lord spun around slowly to look into the agitated auras of those staring down at him. "I understand that there may have been an inclination by some parties to investigate the paths of succession…in case I had not recovered. That is why this body exists! To establish and follow protocol in governing our people and our forces."

There was a silence in the room that reeked of anxious anticipation.

"Beyond those who accepted that responsibility, there are individuals who covet my power, my position, and my throne. They believe that they should rightfully stand in my place." He let the thought echo through the chamber for a moment. "There can be no question and no doubt about who is the supreme leader of this organization, the visionary who can see our path to ultimate victory, and the only one who possesses the power to take us there."

There was scant applause and hushed whispers.

"Lord Doltrim, would you step forward?" shouted Zepallo, his face distorted, his eyes blazing, his lips twisted into a violent sneer. "Keeper Stulton, would you stand? General Valisea would you stand? And a most promising *seer*…I had such hopes for you, *seer* Donica! Why don't you join your comrades?"

One by one, the men stood and spotlights erupted from the darkened ceiling to etch their features with a blue-gray wash framed by ghostly shadows. General Valisea sobbed quietly, which was an embarrassment because he had fought so valiantly in many battles over the years. The others bowed their heads, their arms at their sides, each too proud and too frightened to speak.

"Gentlemen, I present the cabal! The group that would lead you! I offer you a choice. Would you rather follow them…or me?" He screamed, as he spun around the stadium, pointing at those in the crowd.

"The Council rose to their feet. Applause rippled around the circle in a thundering wave, accompanied by whistles and cheers.

Zepallo raised both hands above his head and there was silence. He pointed the index finger of his right hand at the General, who rose into the air and turned upside down, where he remained suspended with his robes hanging down, revealing a crystal dagger sheathed inside his boot. The others followed, each hanging at one of the four points of the compass. The Dark Lord crouched, as he turned, his crooked finger pointing to his victims, one by one. A bolt of lightning seared through the darkness of the hall, striking Lord Doltrim's chest with a ball of blue flame, then Donica, Stulton, and finally, Valisea. The initial charges were not intended to kill but rather to allow them to suffer. Slowly, their flesh began to rot, a foul stench consuming the atmosphere, putrid droplets splashing on the cold stone floor, forcing nearby councilors to move away...until the screams of the convicted became overwhelming and he ended it with four final blasts, saving the last for young Donica.

He turned to the audience, "That concludes our entertainment for the evening. Will there be any questions?"

Slowly, hesitantly, Marcus raised his hand.

The Dark Lord turned to him and pointed, "Yes, Marcus?"

"Will there be any orders?" he asked meekly.

"As you know, we have just reviewed the progress at some of our installations and found them to be satisfactory. I'm pleased with the work that has been done in my absence. Please accept my sincere gratitude for a job well done. That will be all."

Zepallo bowed his head and vanished and the councilors moved out of the stadium in stunned silence.

~

Sammy, the brilliant young Jamaican Keeper in training, stepped from the elevator to find Professor Ponte sitting alone at the dining room table in the dark. The only illumination sprang from the dying embers in the fireplace in the parlor and a small glowing green ball that the old Keeper was rolling back on forth across the wooden surface of the table between one hand and the other, while he hummed absently to himself. He was considering life as it had been, only a few years before.

"Professor?" whispered Sammy.

"Yes, my boy, what can I do for you?" replied Ponte, staring at the grain of the old oak slab, revealed in the halo of soft light as he continued to roll the ball back and forth.

Sammy approached the table shuffling a sheaf of papers, "Are you alright?"

The Professor sighed, "Aye, laddie, I'm fine…just considering the changes that are taking place all around us. It wasn't that long ago that things seemed less complicated and more straight forward than they do today."

"When the Jasmine first pulled into the harbor at Montego Bay, I knew, instantly, that Adrian was a *seer.* I understood that there were mysterious powers that my uncle seemed to use in magical ways and I yearned for a chance to become a master, just like him. I also knew that I didn't inherit his gift and I felt as if I was in some way inferior, until you and Nanchez gave me the chance to learn the science of it…to become a Keeper.

Here we are at the advent of the next level of understanding, of achievement, of combining all of the knowledge from all of the people who have been using and protecting the Crystals through thousands of years. This's like the beginning of the Renaissance! Do you think that someone actually realized what was happening when they launched into their cultural revolution out of the ashes of the Dark Ages?"

The Professor smiled, "I think these things happen because…mankind and, even more to the point, the natural world can not live confined beneath a cloud of darkness. At some point, the resistance builds to a boiling point where the pent-up energies erupt and overflow into the sunshine, like a flower opening from the promise of a bud. These things are destined to happen and, you're right, we're on the first step of a mighty staircase that leads into the promised land, the fulfillment of the unification of The Forces of Light.

The problem is…are we wise enough to master these forces and use them in a beneficial, constructive way or will we follow the historical patterns of the mightiest powers in the real world, each using their newfound knowledge to take one step closer to self-destruction and oblivion? Each advance forces the opposition to explore the next deadly option, endless escalation that can only lead to confrontation."

Sammy was quiet for a moment, while he considered the Professor's insight. "Are you saying that the technology is only a tool and that the teachings and the wisdoms should guide us in its use?"

"That's exactly what I'm saying. We can join all the pieces of this puzzle together in several ways, some more admirable than the others. I should add that the goal must be worthy of the investment and the effort, which means that there is really only one correct arrangement of these new tools. To approach this in any other way is to miss the opportunity to create a legacy that will guide every generation to come." The old man paused, pushed his glasses up the bridge of his nose, and then continued, "Every positive advance that we make is accompanied by the potential for an equally lethal application. For every positive there is always an equal negative."

"As we've seen in the conflict between the Light and the Dark."

"We can create our own darkness, if we're not careful," cautioned the old man. "Now, what was it that forced you to interrupt my quiet contemplation?"

Sammy held up the papers, "I've been monitoring the power on the Dark Vectors since the battle at the North Pole."

"And," inquired the Professor.

"Well, first, there's been a lot of movement in the dark vectors around North Korea."

"A council," whispered the old man. "They're meeting to plot their course."

"Maybe more important than that, the dark vectors have always had bumps in the pattern…I would guess, from what I've learned from you and Nanchez, that these are normal surges and fluctuations that occur because the vectors are always moving, expanding, and contracting."

"That's true."

"Well, over the past few weeks, those fluctuations have calmed down. The dark vectors are acting just the way the light vectors behave, since the nodes were installed."

The ball stopped rolling midway between the Professor's hands. "That's interesting. Have you talked with Nanchez about this?"

"No, I've been working in your laboratory, so I could also help with Raffe on the computers, and Nanchez has been spending most of his time at the domes, so I thought I might ask you about it."

"That's perfectly alright," said the old man, as he looked up at the boy and gestured to the chair opposite him. "Sit down. Now, I must ask you, have you checked all of your data and the *messengers* that you've been using?"

"Of course, that's what you taught me!"

"I admire your work ethic, Sammy, and your technique. You are far more critical and precise than I was at your age. I only ask these questions to eliminate tangential causes or rippling eddies that cloud our ability to see clearly."

"I understand and I wouldn't have brought this to you unless I was convinced that my calculations were correct," said Sammy. "The question is…what does it mean?"

The old man sat back and placed the tip of his index finger on the ball and stroked his whiskers with his left hand, as he moved the green crystal back and forth, its glow lighting the table to the left and then to the right. "It means…that the Dark Forces have found a way to manage their power on a global scale."

"Then, they must have been using this technology when they moved the energy across the vectors to form the hurricane and to melt the ice at the pole."

"Absolutely. Those were experiments…probably using only a portion of their potential but…monumental experiments designed to capture our attention and to solicit our reaction. They learned from the wave that we sent along the positive vectors!" exclaimed Ponte, his face flushed with anger. "It was all theatrics to see what we would do!"

The young Jamaican's mouth dropped open. "All those people fought and died so they could gauge our reaction…?"

"That is correct."

"But…why?"

"Because they're planning something bigger when they've finished their network. We're farther behind than I thought!" He grabbed the green crystal from the table and stuffed it into his vest pocket as he stood and, with the other hand, pressed the clasp of the crystal that hung from a golden chain around his neck. A portal opened in the parlor, "Come along, son. We have to talk with Nanchez and the others!"

~

Simian was surprised to see Coke step from a portal, as he passed through the airlock from the third dome, "Mr. Tierney, I'm so pleased to see you!"

"It's nice to see you too," said the attorney, who was still in his uniform dark suit and red tie, which seemed slightly out of place next to the Jamaican's bright yellow robes. "Is Adrian around?"

"Yes, he's in a *seer's* conference. If you'll step this way," said the old *seer*, "I was going to join them anyway." The attorney was in fairly good shape for his age. He jogged regularly and was careful with his diet, but he was almost in a dead run, trying to keep up with the old Jamaican who seemed to float along the floor.

They stepped through a small airlock, which opened into a miniature dome that was private and secure from the rest of the facility. Sunlight scattered through the water outside the glass, weaving bright patches that moved rhythmically across the cushioned steps spiraling around a circular podium in the center. One hundred people could sit in comfortable intimacy with the presentation in the middle.

Several dozen *seers* gathered close to the two *seers* in the pit, some lounging, others hanging in midair and no one acknowledged the new arrivals.

Adrian did not look up but pointed at his mentor, "For those of you who have not had the privilege, I would like to introduce Simian, a *seer* from Jamaica and one of our teachers."

Simian bowed to the group, "I bring another friend, Adrian's attorney, Mr. Tierney."

The two men walked down a ramp to the center, "I hope that we're not intruding. What are we discussing today?"

Alius replied, "Most of these *seers* were involved in the battle at the pole, so we were talking about things that we noticed about the Dark Forces - their weapons, their tactics, and their strengths."

"I can honestly say that it was the coldest that I've ever been in my life," shuddered the old Jamaican. "Jamaicans are not used to temperatures like that!"

"Here, here!" came a call from Jordan, one of the younger *seers* from Central Africa.

"What have you learned from this experience?"

The *seers* glanced at each other before Jojo, a young brown-skinned, blue-eyed prodigy from Nepal, spoke, "Well, first to wear more clothes!" Everyone laughed. "No, if nothing else we learned to respect their powers."

Simian looked at the boy, "You should always respect your enemies. Never feel superior. Never assume victory. Success is earned. In this case, we earned our victory at the price of our dead comrades and they could have been any of you." He was quiet for a moment to let the thought simmer. "We know that we will face the Dark Forces again. Learn from our history and our mistakes. All of the *seers* must learn to work together as a team, seamlessly.

We face an army trained with discipline and regimentation. They practice the art of killing and their *seers* study the history of The Powers, theirs and ours. Their Keepers have developed systems that are far more advanced than anything that we have at the moment but, no matter how lethal our weapons, in the end, it will always be up to the vision of the *seers* to lead us. Our strength has always come from our belief in The Powers and our ability to use them for the right purposes.

That's why these meetings and the classes that we're forming are so important. Each of you possesses talent and knowledge that the rest of us have yet to master. There are many more who will join us over the next weeks. This is our chance to learn from each other…and we'll all be stronger for it."

Someone started clapping and soon all of the *seers* in the room were gathered around the old Jamaican. Adrian walked over to Coke, "I didn't expect to see you back so soon."

"There's something that we need to talk about," said the attorney quietly.

Adrian walked up the ramp and out through the airlock into the lobby of the second dome. There was no one else near the windows. "Well?"

"The oil markets are moving up, in spite of our efforts to restrain the trend by increasing production. Our adversaries seem to be manipulating the world economy."

"A mentor of mine once said that if Zepallo couldn't take something, he'd buy it, which seems sort of…backwards…unless you understand his ultimate goal."

"In theory, he could control the world by owning key pieces of the most basic and vital industries. I think the move on oil, with the hurricane, the embargo, and his interests in many of the largest oil companies, is just a test of a system that has already targeted other prime industries. With access to a never-ending supply of investment capital, there's no limitation to the potential extent of his holdings," mused Tierney. "You know, I get this weird image in my mind of an octopus that continuously grows new appendages, each reaching out to explore new territory…but what if we followed that trail backwards, to the body of the beast? I think I have a new tact for Raffe and Sammy to use in their exploration of your grandfather's files."

"There's a portal from The Professor's office directly to the observatory. I'm sure no one would mind if we used it."

"Great, let's go," said Coke. Adrian grabbed the lawyer's arm and levitated to the balcony. "That's amazing!"

As they turned into Ponte's office, the Professor and Sammy were stepping through the portal from the observatory, "Oh, Professor?" exclaimed Adrian. "We were just going to find you."

"And I you, laddie."

"Coke's got some interesting thoughts on the financial affairs of the Dark Forces."

"And we…errr…Sammy has come up with some interesting news about the dark vectors."

"Perhaps we should sit down for a moment," suggested the attorney.

"Good idea," replied Ponte as he gestured to the sleek comfortable chairs before his desk. "Let's start with Sammy."

He was still holding the sheaf of papers in his hand, "I've been monitoring the dark vectors since the battle at the pole. Normally, there are fluctuations in the pattern of waves. Since we installed the red crystals in the nodes, the positive vectors are smooth, without bumps or surges. Our sensors confirm that the wave form of the dark vectors is almost perfectly smooth."

"What he's saying is that they've managed to connect all of their vectors into a web that covers the planet."

Coke looked confused, "What does this mean?"

"It means that the hurricane and the melting at the North Pole were merely experiments, trial runs to test their systems…and to see what we would do in response."

Adrian gasped, "We lost many of our friends in that battle…and it was all for show?"

"I'm afraid that you are correct," sighed the Professor, as he sat back in his chair, took off his little glasses, and rubbed his eyes. "Their engineers were watching, when we sent along the wave. We provided them a window into our capabilities."

"I'm afraid that I'm new to this," said the attorney. "What will they do next?"

Adrian looked at Sammy, then the Professor, and finally at Coke, "We have no idea but the things that they've done in the past won't compare."

"I was feeling confident that we were making good progress with the domes, the new systems, and the school. Now, I'm not so sure. There's so much that we need to finish," said Ponte, "and there are so many possibilities…"

Everyone was quiet for a moment as they considered the Professor's thoughts, before Sammy turned to Coke, "What was it that you wanted to talk with me about?"

"I've been studying the information that you sent along with me, the last time that I was here, and in the past few days I've noticed that the oil markets are moving up for no obvious reason. What struck me was that all of this information leads out, like tentacles reaching out to find a new food source. We've been concentrating on their interaction with the real world, when we should be working the other way…back to the source."

Sammy smiled, "I see your point. We could work backwards!"

"Exactly!"

"Come on, let's go to the observatory and we'll see whether I've learned enough to create a program to help in the search." Sammy pressed the clasp on his necklace and the portal opened behind the desk. He turned to the Professor, "I don't mean to run out on you…"

"Give me those papers. I'll send out a call and we'll convene a council day after tomorrow."

"Good," said the young Jamaican as he led Tierney through the shimmering aperture that closed behind them.

Adrian stared at his mentor, "What will you say?"

"To tell you the truth, I'm not sure. We have to be very careful to avoid a panic, while accelerating our efforts. We'll convene a general meeting and then break up into groups to pursue individual tasks."

"The *seers* fought well at the pole but we need to coordinate our talents. Everyone has abilities that could be shared and learned. The clones proved that they have a sophisticated system to train their warriors."

The Professor smiled at his young charge, "You have accomplished many things that I would have thought impossible. You succeeded because…?"

Adrian pondered the question, "Because, I believed in the Balance and the Powers."

"Exactly!" replied the old man as he stood up and shook his finger, "and we would all be well advised to make that the basis for everything we do from this point forward. To lose sight of our purpose would surely lead to defeat."

"Simian mentioned something else that I think is important. He said that their *seers* study their history and ours…"

"Considering the meeting that Raffe had with Marcus, I think that we would be well advised to do the same."

"I'll find Alius and we'll take a look at the Book of Knowledge. She has more insight into the dark energies than any of our other *seers*."

"I think you're on to something. Go find her and I'll send out the call."

~

Adrian found Alius in the third dome with several of the other *seers*. "Could I talk with you for a moment?" he whispered.

"What is it?"

"I've just come from the Professor and Sammy. They've found that the Dark Forces have harnessed the dark vectors. The hurricane and the melting of the polar ice were just experiments."

Alius turned ashen, "We knew that there would be more…but…?"

"We still don't have a clue about what they're planning but I started thinking about what Simian said about the dark *seers* studying their history and ours. You're the only one who's worked with the dark energies. I was wondering whether you might be able to use the Book of Knowledge to gain some insight into their intentions?"

"I haven't summoned the Dark Powers since the day that we met…"

"I know I'm asking a lot but it might be helpful…"

"Of course, I'll help…I just don't want to go back to that…feeling."

"I understand but there is no other way."

"Let's go to the observatory," sighed the beautiful blond *seer*.

"Shall we use the portal?"

"No, I want to fly."

Adrian took her hand and walked out through the tunnels to the beach. The setting sun cast long shadows of the trees along the ridgeline reaching across the island to whitecaps glistening with flashes of yellows and reds. Alius stopped to watch a flock of pelicans skimming just above the waves, searching for an evening meal. "It wasn't so long ago that I didn't understand…and, now, I can't imagine any other way of life."

"I'm glad," whispered Adrian.

"Let's go," said Alius, taking his hand to lift into the deep blue sky.

Ester greeted them at the door, "Why didn't you use the portal?"

Alius smiled, "I just needed some air."

"With so many people coming and going, I don't know who's in the house!"

"We don't mean to interrupt," said Adrian.

"You know better than that, come in, come in," smiled the old woman, her thin lips stretching across her too small teeth. "Your attorney and Sammy just materialized in the dining room and disappeared into the workshops. I think Raffe's still down there too. It's all so confusing, I never know who's where or where I'm supposed to be!"

"We just want to consult the Books, if that's alright with you?"

"They're in their usual place in the dining room. Have either of you had anything to eat?"

The two *seers* looked at each other, "No, we haven't had time."

"Fine, I'll fix you something to tide you over. While I'm about it, have you talked with your parents, Adrian, or your father, Alius?"

"No, I haven't been home since…the day before yesterday," replied Adrian.

"Nor I," added Alius.

"Then tend to that before you get lost in those books."

Jofre's face appeared in front of the *messenger*, "There you are! I thought that I'd lost my daughter once and for all!"

"I'm sorry, I've been busy. I just wanted to check in…"

"I see that you're at the observatory and I'm sure that you have more than your share of responsibilities. I'm just relieved to know that you're alright."

"I'm fine. What are you doing?"

"We've just about got the fourth dome airtight," replied the huge man, as he gestured to the scene behind him. "What are you working on?"

"You might want to have a chat with the Professor, when you have a moment," said Alius.

"I'm going to meet with him in a little while. Is there something I should know?"

"He'll fill you in. I've got to go. I'll see you when there's time."

"I understand," said her father.

The image faded and Adrian said, "House of the Four Seasons!"

Elsie's image appeared on the *messenger*, "Oh, there you are! We worried that you might have forgotten about us!"

"I'm sorry I haven't been home, there's a lot going on."

"I understand," laughed his aunt, her blue eyes twinkling with delight. Your father and George are down at Samuel's working on the next set of beams. The twins are up at the old school, helping Mrs. Green, and your mother is…oh, here she comes now."

Sara appeared, "I've been worried about you."

"I know and I'm sorry that I haven't been home in a few days. There's a lot going on."

"I know. The President…or the Chancellor…called looking for you. He's coming in the day after tomorrow."

"Good, there's a council meeting."

"I assume there's more to this than you are saying?"

"Yes."

"I'll tell George and your father. When will you be home?"

"I don't know but a hot shower and a good night's sleep, after one of your meals, sounds awfully inviting."

"You say when!" smiled his mother.

"Soon."

"I love you, Adrian."

"I love you too." The image faded.

Ester appeared at the dining room table with a crock of soup and some sandwiches. "Come sit down and have something to eat. Then you can begin your work."

"Thank you," said Alius as she sat down at the old table and took a spoonful of the cold potato soup. "This is delicious!"

"Thank you," smiled the old woman. "Now eat up. I'm sure that you have plenty to keep you occupied when you've finished."

Adrian smiled, "We do."

Chapter Seven

Raffe yawned and stretched. He had been monitoring the dark vectors and rechecking the data displayed on the *messengers* lining the workbench in the Professor's workshop. After working through the entire program three times, the results remained unchanged. Sammy was correct, it was time for a break.

He padded out and turned to the left along the corridor into the computer room, where he found Sammy and Coke sitting before the monitors.

"You're getting close," said the attorney, "keep going."

"I wish I knew more about programming," replied the young Jamaican.

"What are you working on?" inquired Raffe, as he walked behind Sammy's chair to check the flat screens.

"We're trying to figure out how to run all of this backwards!" exclaimed Sammy.

"It dawned on me that we've been hunting for the objectives of the investments of the Dark Forces, instead of trying to work the other way to find the source."

"Oh, what a brilliant idea," said Raffe, as he tried to grasp the significance of the data that was streaming down the screens. "I think I saw something like that in the data resources file. Maybe we could jigger it around."

Sammy hit several keys in quick succession and a menu appeared filled with file options. Raffe pointed, "There…in the file that contains the status report generator."

Clickity-clack, clickity-clack and a list of programs appeared. The fourth one down was titled, "Reverse."

The black Keeper pointed the stylus and the file opened with a notice "This file is incomplete and unfinished."

"Well, at least it's a start," said Raffe.

"If I can get to the code, I can figure out his logic and we'll be part way there. Thanks, that really helps!"

"You're welcome," yawned Raffe. "I'm going to see if there's anything to eat in the kitchen. Do you know the time?"

"Oh, my," said Coke, as he glanced at the screen, "it's three in the morning. No wonder Adrian always calls me at strange times. You people have no schedules!"

"Yes, we do," laughed Sammy. "Our only schedule is right now or sooner!"

"Now you're on island time!" Raffe patted the attorney on the back and wandered out of the room and into the elevator. He emerged to find Adrian and Alius sitting at the dining room table with the silver Book of Knowledge open before them. They were both wearing black diamond pendants and Alius looked ashen.

He stepped behind their chairs, "What are you two up to?"

"Alius is exploring the history of the Dark Powers."

"I didn't know that you could see both sides in the books."

"A dark *seer* can read from the silver books, when they're close to a Black Crystal."

"I'd forgotten that you were a dark *seer* before Adrian straightened you out," smirked Raffe.

"This is harder on her than you might think," said Adrian.

"I'm sorry. I didn't mean to interrupt. Is there anything to eat in the kitchen?"

"Yes, there's some cold soup that Ester made for us earlier. She's gone to bed."

"I'll be quiet," whispered Raffe.

"Get out of here and let us work!" said Adrian, swinging an open hand at Raffe's leg as he darted to the kitchen.

"Are you sure you're alright?"

Alius shivered, "I tried to forget the sensation. I always feel cold when I read. I blamed it on being inside the mountain. I guess I've gotten used to the Golden Book."

"What have you found?"

"Well, it seems that while we had a woman guiding our forces for the past thousand years or so, they had a family…a lineage of rulers who have handed the throne from one generation to the next, until the most recent Grand Master, Ptolemy, died during the battle here on the island. His son, Marcus, should have ascended to take his place but Zepallo seized the authority…and here, there's a Lord Petry and a Sigmond…there's a whole list of the inner circle and most of them are related in one way or another."

"That explains the secret meeting with Raffe. Marcus isn't acting alone, he has political and, probably, strategic support within his family."

"Let's go back a bit farther," said the blond *seer.* "Why didn't I explore these things when I was younger and had the time?"

"You're doing fine."

"Show me previous generations."

The figures in the book scrambled across the pages and lined up with names and dates.

"Add to this information, their most infamous achievements."

The list expanded.

"This is amazing. Look here, Marcus' great grandfather belonged to Hitler's inner circle and, at the same time, a cousin was a protégé of Stalin!"

"Somehow, that doesn't surprise me. Working both sides against each other, I mean."

"Look there's more…the Dark Forces influenced the conflicts in Vietnam, Korea…here's the great depression, the assassination of Archduke Ferdinand that led to the First World War, and look, they controlled the companies that produced the guns and bombs for both sides…and, here farther back, they controlled the supply of slaves for centuries. Civil wars and dictatorships in South America, the triumphs and destruction of Greece and Rome…here's the plague! This goes on for pages!"

"Okay, we can assume that most of the great tragedies were the result of their efforts, but somehow, we have to convince the Book to show us something about their strategies."

"I think we already know a little about that…they plant their people in positions where they can influence those who make the great decisions in the real world. Our old friend, the Ambassador, was a prime example."

"That shadow probably falls across every seat of power in the world."

"Right, so the question becomes, what's next? What are they after this time?"

"Ask it about natural disasters."

Alius whispered, "Show me the natural disasters that were spawned by the dark energies."

The figures disappeared and an iridescent globe appeared. Green blotches erupted on the western coast of Africa, formed into circular storms, and sailed to the west, ramming the eastern coast of the United States, or scouring the islands of the Caribbean before crashing through the Gulf of Mexico. Electric yellow surges rippled through the Earth, leveling structures and exposing long fissures where the land cleaved against itself. Blue waves rolled across the Pacific, as Tsunamis slithered beneath the surface rising out of the depths to wash over the islands of Hawaii or Alaska or along the eastern coast of Asia. Bright red volcanoes spewed lava that flowed like a melting ice cream cone, devouring cities and towns as it raced to the sea. Tiny gray splotches appeared here and there and grew, like a slimy mold, to smother broad expanses inhabited land.

"Those were diseases," murmured Alius. The strain of working with the Dark Powers without being seduced and entrapped by them was draining the energy from her core.

"I think this tells us that there is nothing that they have not tried or will attempt in their quest to control the world. We've just witnessed centuries of suffering and death."

"I think the Professor was right when he said that we're not ready."

"I'll have to agree with that," smiled Adrian, as he looked deeply into her eyes and put an arm around her shoulders. "Come on, I think that we've done enough research for one night."

The blond *seer* sat back in her chair, sighed deeply, closed the book, placed it on the shelf above the sideboard, and removed the necklace. "It feels good to take this off."

"Let's see if Raffe found anything to eat. I'm hungry again."

"Well, no wonder," said Alius as she placed a hand on his shoulder to steady herself and glanced to the old grandfather clock that stood in the corner, "It'll be dawn in a little while."

~

Raffe greeted a bright beautiful summer morning, as he trotted up to the ridgeline that spanned the length of the island. He scampered into the trees and stopped in a small clearing to swing his arms down to his feet and back above his head. His body was sore and stiff from spending most of the previous day confined in the laboratory.

Songbirds tittered in the branches and a family of fox trotted through the shadows. He climbed up the rocks until he reached the peak, where he could see the ocean on both sides of the island. This was his secret place on Morgan's Knot, where he could be alone with his thoughts, for it reminded him of the Island of the Children and the strange assortment of native and exotic circus animals inhabiting the jungle. They had become friends and allies, after Adrian and the others introduced the children to The Balance.

Life was far more simple when the children cared for each other. The island provided plenty of food, with a little bit of effort and cooperation, and the cave ensured a warm, dry place to sleep. The only worries were the occasional hurricane or a visit by the pirates, and it was easy to hide from them.

He wondered how he had been transformed from the person who mastered that life to this world where everything depended on protecting the Powers. Raffe never thought about pride when he lived on the Island of the Children, it never occurred to him that he should or could do anything more or less than he did every day. Somehow, when those who taught him to survive and prosper descended into the pit, he accepted the responsibility for the rest of the children without thought or hesitation.

That circle widened as he learned about the Powers and his own abilities because he realized that he was an integral part of something much larger. He closed his eyes and felt the sensations of his first journey through the vectors, learning to levitate, and the joy of discovering that he could read from the Books. Visions of giant slugs beneath the pyramid, the skulls guarding the Crystals in Stonehenge, his time as a hostage in the lair beneath New York, rescuing Adrian, the battle at the pole, and so many other experiences flowed through his mind like the colors streaming through the vectors.

Raffe considered Adrian his best friend and, although there was a tinge of jealousy, he did not resent the position he held. There could be no doubt about who found the solutions to each of their challenges but Adrian always made everyone else feel that they were the most important part of the plan, that they were all merely guardians, dependent on their individual talents and their love for each other.

His breathing slowed as he accepted the image of the world rotating in space and heard Adrian's thought, "It's all about the Balance." Protecting the Earth for every living thing was a responsibility that each of them accepted without a moment's consideration.

Startled by the sound of air moving behind him, he spun around to find Marcus materializing on a flat stone jutting out to the east. Instinctively, he reached into his robes for his sword, as Marcus raised his hand, palm outward, "We went through that the last time we met. I'm only here to talk."

"I still have no reason to trust you."

"That's true but, just this once, let's have a civil conversation and then I'll be on my way. If I meant you any harm, I might have brought some help or attacked you as I moved out of the vectors."

"Perhaps I should just take you back as a hostage. You might be useful."

The dark *seer* smiled, "You'll not be taking me anywhere. Perhaps, someday we'll have the opportunity to face each other in battle…but that day will not be today."

Raffe held the handle of his weapon inside his robes, "What is it that you want?"

"Did you pass along my message to your leaders?"

"It was discussed," smiled Raffe, sensing the jibe.

"And what was the conclusion?"

"That you're probably a renegade who covets Zepallo's power."

"That's true but at least I'd be predictable and, for the first time in our long history of confrontations, I have offered the possibility of negotiations."

"I'm not sure that I see how we could gain anything by having you in his place."

"I have his confidence and I have a plan that might benefit both sides."

"What guarantees could you possibly offer?"

"As things stand at the moment, I think we're approaching what the superpowers in the real world called 'mutually assured destruction.' In other words, if our forces continue to progress at their current rate, we'll both have the capacity to annihilate each other. An all-out war between us would certainly be the end of life as we know it."

Raffe opened his mouth to speak and then considered the sound behind the words that he just heard. He perceived assurance but found no trace of desperation in the tenor or cadence of the dark *seer's* voice. The sequence of thoughts had been carefully arranged to appeal to anyone dedicated to protecting the human race and the natural world.

"We're aware of your movements through the vectors and we've been watching, with absolute attention, to the gatherings of *seers* and Keepers from all over the planet. Whether your people and my people are working on the same projects is irrelevant. The ultimate product will be a weapon or some new way to destroy our enemies...yours and mine. At some point, we have to agree to disagree to create a treaty that will halt the lethal competition. These tools, in the hands of the people who live in the real world...well, you see what I mean."

"I do," said Raffe quietly, "but I still don't see why we'd want to risk anyone for your political ambitions. If you want him dead then you should be the one to kill him!"

Marcus smiled, "We both know that I'm a young talented *seer*, much like you and your comrades, and I understand that there is much to learn before I will truly be worthy of leading my people. If I am to have that chance…if we are to survive…then Zepallo must be stopped and there is only one person who has that power."

Raffe hesitated for a moment and then bowed to the dark *seer*, "There is no way that we will agree but I'll relay your message."

"That is all I can ask," said Marcus as he wrapped his cloak around his body and disappeared.

~

Adrian remained quiet, as Raffe recounted his second meeting with Marcus, and finally said, "What bothers me most, at the moment, is that he arrived on the island without detection. We're watching their vectors, why didn't we see him?"

"I don't know," replied the Professor, "but I'll look into it. Perhaps there are even more planes than we realized."

"I'm absolutely sure that there are but this means that they're using at least one that we know nothing about."

"I think that we should consult Master Jung. He knows far more than any of us about the planes."

~

The Thai Keeper sat motionless, a foot above a Persian carpet on top of an open space above the ceilings of the classrooms in the first dome. He was transfixed by the motion of water swirling past the glass barely ten feet above his head.

Adrian and Alius grabbed Ponte's elbows and levitated him to Master Jung's private meditation platform. Raffe landed softly beside them but the old Keeper turned in midair and settled back onto the carpet. "You are surprised that I can levitate?"

"We've been trying to teach some of our students in the regular school," replied Alius. "There's no reason why anyone couldn't learn, especially someone who is so attuned to the Powers."

Master Jung bowed his head and said quietly, "You have come to learn about the planes."

Adrian's mouth fell open, "How did you…?"

"Ah, that is too easy, my young *seer*," laughed Jung. "I am the expert in the group."

The young *seer* blushed, as Raffe patted him on the back. "I'm ashamed that I haven't come to you sooner."

"Orana told me that, when the time was right, you would require some instruction in these matters."

"There's something that is, perhaps, more immediate," said Ponte. "We've had a breach of security. A Dark Prince visited the island undetected by our sensors. We must assume that he is traveling on a plane that is beyond our understanding."

Master Jung motioned for Ponte and the *seers* to sit on the plush carpet. "Feel the texture. Try to run your fingers down through the pile. You can't because it is too thick. Peal up that corner and count the stitches that form the pattern on the front side. See the richness of the colors, the intricacy of the weave, and the binding along the edges."

Everyone stared at the old man.

"The point is that this object is not just a rug on the floor. It is far more intricate; its beauty arises not only from what we can see but what we know about how it was made…just as the planes that you know represent only a small portion of something much larger. You travel about the world through the plane of the positive vectors and, occasionally, you make a side trip into the world of the animals, but they are only two of many. You know that the Dark Forces use the plane of the dark vectors for transportation and communication but did you ever wonder how Zepallo can move about without showing up on your monitors? Of course, he's using another plane and they're using another set of planes to provide connections between the gaps in the dark vectors."

His guests listened intently, watching his eyes glisten and dance as the light weaving through the water surrounded the old man in a luminous pool of amber.

"Think of the planes as spheres of glass that surround the Earth. These bubbles intersect and overlap. They're not centered on the planet, so one plane might lean out towards the sun, while another is pulled to the moon as it orbits, while yet another might have the Earth in the smallest section of the globule and the rest is stretched far into space. They intersect and change shape constantly."

"Each is unique. Some are tied to the positive energies, some to the negative, while others are totally independent and powered by something far beyond our understanding or capacity."

"When Orana arrived on the island with the Crystal ships, we traveled through a plane the she liked to call The Tropics because the sky is the same shimmering blue-green as the waters of the Caribbean. Conveniently, it also acts as a funnel for the vector winds. Which brings me back to your original question. Certainly, the Dark Forces are using planes that we have yet to discover. Tell me, Professor, have you noticed any patterns in the frequencies that you use to monitor the planes, dark and light?"

The Professor pondered the question for a moment, "Yes, it seems that each is based on the square of a prime number."

"There you have it."

Ponte smiled, "It's got to be one of the primes that we haven't tried."

"I think you've found the solution to the problem."

"But there's more than that…" said Adrian.

"Oh, there is much more than that," said Master Jung. "I'll expect the three of you to call on me this evening and I will begin your training."

A voice called from the plaza below them, "Master, are you there?"

All the *seers* and Keepers leaned over the edge of the platform to find Madame Danali staring up at them expectantly.

"Good afternoon, Madame! How may I assist you?"

"Well, I…ah, Master Adrian, I do want to talk with you. Mrs. Tierney told me that you had employed her services to create a campaign to educate the population of the real world about the environmental catastrophe that awaits us all, if they do not change their ways! I believe that I could be of assistance."

Adrian smiled down at the little woman, who was dressed in flowing red robes that seemed a bit too large for her because the hem spread out on the floor around her feet. "I promised the animals that I would do everything possible to protect their world…or our world…"

"I understand completely. Why don't you and your friends join me? I'm beginning my first class this evening."

The young *seer* turned to look at Master Jung, who said quietly, "I believe that your first priority might be understanding a bit more about the planes before you become involved in saving the world from a self-inflicted demise."

Alius piped up, "I'll go. I'm rather interested in her perspective."

Adrian leaned over the edge again, "I'm sorry Madame Danali, I'm afraid that I'm committed this evening but Alius said that she would like to attend your class."

"Oh, lovely," smiled the tiny black woman. "Tell me, why are you all sitting next to the ceiling?"

Ponte laughed, "We just came up here to inspect the view. We'll be down directly!"

Raffe and Alius took The Professor's arms and slowly descended to the lobby. Master Jung reached a hand to touch Adrian before he followed, "I'll bring Master Chi and Sky. Come to my chambers at eight o'clock."

"I appreciate your time."

"Time is a very relevant commodity. Sometimes there is too much of it and at others there is too little."

~

The air was thin at the summit of the snow-covered mountain. Several of the elder members of the small group, gathered at the chalet, were laboring to breath in the lean atmosphere, although they would not complain to their comrades. To show any sign of weakness was to invite an early retirement from the inner circle of *seers* and Keepers who were invited to the Dark Lord's conferences.

"Our experiment at the pole was not quite a success and, yet, not a complete failure either. I must blame myself for underestimating the vigilance and resourcefulness of our foes but we've gained untold knowledge about their defenses."

Cadeau attempted to interrupt with a comment on the technological trap that had been set but sat quietly, cowering, after Zepallo deflated his enthusiasm with a dark stare. "We proved that our system is functional, if not complete, and that the Forces of Light can be counted on to react with the sum of their technologies. Our Keepers have moved ahead, while they are years behind but I would not be foolish enough to discount their creativity."

The attendees nodded their agreement as he continued, pacing around a blazing inferno within a stone hearth at the center of the circular room, passing Beta and Gamma, who stood apart from the others. "According to our accountants, we are expanding our holdings, step by step, industry by industry, and within a relatively short period of time, we will control most of the key players in the financial world. Our Whisperers are deeply invested in the power centers of the political, religious, and social world and our armies are expanding. There is only one force that stands in our way."

Marcus raised his hand, "With the rapid technological developments and the expansion of our influence in the real world, do we really need to waste our energy combating an enemy that may well become irrelevant in the not too distant future?"

"They will never become irrelevant! They are dedicated to protecting the natural world and they will fight to the last to fulfill their commitment."

Lord Petry interrupted, "We have several accounts of the death of Orana, when she collided with one of the saucers as it crash-landed on the ice. Their chain of command is surely disrupted."

"They do not depend on the strength of one old woman," snarled Zepallo. "She is the past. Adrian and his friends are the future. They're smart, cunning, talented, and dangerous. We will not succeed until they've been eliminated."

There was silence in the group, as each contemplated the powers of the very young Adrian, who foiled their plans and injured their leader on more than one occasion. The invasion of Morgan's Knot cost them dearly and none of this clique were anxious to repeat that mistake.

Cadeau raised his hand, hesitantly, "We've been monitoring their movements through the vectors and, until recently, there has been a continuous flow of *seers* and, one might assume, Keepers to Morgan's Knot beginning immediately after the battle at the pole. In the past few weeks, that number has diminished to almost nothing."

Regis added, "They are organizing themselves for the first time in history."

"Then there is even more reason to consider our options and to move boldly to eliminate their threat before it becomes an insurmountable obstacle," smiled the Dark Lord. "The island is home to a pair of Crystals and it is one of the only places on the planet where the opposing Gems have been harnessed together."

Beta mused, "There is an opportunity for us in their unique situation. Perhaps there's a backdoor into their systems?"

"We'll explore that possibility," added Gamma, "but history shows that they have always reacted to our advances rather than taking the initiative. I do not underestimate their abilities or their dedication but I doubt their capacity to react to so many technological advances all at once. Combined with our expanding assets and the integration of our people in so many power points, I believe that they'll be overwhelmed by the sheer mass of our efforts."

"Well put, young man," replied Jarvus. "The point is that our options to deal with the Forces of Light are limited by our inability to monitor their progress, to see what's happening on that island to gain some insight into their intentions and preparations."

"The population of the island is too small to insert a spy and, like us, they're monitoring the frequencies as well as their environment," said Regis.

"If there is a back door through the Dark Crystal on Morgan's Knot, we'll know everything they're doing," said Gamma.

"Focus on their movements and communications," instructed Zepallo. "Find out what materials are being imported from the mainland. We have people who will supply that information. They've been trying to disrupt our financial assets. Let's investigate their fledgling empire starting with the foundation that took control of World Oil. And finally, let's zero in on every other Positive Crystal on the planet. They've enlisted every *seer* and Keeper, perhaps there's a weak link.

In addition, I want construction of our new facilities to move ahead as quickly as possible. The first phase of the network will be complete within a few weeks. When all of our forces are ready, we'll commence our next campaign. In the meantime, let's try another little experiment."

~

Mighty storm clouds billowed up in the east and settled over the island, dropping torrents of rain that washed out the paths, making transportation all but impossible. Completion of the fifth and sixth domes would slow if supplies and materials could not be delivered from the foundry on schedule.

Ponte and Sammy consulted the international weather reports and found that the satellite images showed clear skies for hundreds of miles around the island with the exception of a tiny squall stalled over Morgan's Knot.

"Well, we might guess that this is another demonstration by the Dark Forces to slow our progress. Dadeus is downstairs checking the instruments," sighed Ponte, as he took a seat on the sofa next to the fireplace. He turned to Sammy, "Let's see whether Sir Isaac can create a portal large enough to move our steel beams from Samuel's to the interface of the fourth dome."

"I'll see to it," smiled the young Jamaican.

"Meantime, it's time for you to go to your meeting with Master Jung," said The Professor to Adrian. "Council's meeting in the morning."

"Oh, you're right. I'll be late if I don't hurry!" Adrian stood up, closed his eyes, and slipped into the vectors. Moments later, he was standing before the third door on the third balcony of the third dome in front of Master Jung's studio. As he reached to knock, the door opened and Sky bowed formally and stepped back to allow him to enter, "Welcome."

"It's nice to see you," said Adrian, hugging the tiny *seer*.

Master Chi was seated on a large pillow before a round table with a blue flame lapping from a hole in the center, three white lilies stood in a slender vase, a perfectly round orange, and seven slender panes of what appeared to be clear glass stood on edge in a row.

Master Jung was seated on another pillow and bowed to the young *seer.* His quarters were unlike any of the other rooms in the domes. *Orbs* on the outside of the structure illuminated sea creatures that slipped out of the dark waters and swam through the blue-green iridescence that filled the room in reflection. Tiers of candles burned in the corners and there was a faint hint of jasmine incense. Two tall palms stood like sentries before the curved window and, aside from the table and plump pillows piled on a large carpet, there were no other furnishings in the apartment.

Sky settled next to Adrian, as Master Chi began to speak. "Each of the Keepers and each of the *seers*, who have joined us, has some unique knowledge or ability. Ours, the three of us," he said gesturing around the table, "happens to be the mysteries of the planes."

Master Jung continued, "Orana, and Lyra before her, felt that by maintaining independent groups to protect each of the Crystals without revealing their existence, let alone their identities, they could protect the majority of believers. She alone kept and protected the secrets. The lessons that you learned at her hand were unique to you. Ours have always been about the unseen world and the powers that exist there."

Sky reached over and touched Adrian's arm, "There is so much more…"

Master Chi pointed at the orange, which rose into shimmering air above the flame in the center of the table, spinning slowly.

Master Jung said, "Let us assume that this is the Earth. It is almost round and we'll also say that the surface of the orange is the first plane. The plane of the real world."

The old *seer* pointed at the first sheet of glass standing upright on the table. It lifted gently, flipping over and over, until it floated above the orange. Slowly the corners began to droop and soon formed a delicate sphere surrounding the orange.

"This is the second plane, the one that we use every day for communication and moving about the world...but remember the first rule of the Powers, for every positive, there is also an equal and opposite negative. Perhaps it might be easier to understand as having two sides...an inside and an outside. We use one plane while the Dark Forces use the reverse." Pointing to the globe, he said, "This is a representation of the changes over time."

The surface of the sphere of glass became transparent in some spots and sooty gray in others with murky areas in between. There was no pattern in the ever-changing swells that expanded and contracted before slithering around the globe to coalesce in a new position.

"While this is only a demonstration, you can see that, over time, the ebb and flow of the Powers has moved back and forth from one side to the other. The waves of energy are generated by the Crystals scattered around the world and transmitted on the vectors extending out into the plane from each."

A second sheet of glass twirled through air and splintered into long slender shards that formed a black web around the first. "This is the plane that the Dark Forces are using to channel their energies."

Master Chi pointed at another piece of glass that changed to a deep green, as it soared above the orange within the globe. It melted to form an egg-shaped bubble that wrapped around the inner sphere, the narrow end pointing towards the sun, just below the horizon.

"This is the plane of the animals, which gathers a little more energy from sunlight than the real world."

A blue pane of glass sliced through the first three and reached in the opposite direction towards the moon. It was larger and more elongated than the others.

"This is the first of the spiritual planes. Orana told me that you could hear along the vectors. Is that true?"

"Yes, although I'm beginning to see and, sometimes, I feel sensations from the vibrations."

Sky smiled, "And those visions and feelings can be overwhelming."

Adrian turned to her, "There's a tone that is the sound of life disrupted by the grating of the dark energies and the cries of death and anguish. Recently, I've been feeling those things and seeing flashes of the carnage…"

The two Masters glanced each other. "Then you've begun the journey that will lead to true understanding," said Master Chi. "It is a long and painful passage but it is the only way to comprehend all that you must know. That is why we are called *seers*."

"You must also understand that it is not within your power to eliminate the suffering of humanity," said Sky quietly, "but you do have the opportunity to begin, to take the first steps along a twisted crossing into the promise of what the world might be. We're all with you because Orana told all of us that you and you alone would see the path."

Adrian almost whispered, "How will I know?"

"You'll learn everything you can from all of the other *seers*, their talents, their tricks…the way they use the powers, and each piece that you add will expand your understanding tenfold. We all have similar sensations, but you're beginning to see…to truly see across the planes…not one but at least two and perhaps more, if I'm not mistaken?"

"I never thought about it but you're right. I can see in the plane of the real world, in our plane, and into the plane of the animals…and I've seen into the plane of the Dark Forces. I've seen Zepallo and his clones several times."

"Have you found Orana's energy?" inquired Master Jung.

"How did you know?"

Masters Jung and Chi smiled, "You're seeing into the plane of the spirit, so you've just added another."

Adrian bowed his head. He found it hard to comprehend how these abilities revealed themselves when, less than three years ago, he had been an ordinary kid who lived in a house by the bay and wanted, more than anything, to sail to Vancouver with his parents on their sloop, The Sparrow.

Silver glimmered off another piece of glass molting into a long tube that curled and twisted into itself, like a tangled metallic snake devouring its own tail. "This is the plane of time. It does not move forward and it does not move backward. This is all the time that there ever was or ever will be...it's infinite and yet confined. As you can see, there are places where time overlaps itself, where it is more than one time in the same space, while there are other areas where there doesn't seem to be time at all."

"I'm not sure that I understand."

Master Jung smiled, "Orana told me that you met yourself as a very old man. How could that be?"

"I assumed that it was an illusion."

"It was very real," replied Master Chi. "Your friend, Kelly, has a watch that takes advantage of this twist in time."

Adrian smiled, "I understand."

"Good, then there are two more. Another pane of glass hovered around the others, a deformed molten glob, issuing hisses of noxious gases from the fires burning inside. This is the plane that contains all the evil, the suffering and destruction...death and war, starvation and cruelty...all the things that life must endure in its struggle to survive. This is the plane that opens during those times when you feel the sensations."

Master Chi pointed and the final sheet of glass turned golden and stretched to form a sphere that encompassed all the others. It grew until it was so thin that the faintest human breath would surely shatter its delicate beauty, quivering and shimmering with a warm glow that might have blessed the dawning of life itself.

"This represents what I like to call 'Hope.' This is the plane that contains the very essence of life, the energy that is transformed into living beings and the place where that energy returns when it has finished. The tone that you have been hearing is a harmony of sounds that spring from this sphere. Many of your powers pass from one plane to another but they all start here."

Master Jung gestured to the orange within the layers of glass, glittering like a gemstone. "This is only a demonstration. There are hundreds of layers, each bearing a unique identity and a distinct set of characteristics. When there is time, we will train you to use some of them."

"Is it possible to move about in other planes?"

"Of course, it is," replied Master Chi. "You've passed through the plane of the animals and, during your training, I assume that you visited others."

"I never really thought about where I was, I just assumed that it was a vision planted in my mind."

"No," smiled Master Jung, "Each of the places that you visited were in different planes."

Adrian pondered the realization for a moment, "That explains a lot of things that didn't really make sense at the time."

"You probably had other things on your mind," laughed Sky.

"Was your Master like Orana?"

"He was one of Orana's honor students. I'm sure that he trained me just as she trained you."

"Only different…" snickered the young *seer.*

Masters Jung and Chi stood. "That will end our first lesson. There is a council meeting in the morning and there will be many things that will require our attention. We'll create an opportunity to continue this discussion but, in the meantime, use this time to learn from the others, to strengthen your powers and your will. We all believe that time is running short and something will happen before we can prepare."

"I'll meet with the other *seers* after the session in the morning…and thank you for taking the time to introduce me to the planes."

"It is our pleasure to share our knowledge with you," said Master Chi, as he patted Adrian on the shoulder.

Sky took his arm and escorted him to the door, "I'll see you in the morning."

Chapter Eight

Adrian opened his eyes to the gloom of heavy clouds and dull moldy light molting through the tree outside his bedroom window. He had not slept in his own bed for days and he rolled over to savor the warmth and comfort of his favorite teddy bear. Presently, he padded to the bathroom, took a shower, and found clean robes in his closet.

He met the twins in the hallway, "I haven't seen you in days!"

Molly and Megan hugged him, "We're easy to find, which is more than we can say for you!"

"I'm sorry. It's just that there's so much going on."

"That's alright, we understand," said Megan. "We've been busy too, helping with the construction and moving things into the domes."

"You might want to take a moment to see Morgan. She misses you," added Molly.

Adrian blushed, "I will. Let's see what's for breakfast."

They scrambled down the stairs and dropped their *orbs* in the caddy to find Elsie and Sara serving platters of eggs, fish, fried potatoes, fresh fruit, and sticky buns, just as John and George came in from the barn.

Adrian sniffed the aromas, "Ah, that smells so good."

"It's been a long time since we all sat together for a meal," smiled Sara, as she hugged her son and kissed him on the forehead. "Now sit down while it's hot."

"The council meeting begins at nine," said George. "Jofre told us that they want to move the construction schedule up."

Adrian nodded, as he stuffed a large piece of sticky bun in his mouth, and mumbled, "It's the Dark Forces."

John laughed, "The Dark Forces want us to speed up our construction?"

"No, no..." said Adrian, struggling to swallow, "We all think that they're planning something and there's no time to waste."

"We're moving as fast as we can, in spite of this blasted weather."

"That's their doing too," said Adrian, attempting to take another bite of his warm roll.

"I might have guessed," said George. "I'm sure that Ponte and his friends will explain all of this at the meeting."

"I'm sure he will," said Adrian. "We found out that the battle at the pole was a test of their systems…and our defenses."

Everyone stared at him for a moment before Elsie said, "Do you mean that all of those who were lost in that battle, were merely expendable, like pawns in a game of chess?"

Adrian looked into her blue eyes, "That's exactly what I mean. They're very close to harnessing all of the dark vectors and they wanted to know what our forces would do if they decided to use that power. The hurricane, the melting of the ice, and the flooding were experiments using part of their energy. The next time, they'll use all of it."

"I see why Ponte has called a council meeting," said John.

"Add the fact that they're expanding their holdings in the financial world, that they have moles buried deep inside the political, military, and religious centers of the world, and the threat suddenly becomes much larger."

Sara put an arm around her son, "Does this mean that you're off on another of your missions?"

"I wouldn't know where to go," said Adrian. "We don't know enough."

"I think you forgot to add the word 'yet' to that sentence," added his mother.

"I've been instructed to begin learning from all of the other *seers,* so I can be better prepared when the time comes."

"And it will come," sighed Sara. "That's what I'm afraid of…"

"Let's deal with what we have in front of us," said John. "It's far more likely that they'll find a way to attack us than the other way around."

"That's the point, I think, that we don't know their strategy, so all we can do is continue developing our plan."

~

The leaves of the great round table in the third dome rose from the floor to accommodate one hundred chairs. Additional seating had been arranged around the circumference of the enormous space and there were few open seats when Adrian and his family arrived at 8:30. *Seers* hovered in mid-air and Keepers gathered in small clusters discussing the current challenges in hushed tones.

Alius waved from the far side of the table and pointed at seats that she was saving for everyone. This council brought together representatives whose responsibilities covered every facet of this multilayered endeavor. Adrian led the clan around the huge table, greeting friends, Keepers, and *seers* along the way.

Just before they reached their seats, Adrian spied Morgan standing alone in an alcove in the curved wall of the room. He excused himself and walked up to her, "I'm sorry I haven't seen you in a while. I've been really busy but that's not really an excuse…"

"I know we all make demands on you. We talked about that on the way back from the Island of the Children, if I remember correctly." She gestured with graceful hands and moved closer, which only reminded Adrian that she was still taller. Her eyes sparkled and her lips curled into a knowing smile.

"Do you know that I've thought about that moment and the things you said to me so many times when I doubted myself. You gave me the strength to see it through."

Morgan smiled and tilted her head forward as she looked into his eyes, as if she was looking up at him. "I've missed you."

"And I've missed you too. I don't know what's coming next but I'll find the time to see you soon. I promise."

Morgan hugged him, as Ponte rang an old school bell to bring the meeting to order, and kissed him on the lips. Adrian pulled away, smiling, and stumbled to his seat.

The Professor began, "I thank you all for coming on such short notice. I understand that each of you has tasks and responsibilities that demand your time, so I'll make this short and to the point."

The rumbling of whispered conversations and the shuffling of the audience subsided.

"Within the past few days, we've learned several startling new pieces of information that concern us all. The first is that Zepallo is firmly in control of his forces, with the exception of a band of phantom mutineers who have contacted us in a quest to seek our assistance in taking out their leader for them."

The crowd laughed.

"You think that I'm joking? I am not."

An embarrassed silence shrouded the hundreds gathered in the vast room.

"The second point is that, despite our best efforts and the help of the whales, the production of clones continues in a new location. Which brings me to another interesting realization, that being that the Dark Forces are constructing new facilities near Black Crystals around the globe. We must assume that their network will ring the planet if their progress continues unimpeded."

There were murmurs and comments among the Keepers around the table and in the gallery.

"The final and most intriguing bit of information is that the battle at the pole, the melting of the polar ice, and the hurricane that ravaged the southern coast of the United States were merely demonstrations." He let the thought settle for a moment before continuing, "It was all a trap to see how we would react and, in response, we gave them a demonstration of our best effort. Unfortunately, they were only using part of their potential power and we would be well advised to redouble our efforts. We know they'll make another try. The question is…how soon?"

Sir Isaac stood, "Perhaps we would be well advised to assist the rebels!"

Everyone laughed, until Ponte raised his hand and said, "There is an old proverb, 'Know thine enemy.' Zepallo is a frightful, yet known, quantity simply because we've seen his tactics and we know that his motivation is driven by an insatiable belief that he will rule the world. To be so focused on a single goal is to miss opportunities, as he has demonstrated in the past. There is no reason to believe that whoever takes his throne will be any less demonic." He paused and turned to Adrian, who was seated on his right, "The only person who has any chance of defeating the Dark Lord is seated at this table and we would not, could not risk his life to settle political strife for our opposition."

Adrian could feel hundreds of pairs of eyes staring at him. He felt like the king who wore no clothes, as if everyone could see right through him.

Master Chi stood, "We must face these various threats individually. There is the problem of the dark vectors and I would suggest that Master Jung might join with you, Nanchez, and Dadeus to form a working committee to seek a solution. Every Keeper in the world is ready and willing to assist in any way they can."

George added, "Just as we can't drop a spy into their midst, neither can they know what we're planning. Perhaps we should give them a subtle hint that we're on the verge of a new technology or a new weapon, even if we don't have one. We can certainly provide them with a reason to hesitate before they move into the next phase of their aggression."

Ponte smiled, "A sleigh of hand? I find that intriguing but we still face the prospect of being prepared when their assault comes."

Madame Danali rose. She was barely taller than the table but her voice carried throughout the room, "I believe that we are misguided if we do not address our weakest and most vulnerable assets. The melting of the polar ice demonstrated that they're using not only the vectors but other planes and the Earth itself. This storm that is hovering over the island is further evidence and we must assume that they are trying to monitor and disrupt our progress."

Dadeus added, "Our instruments show that they created the storm and are directing it from someplace in North Korea. Thus far, our efforts to overcome those energies have failed because we do not, yet, have access to the plane that they are using. I would hope, with the talent available, that we will find a solution within a few days."

The African woman continued, "Thank you. As witnessed during the battle at the pole and the invasion here on Morgan's Knot, the Dark Forces have created new technologies and new weapons. They have a regimented fighting force and, if we are correct, someday, those armies will be populated with clones of the Dark Lord himself.

We were victorious, not because our weapons were superior, rather because we were fortunate enough to have an army of believers, some young heroes, and a gallery of talented and dedicated Keepers. Don't you see, our strength is grounded in our belief in The Balance."

Simian stood, his bright yellow robes glowed in the soft radiance spilling down through the silver waters above the dome, "My friends, we've taken several giant steps in the past few months. We are far more organized than at any time in our history. The knowledge of our ancestors is being merged so that we might use every weapon at our disposal in defense of The Powers. Our *seers* are learning from each other and our network of communications is nearing completion but there is still so much more to do before we're ready to stand against the enemy with any reasonable chance of success. Perhaps, more to the point, we're the only force that stands between the population of the world and the darkness that will descend across the planet, should we fail."

Chancellor Bartlett strode into the room, followed by Colburn Tierney, and walked around the table to take seats next to The Professor, "I do apologize for being late!" Everyone stood and applauded. "Although the weapons of the real world are of little consequence against the Dark Forces, the leaders of the free world have been informed of the multi-level threat and I have solicited their help to maintain some control over the maneuverings of international corporations that are being used to move financial markets across the globe. In addition, Mrs. Tierney and her firm are working on an educational campaign that will strive to reach every citizen of the world with a message of hope and truth."

He scanned the faces around the circular slab, "Many of you participated in the original agreement that we reached months ago and I believe we'd be wise to pursue the course agreed upon at that time. What can we do to defeat the Dark Forces while, at the same time, carrying our message and the promise of The Balance to the citizens of the world?"

Shambala untangled herself from her perch in mid-air and extended her long legs to stand, head and shoulders above the former President, "Sir, I do not mean to interrupt but, as Madame Danali said, our strength is based in our conviction, in our belief in the Powers. Our enemies might have more troops and far more sophisticated weapons but, as we have proved so many times over the past few years, their weakness is a product of their linear leadership and the aura of fear. Everything is decided from the top down, while we have always worked in small dedicated and independent groups, so we can expand and contract as fate demands. As history has proven, so many times, a grand army can be defeated by guerilla raids. I believe that we should build on our strengths, not on our perception of the threat of the enemy that we are sure to face."

Bartlett turned and looked up into the tall black woman's beautiful eyes, "How is it possible for so much wisdom to come from someone so young?"

Shambala blushed, "I am only stating the obvious."

"Well put, young lady." The Chancellor turned to the audience overflowing the room, "It would be easy to panic, to spend so much time and energy anticipating what the enemy might do that we miss the opportunity to do the things that will guarantee our position. Those tasks have been delegated and those who have taken responsibility...whether constructing the domes...and that includes all of the people of this island who have provided labor, nourishment, lodging, tools, and friendship to all of us...organizing the classes that are just beginning, or tracking the movements on the vectors and merging the technologies. Everyone is contributing and we will continue."

There was applause from the crowd before he raised his hands. "From what we've learned, it would seem that there are several new avenues that need to be explored and I'm sure that we have ample talent to find solutions to the problems at hand. We must remain vigilant but we can't lose sight of our objective or our purpose. Before we get on with the technical aspects of the council, I would like our attorney, Colburn Tierney, to say a few words that should be of interest."

Coke stood and took a moment to peruse the gallery, which included hundreds of people...some hanging in mid-air, others looking as if they had stepped from the pages of history or some novel of wizards and dragons. He noticed several young children, who appeared to understand everything that was happening around them. It was the cast of some futuristic science fiction thriller, except all of these characters were real heroes.

He smiled, "I must say that I am honored to be here. I'm certainly in awe of the things that happen in your world and the people who fight to control these forces for every living creature on the planet.

As many of you probably already know, I run the Crystal Foundation which is funded by the inheritance that young Adrian received from his grandfather and by the gold and gems collected from the Crystals around the world. This organization was established in reaction to the growing influence of the Dark Forces in the financial markets and key industries, without which the real world would grind to a halt.

I'm new to the island and to the wonders of The Balance. There's much that I want to learn and even more that I'd like to contribute to the cause but, for the moment, my expertise and contacts are of more value.

Our first effort, after the hurricane disrupted oil production and transportation in the southern United States, was to gain a controlling interest in World Oil, the largest energy company on the planet...which used to be controlled by representatives of the Dark Forces. Through information collected by John's father, we know that they are acquiring companies in other vital industries...weapons manufacturing, aerospace contractors, electrical companies, food production and distribution, and even the water supply in many countries in South America. The list goes on for hundreds of pages and we're moving to offset and disrupt their investments wherever possible.

Within the past few weeks, the markets have moved higher at an alarming rate. When you invest in the stock market in the real world, you make money when it moves up but you lose money when it goes down. The only reason that the market goes up is because there is demand for shares of stock that are owned by somebody who wants more than the current value. There are two reasons why this volatility should be of concern to us. The first is, who on the planet has the capacity to invest sums so large, in ten or twelve different stock markets, that they move the average for all of the stocks bought and sold each day? The second is why? I'll offer two possibilities…either the group behind this movement is buying up shares with the intention of selling them all off at once, when they hit the top of the market…which would cause the value of all stocks to plummet…worldwide, which would cause panic at the very least and a great depression is not entirely out of the question…or…they're buying controlling interest in those industries that are most vital to the stability of the real world."

He paused for a moment, expecting a question. There were none. Everyone was paying absolute attention. "Considering what we've all learned about the suspected intentions of the Dark Forces, I believe the second possibility is more frightening than the first. They've been investing their black diamonds in the world markets for nearly one-hundred years but this is the first time that they've ventured so boldly to control supply and demand for everyone in the real world. This is a weapon against which no bomb, no magic, no single person can stand. It is a challenge that will continue for years to come and, when one entity…one company owns controlling interest in the most vital industries, the world's financial stability becomes dependent on the singular goals of the few.

The Crystal Foundation employs hundreds of people who are, secretly, dedicated to your cause. Each of them is doing their very best to find a way to inhibit the enterprises of the Dark Forces, because we all know that panic and desperation in the real world is their opportunity to take control. We can not let that happen," the attorney looked around the room. "Are there any questions?"

Sir Isaac stood up, "You have explained these complicated matters in language that even we can understand. Every effort will be made to accelerate our collections from the stones for this endeavor and we all thank you for your dedication and expertise."

Coke blushed, said "Thank you," and sat down.

The council continued for two hours, before smaller groups moved through the domes to address particular issues. Adrian followed Alius and Simian through the crowd to the smaller dome, where a large group of *seers* were meeting.

Alius avoided looking directly at Adrian, "I think you should lead this discussion, Simian. You know far more than either of us and, besides, there's a certain respect that goes with being old…er."

Simian laughed, "And I thought that you might be one of my favorite students. I can see that I'll have to give that some additional consideration. Besides, they'll want to hear from the two of you."

Adrian caught up, "I agree with Alius. You lead the discussion and we'll contribute whatever we can."

Simian put a yellow-robed arm around his two protégés, "I don't remember life before I had to worry about the two of you! I am sure that it was far more simple."

They entered the airlock to the small dome to find *seers* dressed in robes in a rainbow of colors. Since the gathering after the battle, *seers* and Keepers copied the style and adapted it to their native customs. They brought bolts of fabrics to Sara and the ladies at the tailor shop with requests for additional garments and many of the visitors were being fitted for diving suits.

A hush rolled across the crowd and then polite applause. Adrian and Alius took seats near the pit in the center of the sphere, while Simian turned in a circle to scan the crowd. "I see that we are well represented and I thank you all for participating in this discussion. Each of us carries with us a unique set of talents and abilities. These are the tools that have allowed us to contribute and to survive and we must find a way to share them with each other."

There were nods of approval.

"The schedule for our classes is ready and while you might be teaching in one class, you will also be a student in others. None of us…not you," he said pointing to individuals in the crowd and then to himself, "and not me, knows enough to stand alone against our enemies. We are stronger when we can depend on each other. If you don't know the person next to you, introduce yourself. That person might save your life in the next battle!"

Quiet murmurs rolled around the room, as the *seers* greeted each other. Adrian gazed at the crowd, which was amazingly diverse. There were old *seers* and youngsters who could not have been more than six or seven, male and female, tall, short, thin, fat, quiet and boisterous, and each had some distinctive tell about their appearance. There was a slender girl with olive skin and black hair in a thick braid down her back who was dressed in saffron robes and wore a single red gem on her forehead. Next to her was a powerfully built young man of, perhaps eighteen or twenty, who had his hair styled into purple spikes that stood straight up above his shaved head. Maze and Lala floated in mid-air, their little hats slightly askew, tittering with each other beside Master Chi, who seemed the wise ancient of the group. There were several Native American Indians who wore a single eagle's feather from a beaded band around their brows. Africans sat with Asians, Europeans with *seers* from South America. The group that encircled the sphere could stand as a portrait of mankind through the ages and each bore some insight, some secret that might save The Balance.

Simian turned to him, "I'd like to introduce Adrian, whom most of you already know."

An English lad called out, "He's been up against the Dark Lord himself! Tell us about that!"

Adrian looked up at the boy and replied, "The only thing that I'll say about that is that I am lucky to be alive and the only reason I can find for that accomplishment was that I believed in all that we hold to be right and true, so intensely, that he could not defeat me. Each of you already has that weapon in your arsenal. Don't forget to use it when the time comes."

"There's more to it than that," said the English boy.

"Certainly, there's more to it than that…facing Zepallo, without understanding that he's the most evil, fearsome, and accomplished *seer* on the planet is suicidal at best! You'll face death, whether you survive or not!" shouted Adrian. "Understand me! I was lucky! I fought a grown man, a *seer* with years of experience and many more weapons at his disposal. He can control the environment with his mind. He can shoot a fatal charge from the tip of his finger. He can reach inside you and know your innermost secrets and fears and twist your perception of reality until you're lost and confused. The only thing that I had that he lacked was that I believed not only in myself but in our cause.

I fought for my survival and almost died but when I considered all that is at stake...all that we are defending, I knew that I could not let them win." He paused, "At those moments when tactics must be decided or the instant when you know you must fight, I always have the same final thought, 'There is no other choice,' because there really is no other choice. The true path has revealed itself. I believe that one absolute truth is enough to guide each of us to fulfill our responsibilities and our destinies."

Alius walked over and stood next to Adrian, "I've been in battle with him and for him. Many of you have faced the Dark Forces and survived. Something that you did or something that you knew within yourself allowed you to be victorious. Those are the things that we must share with each other in a regimented fashion. That's the point of the classes. None of us is a complete *seer* but, together, we might all reach that goal."

Master Chi floated to the center of the chamber, "I see that we have a rather broad range of maturity in this room from the very young," he said, pointing to a young girl with soft red ringlets around a pale white face, "to the very old...and I must include myself in that category...each of us has something to offer and something to learn. Let us undertake this task together."

The *seers*, who had been floating around the room, descended to stand with the other *seers* circling the four at the center. The old Master pointed to Sky, "M'dear would you collect the youngest members? We will assess your abilities and design a course of instruction that will allow you to work with the others in this room."

Adrian noticed a boy of, perhaps nine or ten, walk over to Sky. The bangs of his white hair hung down over piercing electric blue eyes and he seemed a bit hesitant about where he should go. *"It wasn't that long ago that I was that boy. At least he understands and has a chance to learn from the rest of us,"* he thought.

To his right, he noticed a familiar woman with her young son, who might have been three or four. He suddenly realized that she was Suzanne, the young woman who helped with Raffe's rescue in New York. Her son was Tiffin and he had only been a newborn when they first met. Alius' hunch that he might be a *seer* proved correct.

"The remainder will divide into seven groups. Each will be representative of this assemblage with a broad range of ages and experience. If you have friends in this room, find a group that does not include them. Do not choose one of the people that I am about to call to guide you to meet in smaller groups. They will not necessarily be your instructors. Raffe, would you take the first group, Mary the second, Shambala, Simian, Alius, Adrian, and I will take the last."

The seven formed up into a circle at the center of the room, as the crowd moved around into clusters of bodies that swelled up the ramps like the petals of a flower, opening to the dull blue glow tracing through the water above them.

Sky led the children to one of the laboratories that had been installed in the third dome. There they would be gauged on their level of sophistication and assigned to advanced classes that would allow them to expand their skills and their understanding of the Powers, so that they might contribute to the larger groups.

The seven groups followed their guides to theaters and classrooms throughout the domes. Each would have access to every part of the facilities, except the observatory. Ponte and the other Keepers decided that there had to be a place where they could work without interruption.

Chapter Nine

Martina Tierney sat alone at her desk in a sleek modern office that overlooked lights skittering across the Potomac, staring at the large prints tacked to the walls and taped from the floor to ceiling on the windows. Hundreds of ideas had been synthesized down to several dozen, with variations that might appeal to different cultures around the world. The message was so simple…yet convincing the citizens of the world to accept their responsibilities, let alone the potential disaster that would result from their indifference, added another layer to the challenge.

She was startled out of her thoughts by a whooshing sound, as a very tall, black-robed man appeared before her desk. He bowed formally and pushed back the cowl of his robes to reveal a chiseled face with deep hauntingly eyes that burned with an intensity that she found thoroughly frightening.

"How may I help you?" she inquired coldly, from her seat behind her desk.

"I believe it is I who might help you, M'lady," smiled the Dark Lord.

"I assume that you know who I am but I'm afraid that I am at a loss…"

"Oh, but I'm sure that you know me by reputation. Allow me to introduce myself, I am Zepallo, Lord of the Council of Ollapez."

Martina gasped.

"I understand that you have a new client who has engaged your firm to produce a global campaign to save the natural world. I would suggest that you fire your client."

"Why would I do that?"

"Because I will hire you for far more money."

"That is not my only reason for working for any client. I have to believe in the message."

"I understand that you have family still living in Cuba, is that correct? And I know that you have a daughter, son-in-law, and two adorable grand-daughters who live not far from here."

"What are you saying?"

"That you would be wise to accept my offer…for the protection of your…family," smiled the Dark Lord. "I can offer you that protection…"

"Get out of my office!" screamed the raven-haired beauty, as she stood and threw a paperweight in his direction.

"Ah, I'm pleased to see that you have spirit. I like that in a woman," smiled the dark *seer* as he grabbed the glass ornament from mid-air and placed it gently on the edge of the desk. "Spirit is one thing, common sense is another. I trust that you are one of those fortunate few who possesses both?"

"What is it that you want?"

"I want this campaign to end before it begins," he said, pointing with the index finger of his right hand at a poster hanging on the window to his left. A blast sizzled across the room and shredded the paper, leaving smoldering embers smoking on the carpet. "In a few weeks, there will be another promotion that will need your attention. Your firm will be paid handsomely and I'm sure that they'll make a splendid job of selling the message that will be delivered to you."

"And if I decline your…proposal?"

"Then there can be no guarantees concerning the safety of your loved ones."

"I will have to consider my options," replied Martina.

"You have no options, my dear woman. This is life or death. Your choice!" He bowed again, "I would suggest that you pass this message along to your husband. The Crystal Foundation is an inconvenience, a thorn in my side. Pursuing their current line of investments might well endanger the life of his lovely wife. I'm sure that he loves you, so I must assume that he'll understand my simple suggestion. I could have killed you, perhaps more easily than poor old Sir Jonathon, but, instead, I'll bid you adieu. Until we meet again!"

Before she could reply, he pointed with his right hand and a blast ran across the carpet, up the wall, and across the ceiling leaving a smoldering image of a writhing snake with flames erupting from its mouth. He swirled his black robes and disappeared. Her whole body was shaking, as she lifted the receiver on the telephone and pressed the first button on her speed dial. "Coke?"

~

The telephone startled him. It was three o'clock in the morning and he was worried about his wife, who had finally fallen asleep on his shoulder.

He picked up the receiver, "Yes."

His eyes grew wider, as he listened to the voice on the other end of the line, "I understand. Thank you." He hung up the phone and settled back into his pillows with a long sigh.

Martina had been roused from her sleep, "Was that Adrian?"

"No. It was security from your office building. There was a fire, which was confined to your offices. There's nothing left," he hugged her and kissed her on the forehead. "I'm so sorry."

"That bastard," shrieked Martina, as she sat straight up in bed, tears running down her cheeks, "He didn't kill me but he destroyed everything that I've created!"

"I'm sorry I got you into this," whispered her husband, as he stroked her back.

"You didn't get me into anything. I joined because I believe that these people are the only ones who have a chance against the Dark Forces. A year ago, I wouldn't have believed any of this but now the threat has become very personal. We have to find a way to protect the kids and our granddaughters, because now I have something to fight for besides principle…the people that I love most in the world have been threatened. Call Adrian. I want to talk with them!"

She got up, slipped into her dressing gown, and headed for the closet to find something to wear. "We can be there in an hour."

~

Adrian was waiting when Coke and Martina stepped through the portal to the lobby of the second dome, amid a torrent of bodies rushing from laboratories to classrooms to meetings. Some walked quickly, the *seers* flew, and the sphere felt as if it had been overtaken by a swarm of frenzied bees. A sense of urgency and mission had overtaken the facility in the past few weeks, replacing the orderly pace of construction.

He could see that they were distressed and hugged Martina, then his attorney. "From our brief conversation, I interpreted your message to mean that you'd been visited by the Dark Lord himself. Is that correct?"

Martina nodded, "I'm so mad, I'd take him on single-handedly! I don't react well to intimidation."

Adrian laughed, "Well, I'm glad we've got past that…now, he is a frightening man, a powerful *seer*, and, perhaps, the devil incarnates. You're very lucky to be alive."

"He threatened my children and grandchildren and my family still living in Cuba. He demanded that I stop the campaign or he would not guarantee their safety. Then he blew up my studio and all of our work that had gone into developing the message."

"I do like your heart," smiled Adrian, as he took her arm and led her to the stairs. "Let's go visit the Professor and see what can be arranged."

As they walked to Ponte's office, Coke said, "They're on to the Crystal Foundation. He suggested that we find other investment vehicles besides competing in their favorite industries. I think we need to find a way to continue but scattered around the world instead of being in one central location. I'm worried about our people."

"I think that's a great idea and we could probably provide assistance through the Keepers and *seers* who live all across the globe."

Ponte leaned forward in his chair but did not get up, "Adrian told me of your message and his suspicions. Am I to assume that they were correct?"

Adrian nodded, "He threatened their families and blew up Martina's business. He also made an indirect threat against the Crystal Foundation."

"Looks as if we're getting under his skin," mused the old Keeper. "I'm sorry that you were the conduit for this insight but we'll set up a portal to Cuba and you can have your children come in through your office."

"What about the campaign?" inquired Martina.

"Do your people have to be in a big city, like Washington or New York?"

"No, with computers they could work anywhere."

"Then we'll bring them here and set up a studio in the third dome. We can expand your space when the fourth and fifth domes are complete."

"Where are we going to put all of these people?" asked Adrian.

"Aye, Travis and some of the men are converting the village to provide accommodations. It will become a real hamlet after all of these years."

"I hope they don't change the funhouse!"

"I'm sure that it will remain intact, so we can have a celebration when this whole business is finished." He stood up and gestured for Martina to take his chair. "You have several calls to make, if I'm not mistaken. Have you used a *messenger* before?"

"No," she replied, as the large *orb* glowed.

"Right then, just say the number that you wish to call. Speak in a normal voice. On the island, we can see each other but that doesn't work over regular telephone circuits."

~

Adrian levitated up to an airlock, twenty feet above the floor, between the second and third domes. The shiny disk hissed open as he approached and closed behind him. He landed on the second level and found Alius trotting to her next meeting. "Have a minute?"

The blond *seer* turned to face him with an impatient look in her eyes, "I have a meeting and you do too."

"I haven't seen you in a couple of days, that's all…"

She softened, "I thought you had to see Morgan?"

"Morgan will always be special to me. She was the first one to act like a friend when I got here and I like her a lot. Is there something wrong with that?"

"No, I guess not…" whispered Alius, her eyes downcast.

"You're jealous, aren't you?"

"I am not," snapped the blond *seer*, her electric blue eyes blazing. She turned and rushed away, leaving Adrian staring after her in complete bewilderment.

"I'm beginning to understand a few of the mysteries of the Powers but I will never understand that one."

He rose up to Master Jung's meditation pad beneath the glass panels of the dome and settled onto a pillow before the two Masters. "I apologize for being late. I know you have many more important things to attend to…"

"We accept your apology and understand that you have many demands that are being made of you," smiled Master Chi. "Let us begin."

Master Jung inquired, "The last time we met, you mentioned that you could see into the dark planes. Tell us…what did you see?"

Adrian closed his eyes and remembered the visions, "I saw three human forms beneath white sheets. There were red stains showing through the cloth where they had been wounded. They were the three clones after our first battle. I also saw Zepallo's face and he was laughing and staring directly at me. I wondered whether we were seeing each other?"

"That is entirely possible," replied Master Jung. "During our demonstration with the glass spheres, we tried to represent the positive and negative duality…the fact that they occupy the same space in time, like two sides of a piece of fabric."

"Think of it as a window between the planes. You can see through to the other side and so can those who stare back at you. Although this is highly unusual, it has happened before. Orana was a fairly young woman during the Hundred Years War and the leader of the Dark Forces was a Ptolemy, although I can't remember which…anyway, they were both so attuned that they could see each other at will and conversed through the planes. Fortunately, she made the better of it but it took great patience to persevere until she could disconnect it."

"I know how she felt," replied the young *seer*. "When I've faced Zepallo, I felt that he could see inside my soul, that he could manipulate my mind. I've learned lots of new things over the past few days from many talented people but no one can teach me how to use my powers to fight his invasion of my inner person."

Master Chi smiled, "There is no one left who can teach you those things but I think that you already have the power within you."

The boy looked at him curiously.

"Orana told me that your lessons were all about overcoming the demons inside yourself, believing in yourself, and learning to become open enough to take in the energies of the world, so you might use them to your advantage. Is this not correct?"

Adrian thought back to the lessons in the white plane and his conversation with his three-hundred-year-old self. The old Master's words brought the memories into focus. He understood parts of the individual experiences but he had never been able to view them as a whole. "No, that's correct. I never thought about it in those terms."

Masters Chi and Jung were very pleased with themselves. Master Jung smiled, "I think that you have learned enough for one day. Concentrate on this new vision, it will enable you to see your path more clearly and it might provide you with a defensive shield against Zepallo. It has always been there inside you."

"You see far more than you realize. This talent is a rare gift. It can not be taught or transferred to anyone else. Each of us can see, hear, and feel along the vectors to one degree or another but…I will compare it to our ability to speak one or two languages, while you have the potential to understand and converse in every tongue," smile Master Chi. "Orana was correct when she chose you."

"I always wondered about that. Why did she choose me?"

"Because her favorite students told her about you!" laughed Master Jung.

Adrian blushed, stood, and bowed to his teachers, "Thank you for your time and your insight. It has been most helpful."

He levitated back to the floor of the lobby of the third dome, where he found Raffe rushing from one of the labs. "How are things going in the labs?"

"Oh, they'll get there. They've organized into small teams to synthesize projects and ideas to integrate with other groups to build something larger. I just came from a demonstration by Kirsai, that little Japanese girl who demonstrated the ancient art of throwing stars. In the old days, Samurai would carry metal disks cut to resemble pointed stars, which they could throw with extreme accuracy and lethal results. Her stars are packets of power that explode when they hit their targets. Several Keepers are busy working out a process for mass-production."

"That's fascinating!" said Adrian. "I want to try one out."

"Oh, you'll get your chance. What are you doing?"

"I've just come from a meeting on the planes with Master Chi and Master Jung. I have a little time to kill and was going to head up to the village to look around. They're turning it into a hostel for our guests."

"I'm supposed to call Coke from the observatory in an hour. I could go with you."

"Come on, let's get out of here!" laughed Adrian as he levitated up through the tunnel to the beach and then north along the craggy coast to the little marina through a torrent of rain that glistened and sparkled in incessant flashes of lightning. Thunder rolled across the island like a mountain tumbling into the sea. He leaned close to Raffe, "I've got something that I wanted to ask you about."

Raffe slowed and turned to him, "What?"

"Well, I've got a bit of a girl problem. I've never dated anyone and, in fact, I was kissed for the first time a few hours ago."

"By who?" grinned Raffe.

"Morgan," replied Adrian, sheepishly.

"Did you like it?"

"Yeah, I liked it a lot and I'd like to try it again."

"So, what's the problem."

"Well, Alius must of have seen us. I mean Morgan kissed me right in the middle of the council room, just before the meeting. What was I supposed to do?"

"And we all know that Alius has always been in love with you."

"What do you mean 'we all know…'?"

"Well, everyone just sees it. It's kind of hard to miss."

"How come I don't see it?"

"Because you're dense. You're so focused on saving the world that you miss the obvious. It's literally right in front of your nose. Who organized us and led the charge to rescue you from that black *orb* when you were stuck inside? Who's the one who's always there when you need her most, not only with her sword but with her advice and council? And who's saved your butt more than anyone else?"

"Alius…"

"Well…duh! You are brilliant, you're brave and talented, but, sometimes, I think you're a moron."

Adrian was embarrassed and, as he looked down at the ground, which was passing beneath them, he noticed that they were descending ever so slowly. After their lessons with Simian, levitation was second nature and they had never lost concentration before. He tried to pull up but had no control over his movements. "We've got a problem here…"

"We're being controlled by something…or someone else."

The rocks along the bluff were coming up fast and they both turned feet first to take the impact. At the last moment, they slowed even more and touched down gently in a recess in the cliff, out of sight of anyone on the island. Marcus materialized a few feet away. Both *seers* reached for their swords.

The dark *seer* held up his hands, "Please, we've been through this before and I haven't harmed you. I'm here to talk, to discuss the future of the world…perhaps not as an ally but rather as two parties who have a mutual interest that might prove beneficial to everyone."

"I've listened to your spiel," replied Raffe, fingering the handle of his sword inside his robes. "Do you bring anything new?"

"I believe you're seeing the beginning of a major campaign against you and your forces. He's starting with little things…this storm over the island, an inconvenience more than anything, but his way of reminding you that our powers are growing. Then there's Adrian's attorney's wife and her business. Fires are tragic. The Crystal Foundation has produced astounding profits and I'm sure that investigations are imminent in several countries where you do business. Foundations aren't supposed to show a profit. People will wonder where all that money is going and where it came from."

Adrian's mouth dropped open.

Marcus continued, "You have brilliant, talented Keepers gathering from all over the world to create a defense against our threat but you're years behind and they'll not be able to counter our powers in time to save the world. It will be too late."

Raffe countered, "Who is to say that we don't have a secret weapon or a doomsday machine that will react to any attack by the Dark Forces?"

Marcus smiled, "The whole point for the existence of the Forces of Light is to protect the natural world. It would inconceivable!"

Adrian smiled, "Are you willing to take that chance?"

The dark *seer* pondered the question. "Other things will begin to happen, little by little, one by one, your systems will fail. Your Keepers will be powerless to stop the progression once it begins."

"What is it that you want from us?" inquired Raffe.

"There is only one way to avoid this calamity." He turned to Adrian and looked straight into his eyes, boring deeper, exploring the young *seer's* heart and mind, "You have to kill Zepallo."

"Why should I stand against him? You're the only one who gains from that confrontation."

"Because you value life as it exists across the world…because you are the only one on the planet who stands a chance of defeating the Dark Lord once and for all. Certainly, I want to take his place, because I know that I can lead our people to a better life. We have everything we might ever need and we control nearly half the governments in the world. You take your half, we'll take ours. For the first time in history, we could live in peace with each other."

"We won't concede half. We won't concede one country or one city or one village!" screamed Adrian, as he pulled his sword from his robe and extended the blade. "Have no doubt that I could defeat you this very minute."

Marcus held up his hands, palms out, "As I said, I came hear to talk…not to fight. There will plenty of time for that, if you don't accept my proposal."

Adrian held the tip of his sword under Marcus' chin. The energy made his Adam's apple glow. "If Zepallo or any of your people harm one person in the Crystal Foundation or on Mrs. Tierney's staff, I will seek you out and I will destroy you!"

"I can not control Zepallo!" Marcus was shaking. The rain dripped from his straight white hair and the cold light made his pale skin look blue. His eyes moved from Adrian to the sword and back again.

"You're not fit to lead your people. You don't have the guts to stand up for what you believe in! Now go back where you belong. I look forward to an opportunity to meet you in battle. It will be your last!"

Marcus stepped back, bowed, and disappeared.

Raffe exhaled, "I really thought you were going to kill him. Funny how girls affect you!"

Adrian punched him in the shoulder, "That had nothing to do with girls. We both know I'll have to face Zepallo again but I won't be blackmailed into fighting someone else's battle. I guess I've known since the invasion at the pole but I also know that I was lucky to have survived that fight. He is far stronger than he has ever been before."

"Let's find the Professor. We just learned a lot more about their plan," said Raffe, rising into the pelting rain to zoom off towards the observatory with Adrian close behind.

~

Alius was the last to enter the small dome, where their inner circle of Keepers and *seers* were meeting to discuss what Marcus had revealed. Adrian stood awkwardly, as she walked slowly down the broad ramp to the pit in the center of the room. "Sorry I'm late."

"Don't be, we've all just arrived," replied Ponte. "Please, come sit by me."

Nanchez looked at Adrian and Raffe, whose robes were dripping on the carpet, "Well…what did he have to say this time?"

The two *seers* started to speak at once and then stopped, "You go first," said Adrian.

Raffe took a deep breath. "Well, he said that the storm and the attack on Mrs. Tierney's offices were just the beginning. The Crystal Foundation will be investigated in several countries…but the most important thing I got out of what he said was that they know we're constructing a center here and that Keepers and *seers* from all over the world are gathering. He said that they were years ahead and whatever we develop in the short term won't make any difference, once the progression begins. We'll have no defense against their attack."

The Professor turned to Adrian, "And what did you come away with…?"

Adrian hesitated, "I'm afraid that I threatened him with my sword, which might not be the best way to handle delicate negotiations."

"That does not answer my question."

"I felt he believes that this is going to be the final battle between the Light and the Dark. The things he said conveyed a…confidence, as if he knew the plan in detail. He did say that things in our systems would begin to fail, one by one, little by little, until the Keepers had no control. I think they're in our circuits somewhere, somehow…they know what we're doing."

"Yeah, he said that once the progression begins, we'll be powerless to stop it," added Raffe.

The Keepers all looked at each other for a long moment before Dadeus spoke, "I'm only just beginning to understand the depth of the workings of the vectors but it does strike me that this is one of the only places on the planet where the Golden Crystal and the Black Crystal are joined harmoniously. If they've tied every Dark Crystal together, then surely they included the one that lives inside the mountain."

Master Jung added, "Although we've taken every precaution, we know they're using other planes to harness the power of the dark vectors. It's certainly possible that they've found a way to infiltrate our systems through that plane."

Nanchez ran his hands through his scraggly white hair, "We've known they were leaching power since they concocted that hurricane and Sammy's been monitoring the firewalls that we've set up to keep them from entering our circuits. That's not to say that they haven't but we've seen none of the telltale signs."

"From the way Marcus spoke, the words he chose, the attitude and tone of his voice. He knows more about us than we know about them," said Adrian.

"It's time to send most of the Keepers back to be in residence with their Crystals. The remainder will continue the research and development that has been started and the Keepers in training will be moved to production. The *seers* will begin to organize in preparation for battle. We should assume that they will attack the island at some point, so we should inform the citizenry. We'll have to come up with something new," he smirked, "after our last defense, I don't think we can get away with a visiting circus."

"We should inform the animals. We'll need their help," added Alius.

Sara rushed into the dome and walked directly to Adrian, "Have you seen the news?"

"No, why?"

Ponte turned to a large *messenger* that was suspended in midair, "News!"

The blond newscaster's beautiful face glowed before the *orb*, "The Attorney General of the United States announced today that he was calling for a grand jury to investigate allegations of bribery and tax evasion by Wall Street's sweetheart, the Crystal Foundation. Similar investigations are underway in London, Paris, and Hong Kong."

"A representative of the Foundation spoke to reporters this morning."

Coke's face appeared, "The Crystal Foundation was founded on the belief that investments could be used to direct giant corporations to behave responsibly and compassionately toward the citizens of the planet and the natural world. Each of our holdings represents the best that business and industry have to offer. Our goal is to become contributors, innovators, and leaders in changing the way business is conducted. We are dedicated to saving the balance with nature and protecting this fragile world that we all share.

We invite this investigation because we have nothing to hide. No bribes have been offered to anyone, no funds have been secreted into some dummy account or corporation. Every penny that the Foundation has earned has been reinvested to expand our influence in cleaning up the environment, providing for the less fortunate, and acting as a counterweight to protect industries and the financial markets against monopolies.

We would hope that this inquiry will be expanded to include other multi-national holding companies that should be held suspect."

The blond reporter returned, "In other news…power outages in New Delhi, London, and Buenos Aires left hundreds of thousands without electricity. Transportation and shipping are being disrupted by interference with the worldwide Global Positioning Satellite system. Scientists and technicians across the globe are striving to find the cause and a solution but no one is willing to offer a timetable for resumption of normal services."

"We have several unusual weather systems to report, the first in Southeast Asia where a monster typhoon is causing flooding and mudslides. Thousands are fleeing the coastlines from Hong Kong to Thailand. At the opposite end of the spectrum, huge dust storms are raging across the Sahara and the plume of airborne particles is being tracked across the Atlantic. Continued drought is being blamed for crop failures from Canada right through the plains of the United States to the Mexican border."

Ponte said, "Good night!" and the *messenger* dimmed. "I believe that we're seeing the beginning of the next campaign of the Dark Forces. Our first order of business is to find the leak in our system and put a plug in it. We'll be at the observatory if you should need us."

With that, he stood and walked up the ramp, followed by Nanchez, Dadeus, Raffe, Sir Isaac, and Sammy. Alius turned to the others, "I'll go inform the animals and ask for their help."

Sky said, "I'd like to go with you, if you don't mind?"

"Sure, let's go!"

The two *seers* joined hands and disappeared.

Simian sat down and said, "We will not be defeated and we have yet to begin the fight."

Master Chi added, "I'll summon the crystal ships. If there's time, we'll add the innovations being developed in the labs." He bowed and disappeared.

Shambala stood, "I believe that we are left to organize the *seers* and warriors. Shall we go?"

Simian and Adrian followed her out into the lobby of the third dome. Keepers and *seers* were rushing from one airlock to the next, each on a mission. Adrian stopped and watched the flow of bodies, "I almost hate to disrupt this energy…this creative purpose has infected all of us."

"I wish we had more time," smiled Simian. "I'll go and speak with the Keepers in the labs, Shambala, you organize the *seers* into three groups and we'll meet together in the small dome in…an hour. Adrian you go speak with Chancellor Bartlett. I believe he's just arrived and you'll find him in his office."

The young *seer* knocked on the Chancellor's door. A voice from within said, "Come in."

The former President was seated behind a desk, piled with stacks of papers that were vying for his attention. "Adrian, it's good to see you, please come in and sit down."

"I'm afraid that we've learned some unsettling news. The next campaign of the Dark Forces has begun. The storm over the island was just for our entertainment. There's a major typhoon off Southeast Asia, sandstorms in the Sahara, drought in the Midwest, power outages in Delhi, London, and Hong Kong, the GPS systems are failing, the Crystal Foundation is under investigation for bribery and tax evasion, and the Keepers believe that the technicians for the Dark Forces have tapped into our system."

The Chancellor grinned, "I don't mean to laugh but that was quite a list! Now tell me what's being done to meet these challenges?"

"The Professor has taken Nanchez and several other Keepers back to the observatory to work on the systems. He ordered most of the other Keepers to return to their Crystals in preparation for an attack or another display of their power over the environment. Alius and Sky have gone to talk with the animals and to seek their help. Shambala is organizing the *seers* and Master Chi has gone to summon the crystal ships, in case they're needed."

"In the real world, I can use my stature to influence opinions and to join disparate groups together for the common good. Here, I feel inadequate but I must say that I admire the Professor's grasp of the steps that must be taken in preparation for the next confrontation. As soon as Bill and Bob return from their dive to help with the placement of the final beams for the sixth dome, I'll return to my office and then to Washington. I might not be able to contribute as much as I'd like here but I know I can make sure that the investigation into the Crystal Foundation is handled with some restraint. I'll certainly see to it that the corporations controlled by the Dark Forces are added to the Grand Jury's areas of interest."

"You should talk with Coke when you get back, he, Raffe, and Sammy have been working backwards through my grandfather's files. They're looking for the center of the web."

"Is Mr. Tierney back in D.C.?"

"Funny you should ask. Zepallo burned Mrs. Tierney's offices and all the work that was contained inside. We're moving them to the island."

"I saw something about that on the news this morning."

"They showed up here, shaken but ready to fight. When I left, they were calling all of Martina's family to warn them of the threat the Dark Lord made against them. The Keepers are setting up a portal to transport them here. Anyway, the next thing I knew his face appeared on the *messenger* a little while ago."

"He's not known for wasting time," smiled the President. "I've respected him for as long as I've known him and I know that he was your grandfather's best friend. Tell me, do you think that Zepallo is ready to try for the whole world?"

Adrian paused for a moment, to contemplate the question, "Yes…yes, I do. They've been building their systems and new facilities all over the world at least since we discovered them. To tell you the truth, I honestly think he might have the capacity to pull it off and I haven't a clue about how we'll defend against numerous outbreaks in different areas…the financial markets, the weather, the economy and the flow of oil, let alone loosing various factions to pursue conflicts that have been brewing all over the planet…and that doesn't touch the reality that, at some point, he'll move to wipe out the Forces of Light once and for all. He can't leave us with enough power to interfere."

"I'll meet with President Shannon this evening and we'll contact those allies that we believe to be in sympathy with our cause. We'll do everything possible to contain the markets and quell the antagonists before they have a chance to begin the slaughter. We might not be able to stop him but we can slow him down and perhaps that will provide you with an opportunity to take control of the situation. I pray you do."

Adrian did not smile. "I appreciate everything that you're doing, but even more, I appreciate your confidence in me."

"You've earned it, young man. No one can doubt where your heart is…"

Adrian stood, "I'm sorry but there is much I have to do. I hope you'll excuse me."

"Certainly, I'll call you after I've talked with Shannon and you know how to get in touch with me as things develop."

"I'll do that."

President Bartlett reached out his hand. "We're all very proud of you, son, and I know that you accept a lot of responsibility for someone your age. Just know that there is no one on the planet that I would rather trust to do the right thing in a bad situation than you."

"Thank you," said Adrian, turning to leave. As he reached the door, he spun around and said, "You know, it always comes down to the same thought…there is no other choice. That's what guides me."

"Just keep listening to that voice. It won't mislead you."

Chapter Ten

Sky and Alius found Unis and the herd of unicorns grazing in the meadow. It was warm and sunny and big puffy clouds rolled slowly through the deep blue sky. Unis trotted over to greet them, "It's lovely to see you young ladies. To what do we owe the pleasure?"

Alius ran her hand over the softness of the unicorn's muzzle, "I'm afraid the Dark Forces are preparing for a world-wide assault. We're not sure where they'll strike first but we know that one of their goals will be to defeat the Forces of Light. The Keepers and *seers* are preparing but there is only so much we can do, until we learn more."

"This confrontation has been building for years. The previous battles were half-hearted endeavors, lacking a cohesive strategy. It was as if they were practicing for the real battle."

"We came to the same conclusion. The last confrontation at the North Pole was a dry run to learn about our defenses. The next one will be far more violent and I'm afraid this might be the war that determines the future of the world."

Sky added, "I don't think there's any doubt about that. We stand in their way and they have no choice but to try to destroy us."

"You know you'll have our help. We'll open the passage to the island and several other places around the world. We have been aware of the change in the dark energies. We all have much to fear, if they are successful."

"Thank you," said Alius. "I wish we could bring you better news."

"Tell me, has Adrian made any progress with those who are polluting the environment?"

"We've found that many of the biggest offenders are controlled by representatives of the Dark Forces. I believe that our friends are doing everything possible to change the way industry treats the natural world and we have a group working on a campaign to educate the citizens of every country. Unfortunately, Zepallo destroyed their offices in Washington and all the work that had been accumulated over the past few months."

"The truth is hard to destroy," smiled the beautiful unicorn. "It is time for you to get back to your preparations. We'll be ready, when you need us."

The two girls hugged her and turned to leave. Alius took Sky's hand and said, "There's something that I wanted to ask you, while we're alone."

"What's that?"

"Well, Morgan kissed Adrian at the council the other day and I'm afraid I don't know what I should feel about that."

"I know. I saw them," smiled Sky. "Tell me, do you love Adrian?"

Alius blushed, "I honestly don't know the answer to your question. I've never been in love before."

"What does your heart tell you?"

The blond *seer* hesitated, as if appraising her inner core, "I don't know, it's not happy."

"What do you feel towards Adrian?"

"We're so close, I guess we've both always felt it was more like being brother and sister but there's more to it than that. He's saved me and I've saved him. We've faced danger and death together, we can sense each other across oceans, and we depend on each other."

"You can't imagine life without him?"

"That's true."

"And you aren't reacting well to one of your friends showing a romantic interest in him?"

"That's true too."

"Then I'd guess that you are in love with him. You're young and lack the experience to know what these feelings mean."

"But love isn't supposed to hurt…"

"That's not true…it's the greatest joy and the deepest pain and we have no control over the emotions running through our hearts. They are powers unto themselves."

"I appreciate your thoughts but that doesn't really help," sighed Alius.

Sky laughed, "There are many things in life that don't make sense but that doesn't mean that they're not real or that we can avoid the responsibility of dealing with them. Real love is not selfish, although it is possessive…it isn't something that you get, it is something that you give because that's the only way to release it, to let it live inside you. When you happen to be lucky enough to share these feelings with someone else, then you become complete…when two spirits merge into something beautiful and free."

"But what if you don't know whether the other person feels the same way?"

"Then you have two choices. You can be satisfied with the love that you carry inside your heart and wait to see what happens or you can confront the situation and ask Adrian what he feels about you."

Alius stared into Sky's black eyes and saw only truth and compassion in this woman's heart. "I guess I'll wait to see what happens. Maybe she kissed him but…when he turned around he was smiling."

Sky laughed, "And why would he not smile? He's a boy…a young man who is attracted to young women. He can't help that and getting kissed by a pretty girl is fairly exciting stuff. Have you ever kissed him?"

"Well, we've kissed each other a few times, mostly when we were just happy to be alive."

"That's not the kind of kiss that I'm talking about."

"Well, no we've never kissed like that…" blushed Alius.

"Perhaps you should try it sometime."

Alius' face turned bright red and she giggled.

Sky was suddenly serious, "We're facing some dangerous challenges and we both know that you and Adrian are going to be in the thick of it. Maybe you ought to talk with him before all of this begins."

"I think you're right," sighed Alius. They had been in too many fights and, even though they avoided the conversation, they both knew that either could have been killed more than once. Whatever was coming would be no different.

~

Adrian was struck by the last thing Chancellor Bartlett said, "Just keep listening to that voice." He levitated out through the tunnel into torrents of rain falling across the island. There was a voice that he needed to hear and, to find her, he needed someplace quiet. He turned south along the coast and then west into the forest, landing near the stream that provided so many wonderful moments with the animals.

A few birds gathered in the branches over his head and tittered with each other. It would not take long for the news to travel to all the other creatures who lived in the woods. He settled on a large rock above the little brook, closed his eyes, and listened for the sounds.

The gentle hum of the rhythms of life swelled above the grating of the dark energies but the dissonant tones vied in volume and power. His body was wracked by waves of sensations seared in the agony and despair of the lives of the world's victims and a vision of Zepallo guiding his armies like marionettes as they marched through the streets of cities lying in smoldering ruins.

He had witnessed this nightmare once before, when the Dark Lord projected his version of the future into Adrian's mind and he was reminded that alternatives depended more on the course of actions and reactions than any one person's hopes and dreams.

The color of Orana's aura and the warm sound of her energies rose out of the clamor and her face appeared before him, "I see that things are becoming a bit more challenging for you."

"I don't think we should joke about it," replied Adrian. "The future of the world as we know it, as we hope that it might be…that's what's at stake."

"I know, I've been watching. I must say that you're all on the right track. The enemy is far more prepared than they've ever been before. They possess weapons that are far more sophisticated than anything they've shown us in the past and they'll come from every direction when the time comes. That's your greatest challenge, realizing that this battle will be fought on many fronts. Win one skirmish and they'll pop up in another form someplace else."

"The Professor is organizing the Keepers and we're trying to organize the *seers* into combat units that can react to any situation. We just don't know where they'll attack first."

"See this for what it is, nothing more or less. Zepallo's goals remain the same. He wants to rule the world, he wants to transform it into his own personal version of the Dark Ages. Human suffering or the destruction of the environment mean nothing, they are mere inconveniences in his quest."

She paused and then continued, "There is only one force that stands between the Dark Lord and his goal."

"The Forces of Light…"

"Obviously, but, in the end, it will come down to you and him. I wish that there was some other course to win the day but, as I see it, that's the only way this can end. One of you will triumph and one of you will die."

"I think I always knew that it would come down to this…"

"Don't try to see the outcome. I can't, there are too many variables, he's talented and driven, and has far more experience than you…but you have the strength of your convictions, your belief in The Balance, and you possess the power to see the correct path when the time comes. Just be smart enough to understand that he will start on the fringes and work to the center."

Adrian pondered her insight, "Sort of like saving the best for last?"

"He doesn't have to face you head on. He believes he can pick and choose the time and the location for that confrontation. I believe you have an advantage."

"What's that?"

"You can see his visions. You've seen them before and you will find them again."

The young *seer* almost lost his concentration, "I can't say that I enjoy the journey."

"No one said you were going to a celebration. This is war!"

Adrian hung his head, knowing she was right, "I've been trying to learn from everyone else but I still don't feel prepared…"

"You've been learning these lessons since the first day you arrived on this island, since your first introduction to the animals and The Powers. You've faced challenges and adversity and, in every case, you reached inside your soul to find the solution. That's why I chose you to become one of my students and, once you started your lessons, I knew that you were the one to lead our forces, because you showed not only bravery but vision. During your lessons, you moved from one plane to another without thought or concern and you overcame each of the challenges without complaint. That's more than can be said of most of my students."

"I'm not sure I realized I was moving from one plane to another but I never really felt threatened. They were simply problems that I had to unravel, things I had to notice and take into my consciousness."

"They were examples of your fears and demons. Tell me, what did you learn? What was the most important piece of information that you carry with you?"

Adrian smiled, "That my greatest weakness and my greatest strength are one in the same, my love for the people I care about, for the animals and the natural world, and the promise of all the world might be."

Orana laughed, "I am such a magnificent instructor!"

"I wish you were still here to guide us, to lead us…"

"That's your responsibility, not mine. I did my share but I'm here to help you to see the path and I believe I have the easy part. You already know most of it…just carry on and you'll find your way."

"I'm glad you're feeling confident but, then, you don't have to face Zepallo."

Orana laughed and laughed, "Well, neither do you. You could decide to walk away but I'll bet you won't."

Adrian was frustrated, "I don't see why you're laughing."

"I'm laughing because your single biggest flaw is that you don't listen to the voice inside your head until the critical moment! Pay attention, open up to the world around you…feel everything. That's what I tried to teach you but you had to run off to save the world."

"We decided together that I had to go…"

"I'm just teasing you," smiled the old woman. Adrian could feel her aura reaching out to enfold him. He could feel the warmth on his skin, in his bones, and he let himself fall into its softness like a feather quilt.

"I believe in you. If I hadn't, I wouldn't have moved on to the next plane. You have no choice but to do your best, to face your demons, and to defeat the Dark Forces, so there might be peace in the world for more than a few months at a time."

Adrian took a deep breath, "Will you be there when I need you?"

"I'll be there if you need me," replied Orana with the faintest smile in her old tired eyes. "I've fought these same battles through the centuries and it was time for me to continue my journey. I'd been waiting for you for far longer than you might know. It was almost as if I could see you at a great distance but I couldn't know until you arrived."

Adrian felt his aura mixing with hers in a bond that felt so strong, so resilient he sensed he'd grasped some of her strength and her wisdom. He smiled, "I have another question for you."

"What's that?"

"Girls…"

"Well, I am one…or at least I was one once!" giggled the old woman.

"There's a girl that I've liked since I arrived on the island, Morgan…anyway, she kissed me the other day in front of a whole room full of people, including Alius, who's not too happy with me right now. I didn't even know that she cared…like that…I mean, we've been like brother and sister since we fought on the mountain and I never…?"

"You failed to see what was happening around you."

"I'm not sure that I'll ever understand…girls."

"And that is at it should be. We're different than you male people but that's not an excuse for you to stop trying, let alone making some effort to share your love with those you care about most."

"That doesn't tell me anything."

"Well, yes it does…no one can decide who we should love…it just happens. We love because of some mysterious chemistry inside our hearts. It's not a choice but rather something over which we have no control. It's as simple as that. So, who do you love?"

Adrian pondered the question. "I really care about each of them, only differently. I've never felt an attraction like I feel when I'm around Morgan but, at the same time, I can't imagine life without Alius being my constant companion. She's smart and brave and beautiful…and she's always there when I need her most."

"I'd say that you have a dilemma and I'm certainly not going to try to unravel that knot for you. You'll have to find the answer on your own."

"Gee thanks, you send me off to war but you won't help me find the solution to this hopeless personal problem."

Orana laughed and started to pull away, "If that is your greatest problem, then I'd say that you should count your blessings, young man."

"Don't go! There's so much more that I want to learn from you…so many questions."

"There will be time for that," whispered the old woman, as she vanished into a searing point of light.

Adrian opened his eyes to find Daphne's nose an inch from his face. He fell back onto the top of the flat rock, "You startled me!"

"I'm sorry. We were worried about you," said the beautiful deer, leaning down to lick his nose.

Adrian looked around and both banks of the little stream were crowded with creatures from the forest…Beggar and his two sons, Daphne's mate with her yearling and a new fawn, two wildcats, possum, raccoons, five or six young fox, two skunks, squirrels, chipmunks, and rabbits, Harriet the hawk flew above his head with a swarm of cardinals, mockingbirds, bluebirds, wrens, finches, robins, and an old owl, who cooed as he flew.

"I'm sorry, I didn't mean to worry you."

"Well, you always come here with your friends and we found it odd that, this time, you came alone."

"I guess that's why I came…to be alone…to think about the dangers that lie ahead."

"The whale mail says that the Dark Forces are moving troops around. Their submarines have been spotted moving about the globe and the sounds of their energies are filling the oceans. We are aware that something is about to happen and we hope that you know that we're all here to help when you need us."

"I appreciate that. Let's hope the darkness doesn't come to the island…but if it does, we'll meet it head on."

Beggar interrupted, "The vent to the plane of the animals opened this morning. Your allies are ready!"

~

Ponte sagged onto a stool with a sigh, lifted his glasses onto his forehead, and rubbed his eyes, "We've been at this for hours. It's right here in front of our noses and we can't see it."

Sammy said, "That's not necessarily true. We can see that power's being leached from the Dark Crystal in the mountain and we know that to be their entry point. Now where would you go in our system, if you were them?"

Nanchez started laughing, a big roaring laugh, "To catch a thief, think like one!"

Dadeus turned to the *messengers* and started entering commands, "Let's see, the center of the system is the control module, everything goes out from there."

Sammy and Raffe moved to another *orb* and started a chain to explore the communications links connected to *messengers* in the laboratories of every Keeper in the world.

Nanchez and Ponte turned to the power grid, "if they're going to turn off our systems then they'll have to control the core, where the vectors extend out into the web."

Sammy called out, "Hey, look at this! They're wired into our communications just like they used to tap into telephones."

Raffe laughed, "It's rather crude, actually. It's almost as if they spliced a wire into our line!"

The other Keepers rushed over to watch. "Let's see if their trap works both ways," said Sammy, tapping in a small avalanche of code. A moment later they could hear voices crackling and fading in and out.

"Here, let's put a filter over that..."

Several voices could be heard talking over each other, "CC112 to CC108, data packet being transferred...now."

"Roger that."

"Give me status on vector 3117..."

"Positive flow. The system is charging."

Raffe looked up, "What's CC?"

Nanchez smiled, "Command Center. Maybe we can figure out exactly how many they have."

Ponte stroked his chin, "Okay, we've tapped into them, and they don't know it yet, and they've tapped into our system. I believe it's time to construct some inventive communications...Raffe and Sammy, see if you can find a way around their bug so we can communicate with the other Keepers about what we've learned. If that doesn't work, we'll send the message by whalemail, at least we know that's secure."

"Let's get back to our search, if they've found their way into one module, you can bet they've got their tentacles wrapped around the rest of it," said Dadeus.

"At least we know they're fairly clumsy. They didn't do a very good job of hiding their tinkering," said Raffe.

Nanchez laughed, "Ah, here's another one. No wonder we couldn't see them, they were hiding in plain sight!"

~

Adrian had been sitting with the animals for almost an hour when they all sensed someone approaching along the path. A moment later, Morgan appeared and smiled. "No one knew where you were and I just had a feeling that you might be here. May I join you?"

"Of course," replied Adrian, as scooted over to make room for her to sit on top of the flat stone, under a canopy of evergreens. "I just needed some time to think. I hope I didn't worry anyone."

"No, it was just that no one had seen you in a couple of hours, so I thought about where you might go and this made perfect sense."

The animals gathered around. Beggar couldn't constrain himself, "Are you two an item?"

"What do you mean?" laughed Adrian.

"Well, most of us find our mates at a far younger age than you humans and both of you are getting to be old enough…and you're both here alone together in the forest."

Morgan looked around at the menagerie and started laughing, "I don't think that I'd call this being alone together…alone together with twenty or thirty of your friends!"

Beggar pawed his nose, "Well, you could pretend that we aren't really here."

"I think we should drop this subject before it gets out of hand," said Adrian. "You know that Morgan and I have been friends since I first arrived on the island."

"I guess that's true…but you are getting to be pretty old…"

"Beggar! That will be enough," said Morgan sharply.

"Boy, you sound like someone's mother," laughed Adrian. "Remind me not to mess with you!"

Morgan smiled and took his hand, "When we are finally alone, I'd like to talk with you. I know that things are going to start happening and you'll go off on one of your missions again. I just…want you to know how much I care that you come back."

"I think it's time to go," said Adrian, as he stood up. "Give me your hand and we'll fly back to the domes."

"You've never taken me before. Should I be scared?"

"I don't think so, although I did crash this morning but it wasn't my fault."

Morgan extended her hand, "I should be scared."

They bid the animals good-bye and lifted through the trees and out over the fields surrounded by a flock of birds. Morgan smiled, "This is wonderful! I wish I could levitate like you and Alius."

"As we've been trying to teach in our class, it might be possible for normal people to levitate. It's just a matter of concentration and believing..."

Adrian flew along the coast and landed on the bluff overlooking the beach, where they played with the dolphins when he first arrived. Morgan wrapped her arms around his neck and kissed him. It was warm and soft and he did not want it to end.

She leaned back and looked directly into his eyes, "I just want you to know that I care for you very much."

"And you know that I've always cared for you...appreciated the way you treated me the first time I visited that beach...the way you helped me on the way back from the Island of the Children...and all the times that you've been there when I've been injured..."

"I couldn't not be there...if that makes any sense. I was so terrified that you wouldn't come back or you wouldn't recover...that you might never know how I felt..."

They kissed again. Adrian pulled back, "I don't know what's going to happen in the next few weeks...it might be the end of everything we've known or we might find a way to defeat them. Either way, we'll all have to fight in one way or another." He paused, "I don't want this to end before I learn enough to understand what these feelings mean but I have to concentrate on what's coming."

"I know," smiled the tall girl. "I'm glad we had this little talk and I hope we can do it again soon...that's if you can fit me into your schedule now and then?"

"I'll do my best," said Adrian, standing on tiptoe to kiss her again.

Chapter Eleven

Eighteen black mini-subs surfaced inside a bunker bored into cliffs along the eastern coast of North Korea, invisible to monitors in the heavens. Two-hundred Whisperers disembarked and boarded several large saucers that whisked them to the Command Center in the bowels of a desolate mountain. Groups boarded elevators that plunged one-thousand feet beneath the surface to the giant dome, where they were escorted to a large platform surrounding a sphere suspended at the center of the enormous chamber.

As soon as they were seated, Zepallo appeared, flanked by Beta and Gamma. He raised his hands above his head, "I bid you greetings and offer my sincere appreciation for the inconvenience that you have suffered in order to be here this evening. I believe you will find the journey worthy."

The two clones smiled and moved to stand on either side of their leader. He continued, "Operation 'Sacred Mission' has begun."

The audience applauded.

"Although some of our previous efforts did not find complete success, in each case we gained experience and knowledge. We tested the limits of our technologies and our strategies, we pushed against the defenses of the Forces of Light and gained an insight into their capabilities, and, while they were busy fighting off our aggressions…we continued to build our command centers across the globe."

He turned and waved a hand around the room at the technicians manning the purple bubbles floating from one screen to the next like moths flitting from one light bulb to another. "Our systems are nearing completion and they will offer access to every communication and power grid on the face of the planet. As we have demonstrated, they also allow us to control the weather…and, perhaps the most interesting benefit is that they will provide us with a clear look inside the web that has been constructed across the positive vectors. At this moment, we are monitoring their communications, their power distribution and consumption, and the inner workings of their code."

Again, the audience rose to their feet and applauded.

"Our financial mission continues with even more velocity than we might have hoped and we now control the largest corporations in most of the critical industries in every country in the world. The markets are dependent on our investments and I have many of you to thank for your creative and dedicated service. As you might know, the markets have been creeping up as we've driven the prices for our own stocks higher. Tomorrow, we'll collect our profits and start an avalanche that will allow us to capture many more of our targets. I'm sure that each of you will become scandalously rich in the process."

"I would like to thank Mr. Paul James for laying the groundwork for the investigations that are under way in four financial capitals into the dealings of a certain foundation that has been an irritant and a distraction. Mr. James, would you stand and take a bow?"

A short muscular man with a large white moustache stood and bowed slightly. The Whisperers clapped and patted him on the back.

"So that you might be forewarned, electrical power will begin to fade in the most remote parts of the world tomorrow night. The wave of darkness will sweep from south to north across the southern hemisphere, ever so slowly, as circuits overheat and fail due to a mysterious extraction of energy. Industry and commerce will cease to function until we decide to turn the lights back on and, as you might guess, we'll be very selective in restoring the elixir to our friends. In the meantime, our troops will begin to take control of the southern continents. If the industrial powers of the north do not capitulate, then we'll continue our campaign as necessary."

A voice in the crowd called out, "What about the Forces of Light. Surely you do not expect them to stand idly by, without some sort of reaction?"

The Dark Lord smiled, "First, their systems will begin to fail, little by little, bit by bit, until they have no power to work with. At that point, our technicians can take control of the positive vectors and, for the first time in history, we will control The Powers…all of The Powers!"

The audience cheered.

"Certainly, we'll have to finish the task but I'm in no hurry, let them suffer through the frustration and terror of not being able to see out into the vectors. They'll have no way of knowing when the attack will begin or where. I believe there are other targets that we should attend to before we get to Morgan's Knot."

~

Alius and Sky landed in the lobby of the third dome just as Adrian and Morgan flew through the lock, settling gently on the floor. Adrian was still holding Morgan's hand when he asked Alius, "How did it go with Unis and the animals?"

Alius remained silent, her cheeks burning a deep crimson, as Sky replied, "We'll have their help."

"We just heard that the vent opened on the ridge."

"And who told you that?" inquired Alius.

"Beggar," said Morgan.

"Ah, so you've been hanging out in the forest, while we've been off trying to find some help for this battle that's coming," snorted Alius.

Sky took Morgan's hand and started to lead her away, "I think we should check and see what needs to be done next."

Adrian watched them go and then stared at the floor just in front of his feet, "I think we need to talk."

"I'm not sure there's much to talk about."

"There's too much at stake. I need you and they," he said gesturing around the dome, "need us. This is not the time for us to…be angry with each other."

Alius started to walk away and then turned around, "Something's changed between us. We've always been honest with each other but I don't feel that you've been truthful with me."

"I didn't plan any of this, especially now!"

"Just because you didn't plan it doesn't mean that you haven't participated…obviously willingly."

"My feelings for Morgan don't compete with the way I feel about you. You know that. We've always been…more than brother and sister or best friends or whatever. I've saved you and you've saved me. We couldn't have defeated the Dark Forces if we hadn't been together. One of us would surely be dead by now."

Alius softened, "We both know that the battle's coming. I'll be there for you, when you need me, but don't expect everything to go back to the way it was…before."

"I don't want it to change," said Adrian quietly.

"That's a decision you'll have to make for yourself," said the blond *seer*, turning to march defiantly through the airlock.

Professor Ponte waddled down the staircase and across the stone floor to Adrian, "My boy, I think we've found out how they invaded our systems. Raffe and the other Keepers are working on a trap that will allow us to make them think that they're still in control, while we take a peak into their communications."

Adrian smiled, "I'm glad something's going our way."

The old man patted him on the back, "Tell me, what have you found?"

"I went to the forest to meditate and had some interesting insights. I believe they'll start on the edges and work their way to the center…with something monumental in the financial world and then with the Positive Crystals. I also believe that the only way to solve this once and for all is for me to face Zepallo, one on one."

"We've not reached that point yet and I would prefer to explore every other possibility before allowing you to take that chance."

"We both know the final solution."

"That may well become the only option but I forbid you to take any action without my approval. Do we understand each other?"

"Yes, sir."

"Good, now have you checked to see how the organization of the *seers* is progressing?"

"No, I just got back. I was headed there now. Do you want to come?"

The Professor put an arm around his shoulder, "No, I have to get back to the observatory. Things in the laboratories seem to be running smoothly and a majority of the Keepers have returned to their Crystals. If I were one of the bad guys, I'd want to start my attack with the easiest parts of the puzzle, sort of like picking the corner piece first. That would be far less dangerous than a frontal assault here."

"Then we agree," said Adrian. "I think we should take a look at the most vulnerable Crystals and station our troops according to our best guess."

"That's not a bad idea. We have the three crystal ships, which are being outfitted with some new weapons and supplies. We could send them out independently."

"I'll go see what Shambala and Master Chi are doing."

"Good, come by the observatory when you've finished. We should have more to report by then."

"Okay, I'll see you in a little while."

The Professor held up his index finger, "There is one more thing that I wanted to ask you about. Although it shouldn't be any of my business, what's going on between you and Alius?"

"Alius saw Morgan kiss me the other day and she hasn't been happy with me since."

"I can't say that I blame her!" laughed the old Keeper. "Might I suggest that you find a way to smooth things out as soon as possible? You know that we're all depending on both of you."

"That's what I told her but I don't think it was what she wanted to hear."

"No, I'm afraid you're right about that," mused Ponte. "They are such powerful creatures, women I mean…and, perhaps, we are the weaker sex because, no matter how old we become, we never quite figure out where we stand with them. I'm afraid that mankind got it backwards when he assumed that the male was the dominant figure in the mix."

Adrian smiled weakly, "I wish that made me feel better but I'm afraid it doesn't."

~

It was three o'clock in the morning, when Adrian finally excused himself from a meeting with the other *seers* aboard the crystal ship Hope, which was birthed in the interface of the third dome. Workers in multicolored robes crawled over every surface of the gleaming ship, installing new crystal cannons, an alternate communications system, an advanced shield, and accommodations for scores of *seers* and fighters, who would man her next voyage.

He levitated to the observatory and entered the front door quietly. He was not sure who was awake or asleep and he didn't want to disturb anyone. He tiptoed through the dining room to the elevator and descended to the white room and the gigantic spinning crystal. It seemed to be moving at a normal pace and he paused to bathe in the energies for a moment, meditating on the most basic loyalties.

Turning right along the corridor, he found Nanchez, Dadeus, and the Professor in the workshop. "What's happening here?"

"Well, we think we've isolated their bugs and we've managed to do a workaround to control the system no matter what they try to do. We've pretty well moved the sensitive communications to a new grid, so they can still see part of the traffic, but there are still some things that need to be adjusted."

"Good, I was worried that they'd actually be able to take over the positive powers."

"That's exactly what they intend to do and we'll allow them to believe that they're succeeding. Ultimately, they'll probably be a bit frustrated," smiled Nanchez.

"Where are Sammy and Raffe?"

"Oh, yeah…you should go check with them. They're in the computer room. Something about the markets making odd moves."

Adrian ran to the next room, where he found Sammy and Raffe seated in front of the giant screens, tapping away frantically. "What's happening?"

"The markets moved up dramatically just after opening in Tokyo and Hong Kong, now they're taking a nose dive. This could be a disaster," replied Raffe without looking up.

"Have you talked with Coke?"

"No, it's three o'clock in the morning here…earlier there."

"Call his home," instructed Adrian.

There was no answer. "Try the foundation."

Presently, the attorney answered the private line to his office, "Hello."

"What's going on?" asked Adrian.

"Oh, we're seeing Zepallo's holdings selling off en masse. They're taking their profits at the peak and the markets will start to tumble. I'm not sure that any group could stop this once it starts rolling."

"What does that do to us?"

"Because we have continuous outside income to invest, I don't think it will have any long-term effect. We have controlling interest in a number of companies that will continue to do business," Tierney paused, "and there's an upside to all of this, probably exactly what the Dark Forces are going to do…now that I think about it."

"What do you mean?" inquired Adrian.

"I mean that when stocks tumble, the prices reach levels that are far below their actual value. Don't you see, Zepallo is taking out his profits this morning, by the close, every stock on the board will have dropped. Tomorrow or the next day, they'll buy back in at a reduced rate with the money they made at the peak and they'll take control of more corporations."

"I'll get Raffe and Sammy to run the list and see which companies they would find most appealing. Buy everything you can, when the time is right."

"We've already got some targets, so we'll start working on it on this end," said Coke.

"What about your people?"

"I held a general meeting a couple of hours ago and explained the situation and our preference that they be moved to safer locations. They all refused to leave the building until the crisis has passed."

"So, you're staying?"

"Yes, at least for the time being. There's too much to be done."

"What about Martina?"

"She should be arriving there with a crew of family and her staff. We spoke a little while ago and she was in Cuba with Simian."

"Ponte said that they'd found space in the second dome for the new offices and Travis took one of the trawlers to pick up their supplies. Do you need any…protection?"

There was a pause, "I'm not sure how that would work. For the moment, I think we're okay but I'll call you if things change."

"Alright, take care."

"One more thing. Is Raffe there?"

"Yes, I'm here."

"How are you coming on the reverse list?"

"I think we're getting closer. The machines have been churning for hours and, if I got the code right, they should produce the name of the company at the center of all of this."

"Call me when you've got it. Bye." The line went dead.

Raffe was running the list that Adrian's grandfather had gathered of the financial investments of the Dark Forces. Sammy filled screen after screen with code to sort the data into groups of critical industries that might suffer the greatest deflation in value. Then it would identify those companies that appeared the most essential targets. The list was also being analyzed to find the spider's lair at the center of the web in the background.

The young Jamaican turned to his friends, "When you think about it, worldwide commerce would cease with the crippling or domination of only a handful of industries…oil and energy, steel, food production, transportation, communications…that would be enough."

"You're right," said Raffe. "With the right combination, he could control all the others."

"That's definitely what he's after. Let's see what the program produces and send it to Coke. I've got to get back to the domes."

"I know that this is a silly question but do any of us get time to sleep anymore?" asked Raffe.

"I don't remember what that's like," yawned Sammy.

"There'll be time for that when this is finished," laughed Adrian, although the thought of a few hours in his own bed was tempting.

He landed in the lobby of the second dome to find Alius and Morgan at the front of a gaggle of seers and Keepers staring at the large *messenger*. No one was saying a word. Adrian walked through the crowd to stand between the two girls, "What's happening?"

"It's started," replied Morgan in a whisper.

The blond reporter looked more serious than usual, "The stories that we've been following include one of the largest drops in the value of financial markets since the dot-com bubble burst years ago. Investors cashed out, moving their funds to bonds and precious metals. Gold reached an all time high this afternoon."

"Power and communications have ceased functioning in southern Chile and Argentina, from the Congo to Cape Town and in southern portions of Australia. There are unconfirmed reports through amateur radio operators that major cities are being occupied by troops wearing black uniforms. Again, these are unconfirmed reports, but no other nation claims responsibility."

Adrian flashed to the image of the black robed troops marching through the ruins of cities all over the world. Orana's voice whispered, *"The first drop of water portends the coming flood."*

He turned to the others who were gathered in front of the *messenger*, "Our time is up! Ready Hope and Grace, gather our troops and the *seers* in groups one and two. We'll hold the Destiny for a counter strike."

The group scattered to the airlocks and down through the interface. He grabbed Morgan's hand, find my father and George and tell them to ready our defense. Alius, you make sure that everything goes smoothly with the preparations with the ships. I'll go back to Ponte. They've isolated the bugs in the system and they're working on ways to make the Dark Forces believe they're controlling the light vectors."

Adrian levitated up to Ponte's office, pressed the clasp of the golden crystal hanging from his neck, and stepped through the portal to stand just outside the workshop. Ponte was just opening the door and said, "Oh, I thought you'd left?"

"I did but I'm back, have you been watching the news?"

"No, we've had other things to attend to."

"It's started. The stock market crashed this morning and power and communications are out in the southern hemisphere. There are unconfirmed reports of troops in black uniforms taking control of all of the major cities. I told the other *seers* to prepare Hope and Grace."

The old man turned back into the workshop and started yelling, "Nanchez, finish that patch! We've got to begin the progression!"

Dadeus interrupted, "Before you begin your work, we'd be wise to contact the other Keepers, especially those in the southern hemisphere."

"Right, right," mumbled the Professor, as he turned to the *messenger.* "Run bug check 372. Numbers and symbols flashed through the glow before a beautiful eyeball filled the screen and winked. "Right, we're clear. Open alternative circuits to all stations."

The eye disappeared and was replaced with a globe spinning slowly. A web of yellow lines unfolded around the planet, intersecting and connecting in the laboratories of each of the Keepers. After a few moments, the lines turned bright green.

Ponte spoke quietly but firmly, "Gentlemen and ladies, it is time to proceed with our program. If any of you are not aware, the Dark Forces have shut down power and communications to the lower reaches of the southern hemisphere. There are reports of black uniformed troops over-running the major cities.

We've been debugging the system and found several programs planted by the Dark Forces in an attempt to take control of the positive vectors. We'll delay sending a counter pulse until the proper moment. When our forces are in position, let us focus a portion of our power on those networks to see whether we might counter their security. We're running tests, at the moment, and we'll forward the pertinent instructions as soon as the calculations are complete. It shouldn't be more than a few minutes. Please stand by."

Nanchez turned thumbs up to the Professor, "The patch is functioning. Let's see whether they've started invading our system?"

Dadeus was already exploring the most important question of whether the Dark Forces were overwhelming the power grid in South America, Africa, and Australia, or pulling power out. The second question was, where was it going? That much power could not be stored, so the final question was, where was the focal point, the target for their blast? Any chance of success in this effort depended on that information.

Ponte knew better than to interfere when Dadeus was so totally focused on his work. The old Keeper was a genius but the Professor couldn't help drumming his fingers on the workbench.

~

Beta and his forces swept across southern Africa and found the conventionally armed tribes and armies no match for the futuristic weapons of the Dark Forces. In little more than twenty-four hours, they controlled the major cities from the Atlantic to the Indian Ocean as far north as Zaire. There was no need to confront the rural population when they ruled the seats of government and the centers of commerce, communications, and electrical power.

Gamma found similar success in South America, moving into darkened cities in the dead of night. Saucers deposited tactical squads at critical targets that were overtaken within minutes. Even Argentina's sophisticated military was helpless, without power and communications, their armies were defenseless to impede the Dark Force's seizure of La Paz and Rio de Janeiro.

Zepallo stood on the circular dais, floating like the rings of Saturn around the sphere at the center of the command center in North Korea, watching communications links with his clones as they reported one victory after another. With the new imaging programs that tapped into signals from spy satellites looking down from the heavens, he could watch their progress, a dark shadow creeping slowly, steadily across the maps on the giant screens that encircled the enormous cavern. He absorbed their emotions, the depth of their commitment, and the steps in their logic, as they moved through each step of the operation. He could feel their elation long before they reported through normal channels.

"Splendid!" he cried. "What information have we concerning the reaction of the Keepers of the Forces of Light?"

"So far, we are only observing normal traffic, M'Lord."

"What of the powers across the light vectors?"

"Again, we are not seeing any surges," replied a technician within the sphere. "Our instruments show no reaction or movement."

"I don't like this!" said Zepallo. "They will respond. Be ready to begin deconstructing their system. It won't be long now."

"Yes sir. The circuits are open and ready on your command," replied Cadeau.

"We'll wait until our adversaries begin their counterstrike and then we'll slow them to a crawl."

"As you wish," said Regus, bowing as he backed away.

Young Marcus levitated from the floor to the sphere, "I see that we've made substantial progress, M'Lord. Beta and Gamma are proving themselves worthy field generals."

"They should!" exclaimed the Dark Lord. "They have my brain, my instincts, and my determination. They will not fail!"

"I'm here to report that our troops can be in position for an assault on the Island of the Children on your orders."

"I'm sure you are aware that the prize is not the island but the subsurface world they've constructed."

"We've planned to invade through the city and the interface to the ocean at the same time, forming a pincer to leave little room for defense or escape. The population will be decimated and the facilities destroyed before the Forces of Light have time to react. The invasion should be over in a matter of hours and we can move on to the next objective."

"I'll have the technicians send a wave through the island before you arrive to disable their systems. That should give you a slight advantage but do not underestimate their strength, resilience, or resources," cautioned Zepallo. "They'll not fail without a fight."

"Then a fight it is!" smiled Marcus. "We are more than ready."

"Commence the campaign when we take control of their systems. It shouldn't be long now."

Chapter Twelve

Hope and Grace floated over the beach above the domes as the last rays of golden sunlight slipped under the cloud cover at dusk, painting the ocean and the crystal ships with splashes of shimmering scarlet. Fat droplets of rain flashed like liquid fireballs streaking from the sky, splattering through the rigging and limp sails of the two ships, which had been fully outfitted with new weapons and innovations. Each with a crew of three-hundred joining local warriors on the ground, Grace would approach Cape Town from the south, while Hope's attack from west to east, employed the Andes mountains as a shield, launching their troops to cut the supply lines of the Dark Forces.

Raffe, Mary, Shambala, Simian, Master Chi, Lala and Maze, Sky, Alius, and Adrian stood in a circle around Master Jung, Dadeus, Sammy, Nanchez and Professor Ponte, who was dressing in a black coat with long tails, a white shirt with a high collar and a bright yellow bow tie. "This is not the moment for contention. Each of you wants to crew these ships to confront our enemies but some of you will be needed to man Destiny and to help us coordinate here."

"I have to go!" said Alius adamantly.

Ponte frowned, "Alright, M'dear. As much as I value your insight and vision, you'll be in charge of Grace because, most of the time, you are a perfectly graceful young lady."

He spun around to Raffe and Mary, "I would appreciate it if you both would stay. Your talents with the computers and our systems would be far more useful than having you wielding a sword."

The *seers* from the Island of the Children stepped out of the circle. "Sky I would appreciate it if you would coordinate our efforts with the animals. Master Chi, I believe that your knowledge of the planes in combination with Master Jung's expertise would be most helpful. Shambala would you accompany Alius, while Simian will be in charge of the Hope with Lala and Maze."

He turned to Adrian with an air of frustration, "You'll be staying here to command Destiny, should she be needed."

Adrian nodded reluctant agreement and stared at Alius. He had never seen her act this way. It was as if she would rather face death than…be forced to work with him. He had never felt the pain flowing through his heart, an overwhelming need to protect her, while searching for some sign to disprove the impression that she was running away from him. She did not allow her eyes to meet his, before she turned and strutted down the beach through a glowing mist to the Grace.

The other *seers* hugged each other and turned to their duties. The two crystal ships lifted into the clouds and disappeared into the glow of a rising moon behind the mist.

Master Jung smiled, "They're traveling through Orana's favorite plane, The Tropics, with the blue-green sky. The vector winds are favorable and they'll be invisible to the Dark Forces until they're right on top of them."

Ponte turned to the group, "Sammy, you take Raffe and Mary to the observatory. We have to watch everything from the vectors to the financial markets. Let me know if anything drastic happens."

"Dadeus and Nanchez, you monitor the systems. We know their assault will begin as soon as they see resistance. We have about two hours to prepare."

Nanchez clapped Dadeus on the back, "That'll keep you outta mischief for a little while!"

"I'd like to consult with Masters Jung and Chi about the planes, which leaves Adrian. Would you see to the Destiny?"

The young *seer* felt awkward being sent to organize the chaos around the beautiful ship, instead of leading the fight but he lifted off and soared along the beach to the entrance of the third dome. The future of the world might be decided in the next few hours but he knew that the Professor was reserving him as a weapon and making every effort of avoid falling into a trap. At the same time, he felt that Ponte was using this opportunity to teach him a lesson.

The beautiful ship floated just above the surface of the water and he walked up the ramp. Captain Maniford Ruhl was going through a checklist in a worn leather binder. "How are things coming?"

"Aye, we'll be finished in an hour or two, the hull is bulging with new weapons and supplies, the shields have been replaced, a complete second communications system has been installed…one for our chatter and one that the Dark Forces can listen to, if we want…and the crew is on standby. We're ready to cast off when you are."

Adrian smiled, "I'll tell Ponte."

The Captain turned to an *orb* on the bridge, "The other ships are making good time. They'll fall out of the plane in the same instant, shouldn't be more than an hour or so."

Adrian spun around and ran down the ramp, "I'll be back."

He almost collided with Morgan, Josh, Ian, and Kelly who were following the twins through the central hall of the third dome, "Where's everybody going?"

"Your uncle is going to close down the interfaces of four of the domes and they need help moving the diving gear to a central location," said Morgan. "Where are you going? You don't look…yourself."

"Hope and Grace just left and I had to make sure that Destiny was ready. I've…got to have some time to think…"

Morgan looked into his downcast eyes, "Alius went without you, didn't she?"

"Yes."

"And you're worried about her?"

"Of course," said Adrian shyly. "We've always fought together not with each other."

"Maybe she has to prove something to herself."

"Or maybe she's just doing it in spite."

"She can't help loving you," smiled Morgan. "I know, I do."

Adrian blushed, "Get going. I'll see you later."

Morgan followed the others through the lock, as the young *seer* rose to Master Jung's meditation platform where he could be alone. He settled onto the carpet and closed his eyes. Visions of Alius flashed through his mind. The fierce look on her face as she attacked him that first night on the mountain, or the pride in her eyes when he realized that she had rescued him from the command center in the Caucuses, or all those times that she materialized at the exact moment he needed her help...but he could not understand the way she looked away and avoided returning his gaze.

They were closer than brother and sister or friends...maybe even twins because they could feel each other over great distances, they could know what the other was experiencing, and they were stronger when they could feed off each other's strengths. *It can't end this way.* He focused on her eyes and let himself drift into deep meditation. *"You know that I love you, that I need you, and that I care for you. That's all I can offer right now but it's honest and true."*

Adrian started to let his mind move on to the sounds and the energies, when his mouth filled with an overwhelming taste of chocolate, just as she sent the flavor to him across the island when they first started learning to meditate. *"Our hearts and our minds touch through great distances. Be careful."*

~

The color of the sky was enchanting, the deep blue-green of a tropical ocean flowed away from a full moon, the golden light reflecting off the masts and rigging restraining billowing sails filled with the vector winds. Grace flew south, a shimmering jewel streaking through the stars, tacking occasionally to right her course. She was the stuff of children's dreams and few would have suspected that her gleaming hull was crammed with weapons and warriors.

No one had informed Alius that the Captain of this fair ship was Cappy, the bus-driver from the island. He cackled, "Aye young lady, if I can drive that bus, I can pilot this ship. Just don't you worry your little head about that part of it, I'll get you there. You've got enough ahead of you!"

Alius calmed her senses and fell into a meditation. She had not mastered the ability to see along the vectors but she was beginning to distinguish the sounds. When she reached total concentration, she could sense things about those who were close to her and see danger before it arrived, just as she had known that Adrian was in danger when he went to his grandfather's funeral in Washington, D.C. They had always shared that bond.

She allowed herself to focus on the young *seer*. Images of the dangers they faced together, the moments of quiet, the relationship that had grown over the years pulled at her heart. The little blond *seer* sensed frustration and pain in his soul. Leaving without saying goodbye had been cruel but his affection towards Morgan hurt more than she could have imagined. Leading the assault on South Africa would allow her to contribute, while giving her a chance to concentrate on something other than the pain and anger. It was almost as if she had to prove to herself that she could function, that she could lead and fight without him…but she missed him already.

Adrian's voice drifted into her mind, "You know that I love you, that I need you, and that I care for you. That's all I can offer right now but it is honest and true." The beautiful *seer* smiled and thought about the deep, rich flavor of chocolate.

Clearing her mind, she focused on the structure of the columns of the Dark Forces that were moving from south to north. The highest concentrations of troops would be advancing on major cities and the critical targets of power stations, ports and airfields, seats of government, and military installations. Between those points, the Forces of Light would find little resistance, providing the opportunity to join with the animals and local tribes who knew the terrain and the vulnerabilities of those points already seized.

A vision of the battle over the tidal pools in front of the Lincoln Memorial flashed through her mind. She could see Alpha soaring through the air to meet Adrian, Gamma, the third clone, turning away, as Beta flew straight for her, firing blasts from his sword. She could see cold, calculated determination in his dark eyes, a lethal smile on his thin lips, and a supremely arrogant belief in his own powers. That was his weak point and she caught him on his third pass with a mighty blow across his thigh. In spite of the near mortal wound, he kept attacking until Alpha fell out of the air with Adrian, crashing into the reflecting pool.

She realized that he was so confident in his plan and his abilities that he would not hesitate to push his troops too far too fast, stretching the limits of supply and reinforcement. The soft spot would be found in the links between Cape Town and the front lines, vulnerable threads transporting the lifeblood of the advancing forces.

Alius opened her eyes to find Shambala hovering a foot above the deck. The beautiful black woman smiled, "I believe that we are seeing the same path."

"The word that comes to mind is disruption," replied the blond *seer*. "They might be able to use their saucers to move troops and supplies but that task becomes more difficult as the distances and the quantities increase."

"Exactly," smiled the tall black *seer*, as she untangled her arms and legs to stand. "We should begin by sweeping across Namibia, Botswana, Zimbabwe, there are few major cities, even fewer paved roads, and there are plenty of tribes willing to help. I have relatives across the continent."

"Why doesn't that surprise me?"

~

Hope slipped out of the plane of the Tropics and skimmed above the waves of the Pacific twinkling reflections of the millions of stars scattered across the heavens. Ponte's information indicated that the Dark Forces moved around Chile rather than dedicating troops across the length of the Andes Mountains for a thin sliver of land that could be taken after the rest of the continent had fallen.

The Crystal ship slipped across the Atacama Desert and up the peaks of the mountains into the crater of the Socomba volcano, which formed an enormous amphitheater when the side of the mountain blew out seven-thousand years ago. Other than copper mining to the east, the area was rarely visited by outsiders and provided access to Argentina.

Simian stared into the darkness, sensing motionless herds of animals and the auras of hundreds of people, who blended so perfectly with the rocks they would never have been seen during daylight, much less under a full moon.

Lala and Maze started giggling, "Thought you weren't going to find them for a moment there!"

The little people tipped their hats and a cheer rose out of the night, as the animals and warriors rushed to surround the glowing crystal ship. Simian rose into the air, where he could see everyone, "We'll unload skimmers and a cache of weapons here. Lala and Maze will lead you in a sweep down through the river valleys from San Miquel de Tucuman to Buenos-Aries, cutting a swath through their supply lines. We'll take the ship to pick off any aerial support that the Dark Forces might muster against you and then we'll sweep into Buenos Aires from the north."

"What about the animals?"

"We don't have enough skimmers to move everyone, so I'd suggest that you send a message along to your friends and relatives along our route. We could certainly use their help. In the meantime, the animals can set up a cordon along the border to make sure that the Dark Forces don't have a chance to circle around and move down through Chile."

A cheer went up as all hands joined to unload the skiffs and the cargo from the deep hull. The calls of the animals could be heard echoing between the mountains as the message moved north and south along the Andes.

The old Jamaican felt that he should have been surprised to find Travis as Captain of the good ship Hope but, after the journey from Jamaica to Morgan's Knot, he had every faith in his abilities. Travis laughed at the astonished look on the old *seer's* face, "Addicus Belsley was hospitalized in London, so I'm your next best choice! I might not be a *seer* or a Keeper but I know how to sail!"

Simian paused to reflect on Alius and Shambala aboard the Grace. The crystal ship was moving across the Namib desert, above miles of writhing sand dunes, over grassy plains to land near the Etosha Pan, a hundred-mile patch of hard-packed clay that provided water and a gathering place for elephants, black rhinoceros, kudu, springbok, gemsbok, and herds of other desert animals. Guides from several tribes would lead the skiffs to their targets, while Grace moved south to search for the command center. They could only hope they would not be out in the open long enough to provoke the Dark Forces, so far from their lanes of travel. At least not immediately, because they all knew that as soon as they dropped out of the plane, sensors would track their every move.

The captain motioned for Simian to join him at a console on the bridge, which showed two large blips approaching from the south. "That would be our greeting party. We should get moving."

The Jamaican called from the rail, "Hurry, the Dark Forces are coming. We must be gone before they arrive!"

One skimmer sped off into the night, then another and another, until all the warriors and supplies were being ferried to the next rendezvous, where they would join with the animals and build a legion to roll down the mountains to the southeast. The message spread through the jungles and the plains like a wave rolling out ahead of a ship instead of a wake following along behind.

A sailor ran up to the captain, "The gear is stowed and everyone is back aboard, sir!"

Travis bellowed, "Hoist the anchor! Fill the sails! Make speed to the north!"

Within moments, the crystal sails bowed with vector wind and Hope darted into the night.

~

Adrian could feel the progress of his friends aboard the two ships, he could sense the danger approaching but there was something else in the background…a threat, growing quickly. The vibrations of Zepallo's excitement and anticipation were strong. The disruption was deep blue, rolling beneath the surface of the ocean, a wave that would rise up to topple a…pyramid? There were pyramids in Egypt and Central America but this one seemed pink in the bright sunlight. The Island of the Children!

He collapsed on the pad and scrambled to the edge, almost losing control as he plunged to the floor of the dome. "Raffe, Mary, Dadeus…!" He flew to Ponte's office, pushing the clasp on the golden crystal that hung around his neck as he burst through the door and stepped through the portal to the observatory.

Ester met him in the dining room with a hug, "Are you alright, dear?"

"I know where they're going to strike next," panted the young *seer*, "The Island of the Children. I have to warn Raffe, Mary, and Dadeus and everyone on the island."

The old woman patted him on the shoulder, "They're all downstairs in the workshops."

Adrian ran to the elevator. Although it moved at an astonishing speed, it was not quick enough to satisfy his trepidation. The doors slid open and he turned into the computer room to find Raffe and Sammy at the console, "I know where they're going to strike next! They're not coming here, they're going to the Island of the Children!"

Raffe's face drained of color, "It makes perfect sense. I have to tell Mary and Dadeus!"

The three boys burst through the door to Ponte's workshop and screeched to a halt as Dadeus smiled, "They're sending a mighty wave and troops to the Island of the Children. We'd best see if we can help."

"How did you know?" stammered Raffe.

"We tapped into their communications, sort of reversed the flow. They're seeing what we want them to see and we're listening to everything they're broadcasting. They should be hitting the first barrier in about twenty minutes."

"I'll get the Destiny ready to go!" said Adrian.

"We'll take Dadeus and meet you there," said Mary.

"Can you handle things here without us?" asked Dadeus.

Nanchez smirked, "They'll be trying to shut down our power at the same time they launch their attack and we certainly don't want to disappoint our dear friend Zepallo. The least we could do is to provide a grand illusion for him. We're ready."

Ponte started shuffling people out the door, "Be on your way, there's no time to lose!"

Raffe and Mary grabbed Dadeus' arms and moved into the vectors followed by Adrian, who landed on the dock above the interface of the third dome and scrambled up the ladder to the bridge of the beautiful ship.

Captain Ruhl turned to greet him, "We're loaded and manned, just give me a destination!"

"The Island of the Children. The Dark Forces are about to attack."

"Oh, I do love a surprise," smirked the old man, as he stroked his gray beard with an amused twinkle in his eye. "You might not have noticed but, I believe, there's someone waiting to see you off."

Adrian turned to find Morgan standing alone on the platform on the starboard side of the ship. He slid down the ladder and wrapped his arms around her.

"Do be careful," whispered the tall beauty. "I want you to come back alive."

"I will, I promise," replied Adrian. "Tell my mother that I love her and I'm sorry I didn't have time to say goodbye."

"Don't worry, I will."

"Oh, and get Spot and Dusty and Magnus to send out a distress call through the whale mail. We're going to need all the help that we can get."

Adrian kissed her on the lips and levitated back onto the ship, as the captain punched several buttons on his console. A huge bubble formed around the crystal ship, as she leapt into the sky.

~

Zepallo pursed his lips as he stared at the screens. Two ships had dropped into the open for a few minutes and it could only mean that the Forces of Light were about to begin their resistance. The crystal ships were depositing troops and supplies and their intent would appear to be a sweep from west to east across Africa and South America, cutting the supply lines from the south.

He turned to a technician in the pod, "Get secure lines to Beta and Gamma!"

Their voices crackled a moment later, "Beta here," and then "This is Gamma."

"Be prepared for a counter strike across your supply lines. There is at least one crystal ship on the west coast of each continent. They appear to be dropping forces and supplies."

"We're ready," said Gamma calmly. "We've been expecting them."

"Likewise," laughed Beta. "We've set out a welcoming matt at the front door."

The Dark Lord smiled, "I just want you to know how proud I am of your accomplishments. As soon as they're out in the open, we'll begin taking control of their systems. Now get back to work, the next phase begins in a few hours."

~

The Hope deposited another group of fighters along the coast just north of Bahia Samborombon, then headed west to intercept two blips moving north. Simian watched the advances of the skiffs on the *orb* on the bridge of the crystal ship, as they skimmed through the river valleys, stopping occasionally to meet briefly with the leaders of the local resistance. Like a vine of freedom spreading out across the countryside, touching down to set new roots and absorb nourishment that would allow it to reach out in new directions…a massive army of animals and humans was growing and moving to the east.

Captain Travis nudged the Jamaican, "There they are, just to the west. I don't think they can see us in this plane. We should thank the Keepers for their new inventions!"

"What do you think about dropping in behind them? Maybe we can pick one off before they know we're there."

"They're quicker than we are but I agree," said the grizzled old sailor, as he turned and yelled, "Battle stations! All hands on deck! Prepare to tack hard a-starboard, full speed ahead!"

Chapter Thirteen

Colburn Tierney stepped through the portal between his office in Washington and the lobby of the second dome and noticed that the usual rush of bodies was absent. The dome was silent. He ran up the stairs to the third level, along the balcony, and into his wife's temporary office. She was alone at a workstation and swung around on her stool to hug him. "I'd be thankful that it's Friday night but I'm afraid this weekend will be one we won't forget."

"Is everyone safe?"

"Yes, they're all here but they've gone to help with the preparations for the invasion. All of the local people are moving weapons and equipment all over the island. The babies are with Elsie at the House of the Four Seasons. I thought I'd just finish up some design work. Who knows, if the *seers* and Keepers are successful, this campaign will need to be ready."

Coke hugged his wife, knowing that, when she was upset or frightened, she would bury herself in her work. It was the one thing that could totally occupy her mind, blocking everything else out and giving her a few minutes of peace. "Well, for the moment, I'm glad that you're all safe."

"How's everyone from the foundation?"

"We finished the week without incident and I sent everyone home until we see what's going to happen in the Southern Hemisphere."

"What did you find out?"

"Well, the markets closed down when the invasions were reported but until then, we were making some headway. With the information the boys pulled from Sir Jonathon's files, we've peeled back layer after layer of investment structures, corporate divisions, and endless bank and market accounts. It seems that there's a cluster…a small group of companies in countries around the world, that are all controlled by a Swiss corporation that uses a bank as its mailing address. Everything else flows through that one account."

"What's it called?"

"Le-Plazo."

"It sounds like the Plaza?"

Coke smiled, "As you know too well, the plaza was the center of every ancient city, the marketplace, the point where everyone's paths crossed, where goods and services are bought and sold, where money changed hands, and where connections were established. More interesting is that if you untangle the letters of the words, they spell 'Zepallo'."

Martina smiled, "You've done well."

"I sent word to Bartlett. I'm sure that the investigation will be expanded."

She glanced at the layout on her monitor, then at her husband, "Everyone's gone. Alius took one ship to Africa and Simian another to South America. We haven't heard what's happening. Dadeus, Mary, and Raffe left for the Island of the Children and Adrian took the third ship to defend them. They think the Dark Forces are going to attack there first."

"I'd better go see the Professor. Is he at the observatory?"

"Yes, I think Nanchez and Sammy are with him."

Coke rushed to Ponte's office and pressed the clasp on the golden crystal hanging around his neck. The portal opened and he stepped through to find Ester, who had just coming from the kitchen. "Dear, I'm just not used to people appearing through that portal. Having the *seers* flying through the air and disappearing into the vectors is one thing but regular people, like you and me...well, it's just unsettling. You'll be wanting Ponte and they're down in the workshops. Tell him that I've got a pot of stew brewing, when they're ready."

The attorney hugged the slender old woman and stepped into the elevator, which zipped down to the white room and the Golden Crystal. He stopped for a moment to watch the light glinting off the facets, as the huge gem rotated a foot above the floor, and consider all that these people had learned over the centuries and all they were trying to accomplish. In victory or defeat, he was proud to be considered a part of it all.

As he turned to the workshops, Sammy marched out of the computer room, "Oh, I'm glad you're here. There's too much going on!"

"Well, I think we found the central core. It's called Le-Plazo, a small, tightly controlled company that has a Swiss bank as its address. Everything leads back to them."

"That's great. Now we have a target."

"I've already told Chancellor Bartlett and he said that he would see that the investigation into the Foundation is expanded. It's time for the financial world to see the truth."

"When there's time, we'll dig through Sir Jonathon's files in the computers but, at the moment, I think we're more concerned with whether there will be a financial market to appreciate our efforts. The battles are about to begin in South America and Africa and the Dark Forces are set to launch an invasion of the Island of the Children. The next few hours will be decisive."

"Let's go see the Professor."

Ponte and Nanchez scurried up and down the length of the workbench, connecting cables, flipping switches, and checking circuits on *orbs* scattered at odd angles.

"Why don't you use the equipment in the domes instead of rewiring this old gear?" asked Tierney.

Nanchez snarled, "Because we've set up two independent systems, one that the Dark Forces can play with and monitor and, the other, through here. We know how this works."

Ponte turned to the pair, "We're approaching the moment of truth. If we have, indeed, got it right, they'll begin to take control of The Powers. At least, they'll believe that they have the keys to the positive vectors." He paused, "If we've got it right."

Coke looked up at the *messengers.* The first was covered with lines and symbols that had no meaning to him. The second showed the beautiful blond anchorwoman on the international news, without the sound. At the moment, they were showing maps of South America and Southern Africa, the lower half of each continent was darker than the north, indicating the loss of power and the progress of the invaders.

Another large monitor was split into four windows, each showing the circuits that the Keepers were working on at the moment. A fourth showed an overlay of the positive and negative vectors. The golden arcs seemed calm, while the deep purple curves vibrated and flickered, as if great surges of power were running to and from points across the southern hemisphere. The last displayed the progress of the three ships...Hope in South America, Grace sweeping south along the western coast of Africa, Destiny approaching the Island of the Children...and the movements of the Dark Forces.

Nanchez pointed to the *messenger* with the vectors, energy was being drawn from the countries to the south to overload the power-grid just to the north of the advances of the Dark Forces, "We've got to do something about that before they get much farther."

"We wait. Until they attempt to take control of our systems, there is nothing more that we can do. It won't be long now."

The huge Keeper was anxious, "There's a surge heading towards the Island of the Children. I'm sure that Dadeus erected protection but we should warn him!"

Ponte punched several keys and Dadeus' face appeared before one of the *messengers*, "There's a major surge headed your way."

"I see it. We're ready. Their troops won't be far behind. I see that Destiny is approaching. We'll need the help."

"Adrian and his crew might not get there before the Dark Forces."

"We can hold them off for a little while. I've set up a shield and closed off the interface. From the surface, it will appear that we've lost power."

Ponte smiled calmly, "This is our true test. Either we prevail or everything that we've fought to preserve will be lost."

The *messenger* blipped and Dadeus was replaced with the four windows.

~

Simian stood on the bow of Hope staring into the darkness at the black silhouette of Buenos Aires under a magnificent star field.

Several small saucers circled the city on patrol above a deep magenta glow in the heart of the capital that was the only light to the horizon. The crystal ship hovered on the edge of the plane, invisible to two large saucers patrolling the coast.

He spoke quietly into a *messenger* on his wrist, "Is everyone in place?"

Lala's voice crackled, "Roger, One."

"We're here, Two."

Waves of natives and animals from the countryside blended into the landscape, anticipating the signal, replied with similar responses in rapid succession.

He pressed a button on the wristband, "Ponte. We're ready when you are."

Pontes voiced crackled, "They've started invading the dummy systems. I'm expecting a wave of negative energy to sweep through the circuits momentarily."

In the background Nanchez yelled, "Here it comes!"

The connection clicked and buzzed and then went silent. "Professor? Professor can you hear me?"

Suddenly the lights in the city flickered for a moment before darkness returned. Another glimmer and lights began to glow in small pockets across the bay from the crystal ship. "Go! Go! Go!" yelled Simian. Hope dropped out of the plane and flew across the Rio de la Plata, over the harbor, and into the city center.

Four large saucers rose between the buildings, firing at the crystal ship racing towards the command center near the Teatro Colon. At the first salvo, Simian ducked instinctively. The Captain roared with laughter, "They weren't the only ones to learn from our battle at the Pole. We found the frequency of their charges and set up a shield that radiates the energy. Watch, they'll fire again."

Purple flames erupted from the cannons on the saucers and charges streaked through the sky, striking an invisible bubble that flexed with the shock and devoured the energy.

Travis bellowed, "Starboard guns…Fire at will!"

Eight crystal cannons fired in sequence, tracers burst through the fabric of the shield and arced in pursuit of the fleeing saucers. One of the craft erupted in searing flames and a cascade of shards showering the street below. Another slipped behind the spire of an ancient cathedral just as a stream of golden charges ripped past. A third settled at an odd angle on a plaza, smoke and troops pouring out of the smoldering remains. The fourth appeared soaring out of the first glimmers of the rising sun with guns blazing on a collision course with Hope.

Travis cried, "Aye, you want to play chicken. We'll see who turns last! All ahead full!"

The giant ship lurched as the sails caught the vector winds and soared across the city, taking aim on the sleek black ship streaking through moonlight. Simian was beginning to feel a little bit anxious and clung to the rail with both hands as the two ships closed at breakneck speed. At the last possible moment, the wily captain spun the wheel hard to starboard and the port guns opened up with a thunderous roar. The saucer banked hard, exposing the gleaming belly of the beast, and exploded in a massive shower of sparks and flames that showered past Hope into the bay.

Simian smiled, "Now, let's see who's minding the store! To the Command Center!"

Travis tacked Hope into the vector winds and Simian called the *seers* and fighters to the bridge. Several hundred gathered below the bridge. "We've had the opportunity to learn from each other, over the past months. Now those lessons will be put to good use. Believe in yourselves and the Powers and trust in each other. Understand that we are the only force on the face of the planet who have any chance of thwarting their invasion."

"We don't have to kill every warrior who wears dark robes. Our mission is to disrupt, sabotage, and take control wherever possible. You have your assignments but know that I'll take clever over heroic in any battle. First priorities are the defensive positions. We have no idea of how many of their troops are in residence. We believe that most have been sent to the front lines or to secure high value targets. Our second objective is to cut off or destroy their communications control. Third will be transport and supply, and, finally, the Center itself."

"I have every faith in you. Have faith in yourselves."

The crowd cheered as the old square-rigger settled gently to the pavement in front of the Teatro Colon amid a hail of fire.

~

Eight small saucers dropped out of the dark plane to seek out and destroy defenses before the invading force landed in two large carriers. A dozen mini-subs rushed through the ocean from the east, on course for the interface and the Ruby Crystal beneath the pink pyramid.

Initial reports showed no signs of life, let alone resistance, as Marcus piloted one of the smaller saucers to the edge of the plaza at the foot of the pyramid. A panel opened with a hiss and he emerged to walk along the path and up the steps to the promenade at the peak, where he could look down on the white stone of the growing city. *"What a shame to destroy such a lovely setting,"* he thought, sarcastically, realizing that there were no fighters waiting in defense, no animal sounds, no sign of movement to the peak of the ridgeline that rippled like a jagged fin along center of the island to the south, he spoke into the *messenger* suspended near his mouth by an earpiece, "It's a trap. Be prepared for a counter attack."

All power within the domes had been extinguished and the single *messenger* displaying the movements of the enemy provided the only light in Dadeus' workshop. A wave of energy swept through the vectors and passed over the island without damage to the system.

The submarines were approaching the boundary and…a moment more…he punched a button on the console and power surged through the complex, energizing guidance controls to crystal canons that had been installed at strategic points across the island and throwing up an energy shield that trapped the subs at two hundred feet below the surface. Better to draw the enemy into the snare by allowing the saucers to attempt a landing and Dadeus was confident they would not be leaving. He chuckled, "That ought to even the odds a little bit! Soule and

Amy will lead the divers to the subs and join up with the sea creatures. That ought to be a battle!"

Raffe smiled, "I'm off to meet the enemy. It'll take them a while to find the entrances but it might take them longer if they're under fire!"

"I can provide that for you," replied Dadeus, as he spun around to several *orbs* floating above another workstation. He flipped several switches and one of the *messengers* displayed the troops of the Dark Forces emerging from a large saucer perched at the far end of the little boulevard through the center of the tiny city. A moment later, four concussions resonated across the island and warriors scattered in every direction.

Raffe bounded through the tunnels to join the squad of fighters hiding behind the waterfall. He pressed through his friends, "They've landed two big saucers of troops, one at the far end of the plaza and the other on the beach on the east side of the island. There are also smaller saucers looking for a target, so stay down. Mary's taking another group to cut them off along the ridgeline. Let's deal with the closest first!"

Blackbeard, the monkey, appeared and led the fighters down the rocks, along the path to the overlook where Adrian, Molly, Morgan, and Tic witnessed the ceremony that sent Ponte to the underworld only three years previously. Troops in dark robes were moving cautiously around the plaza, entering and securing one building after another. "That's where we'll meet them, in the open," whispered Raffe. He touched the arm of the glasses that Dadeus provided, "Do you see this?"

"Oh, yes! I'm waiting for them to move away from the buildings."

"We'll meet them at the column. Give us some cover."

Suddenly, two small saucers swooped over the trees, spinning to strafe the ledge. Blackbeard screeched as charges exploded all around them, forcing a retreat under fire into the cover of the jungle. "Anyone hurt?" called Raffe.

A voice replied, "Two down but they'll live."

"Take care of them, while we work our way down through the forest. We grew up on this island, let's use it to our advantage."

Four loud explosions tore through the plaza, as Dadeus opened up with crystal cannons erected in the perimeter of the forest, just as the squad ran into the open.

Marcus stood alone, at the precipice of the pyramid, talking calmly into the *messenger* to order his forces, "Regroup! Regroup! One squad is about to emerge from the trees to the southeast and another is coming up from the west side of the city. Cover One and Two, take out those cannons!"

A pair of gleaming black saucers screamed around the tip of the pyramid and took aim on the crystal guns, hidden in the trees on either side of the plaza. One exploded, just as it fired a blast that tore through a mass of soldiers, and the other crumbled in a shower of sparks. A third cannon spun around and fired two blasts, striking the saucer to the north. The sleek craft exploded in a burst of icy embers and deep purple flames, tumbling wreckage scorching through the forest at the base of the pyramid.

Raffe led his troops into the throng of dark troopers, as Gabrielle's group charged the white stone plaza from the west. The old man's eyes blazed as he shouted, "We will not be invaded again! Remember the pirates!"

Lions and tigers, leapt from the foliage and elephants charged the huge saucer hovering just above the ground at the far end of the concourse, causing it to swing back and forth like a huge, sharp pendulum at the end of a string. The static pulse of the force field only angered a bull elephant, who rammed the ship again and again until it pealed like a church bell.

Marcus screamed into his *messenger*, "Back out and swing around to the pyramid. We don't want to damage the ship!"

Sleek saucers streaked through the air above the din on the plaza, unable to fire into the roiling swarm of fighters. Blue and gold sparks erupted from hundreds of swords and the air vibrated with the racket, heavy with the smoke of blasts fired at point blank range. Bodies fell in piles on the pavement, neither side willing to concede. The remaining guns tracked the saucers, taking out two before being blown to bits in a hale of charges.

A second company of dark robed troops force-marched through the jungle and moved into the first valley. Dadeus fired a volley of charges from cannon hidden on the peaks of the hills that ripped through the fighters. Mary dispatched two groups of warriors who lined up on either side of the ditch to fire freely, driving the enemy down the trough. Rats, dogs, cats, squirrels, iguanas, mice, a few porcupines, raccoons, and snakes scurried from beneath rocks and foliage, nipping and biting at the rampaging warriors. Monkeys, chimpanzees, wild boar, mountain goats, bear, lions, tigers, panthers, jaguars, cheetahs, and elephants appeared to block the far end of the gorge.

Suddenly three saucers appeared in the sky above the mêlée, firing into the tree line at the top of the ridges. The Dark Forces broke their retreat, turning the attack on the island fighters who charged down the hillsides. Cannon fire raked the little valley, billowing smoke obscuring any hint of an advantage that either legion might be taking in a slaughter decimating both forces.

Mary hovered at the peak of the western ridge, firing charges from a hand cannon at the saucers. The screams of humans and the roar of the animals echoed through the little canyon with the intensity of thunder. She touching the arm of her glasses, "I don't think we're winning here!"

Raffe's voice crackled through her headset, "I hate to admit that we could use some help on this end!"

Dadeus replied, "The cannon in the plaza are finished and two on the ridge have been taken out. Destiny should be here at any moment!"

~

Grace dipped low over the cold waters of St. Helena Bay, along the western coast of South Africa. Communication with Ponte and the other Keepers ceased almost an hour earlier and they could not reach Hope or Destiny. From the deck of the mighty ship, the crew could see the lights of Cape Town shimmering in the distance, glimmering beacons confirming that the Keepers were doing their best to restore local power. Large saucers ferried troops and equipment in and out of a

Command Center that had been nestled into the hills above the main highway to the north.

The bands of defenders joined with native tribes and animals to overrun supply depots, small command outposts, and somehow managed to hijack two small saucers and several ancient Russian fighter aircraft. They could only hope that their efforts would slow the advances of the Dark Forces until they could take control of the power grid.

Shambala reached to take Alius' hand, "It is our time."

Alius looked up at the tall woman's dark eyes. There was no fear, no hesitation in the clarity flowing like silk from her deep golden aura. "It isn't that I'm afraid. I'm more concerned about everyone else, I guess I never appreciated how hard it is to accept that responsibility. Adrian always directed the final moves in our battles but, somehow, he seemed to find little islands of wisdom to focus his vision and guide his decisions at the critical moments."

"Have you forgotten our invasion of the Caucasus? You and you alone led that attack. You formulated it in your mind and allowed the Powers to guide you. This is no different," whispered Shambala. "You are the most powerful woman *seer* on the planet. If Adrian is the chosen one, then you are certainly his equal! We all have faith in you."

Alius blushed and turned to Cappy, who was wearing his leather flight helmet and goggles, "It's time!"

"Right you are, lassie! All hands on deck! Man your battle stations!"

~

Destiny slipped out of the aqua plane of The Tropics and deposited a large force of fighters between the tiny city and the small lagoon. *Seers*, in robes of every color, levitated over the trees and into the battle in the plaza like a swarm of butterflies firing blasts from their swords and hand cannons. Fighters of every description charged through the forest and into the melee on the white pavestones already glistening with a deep shade of red.

Adrian hovered above the edge of the rampaging fighters and spied Raffe on the far side of the square, surrounded by a curtain of dark robes. He flew through a volley of charges that ripped through acrid smoke rolling across the plaza and landed beside his friend, who was holding off a pack of troopers.

"Nice of you to show up for the party," screamed Raffe.

"Sorry we were late but we're here now!"

"Mary's got her hands full down in the first valley. Send the Destiny to help."

Adrian swung his sword with his right hand, while trying to talk into the *messenger* on his left wrist. "Captain! Destiny is needed in the first valley on the east side of the ridge!"

Above the screams of the desperate and the dying, he could not hear the reply. The two *seers* charged the dark fighters, killing two and wounding another three in fierce combat amid waves of guards rolling in to replace their comrades.

Marcus' first company was pinched between island warriors and the reinforcements from Destiny. Suddenly, two sleek saucers raced above the plaza, firing charges at the Forces of Light, scattering the defenses. A blast hissed past Adrian and raked Raffe across the chest, just as he turned to point at the pyramid. The *seer* collapsed on the ground, blood gushing from his robes. Adrian knelt down and put pressure on the wound to stem the bleeding, "You'll be alright. Just hang on!"

Raffe grabbed Adrian's robes and pulled him down close to his face, "Mar…cus is…on the py…ra…mid. He's directing…the Dark Forces. You have to stop him…"

The wounded *seer* passed out. Adrian grabbed the glasses, as two *seers* seized the shoulders of Raffe's robes and lifted him out of the battle. Adrian turned to stare at the lone figure, silhouetted in moonlight on the top of the pyramid, his dark robes billowing in the breeze.

~

Grace swept out of the plane directly above the Command Center, which was illuminated by rows of immense black *orbs* pointing straight up into the sky like flaming pillars. In the distance, the lights of

Cape Town surged and faded, only to glow again and, here and there throughout the countryside, pockets where the power had been restored.

Cappy crooked a finger at Alius and Shambala, "You ladies might want to look at this."

The golden *orb* displayed the waves of positive and negative energy, churning through the vectors across the southern half of the continent in a titanic struggle for dominance.

"Now we know why we've lost communication," said the old man, pointing to the sky.

Brilliant gold and deep purple waves smeared the heavens, roiling over each other, swirling and twisting like the curtains at the window as the first wind rushes out of stillness before the storm.

Alius turned to Shambala and then to Captain Cappy, "We have to move now!"

"That's the spirit!" laughed the old man, yelling to the crew, "We've some fighters coming in off the starboard bow! Fire when ready!"

A half-dozen black saucers whizzed around the boundary of the shield, firing charges that sank into the bubble and disappeared with a dull flash. Eight cannons let loose a volley from either side of the ship, destroying three of the sleek craft, as the Captain coaxed the huge vessel to settle slowly into the ravine behind the complex. At the last moment, he spun the huge wheel to turn her broadside to the enemy. The portside cannon opened up on the encampment, while another eight fired up through the rigging at fighters diving out of the sky.

The *seers* and warriors slipped over the starboard rail. Alius gathered her troops together, "This is our time. Remember, hit their defensive positions first, then communication. Shambala will lead half of you to their landing port to disrupt and destroy their ships and facilities. If we can ground their transportation, we can cripple their advances. I'll take the rest of you through the other side of the base to the Central Command Center." She paused, "I believe in you and you must believe in yourselves and each other. We will succeed!"

~

Ponte's expression was grave, "It's a tug of war! They've amassed enough energy to fry every electrical system on the planet!"

"We're holding them," growled Nanchez.

"That's true. They're not gaining," added Sammy.

"And neither are we!"

The monitors showed the advances of the crews from Hope and Grace, as masses of fighters and animals charged the Command Centers. There was no communication from the Island of the Children nor could they allow direct contact with anyone outside the workshops, although word had gone out to the other Keepers around the globe, who were focusing all of the energy from the positive vectors to equalize the imbalance in the southern hemisphere.

The Dark Forces controlled the advanced systems that had been installed in the domes, shutting down power in measured increments. So far, there was reason to believe that they would not discover the ruse of dual structures before the *seers* and their friends could take down the hubs of field operations. Breaking their silence would certainly tip off Zepallo's technicians.

"I'm not sure how long we can hold this level," growled Nanchez. "The positive vectors are surging and vibrating. The whole system could implode!"

Sammy whispered, "I have faith in both of you, don't let me down now!"

Ponte and Nanchez's laughter exploded through the little workshop, "All right lad, you've made your point. Let's get back to work."

Coke held the door, as Ester entered her husband's inner sanctum, "I've a pot of stew on the stove, if any of you gentlemen are hungry."

Ponte walked over and hugged her, "I'm sorry, we've had some distractions down here."

"What's happening," asked Coke, who had been working on Sir Jonathon's computers in the next room.

"Well, at the moment, it's a stalemate. We're pouring power into the southern hemisphere and they're pulling it out at an equal rate," replied Nanchez.

"They're using it to short circuit the systems just in front of the advancing forces," added Sammy, "disrupting any defense that might stand against them."

"Hope and Grace are moving in on the advance cores but we haven't heard a word from the Island of the Children," said Ponte quietly. "There isn't much more we can do, until our troops take their targets. Unfortunately, it won't be long before their technicians realize that they don't actually have control of both systems. At that point, they'll send a force to find out why."

Ester kissed the Professor on the cheek, "I'll just bring the stew down here for once. You all need some nourishment. Mr. Tierney, would you be kind enough to give me a hand?"

"Of course," smiled the attorney. "I'm certainly no use in the lab at the moment."

~

Troops from the Hope rushed through the streets of Buenos Aires to join waves of animals and local fighters in the attack on the command center hidden in Plaza LaValle, a long city park surrounded by perfectly square blocks of multistory buildings. Travis piloted the giant ship into the air and tacked to the south for a run on the transportation hub in Reserva Ecologica Costanera Sur, an ecological reserve on the coast, through a screen of seven small saucers and two large gunships.

Simian was pushed along by the surge of fighters and animals stampeding through the boulevards. A stream of charges ripped across the pavement, through the advancing army, and Simian lifted above the rooftops, where he could see fortifications blocking every entrance to the enormous plaza.

In spite of the casualties, the throng surged ahead, *seers* and fighters firing hand cannons and lobbing crystal grenades in response to a fierce fusillade of charges from the rooftops. Herds of capybaras (one hundred and seventy-five-pound rodents) swarmed ahead of the humans, leading packs of maned wolves, slithering caiman, puma, and jaguar into the square overwhelming dark robed troops at their stations.

Simian spied reinforcements spilling out of the buildings and fired charges from his sword, as he swooped down over his warriors, to join other *seers* on the attack. A blazing purple charge ripped through the sleeve of his robes, as he darted to his left to blast troopers manning a cannon emplacement on top of a tower.

The vast square was shrouded in smoke, illuminated by numbing explosions and brilliant cascades of sparks, as the two sides clashed together in mortal combat. Casualties from both sides littered the smooth stone pavers and the screams of the injured blended with the incessant concussions of the cannon, the clash of swords, the high-pitched drone of the saucers soaring overhead, and the shrieks and howls of the animals.

The old Jamaican spied Lala and Maze leading more fighters into the din through the narrow street next to Teatro Colon, as a pair of dark *seers* flew up at full speed. Blasts from their swords ripped through the air around him. He twirled in place, extending his sword to meet the attack, slicing one of them across the back. He flipped over to face the return of the second, as a sword sliced through the yellow material of his other sleeve, the tatters smoldering and smoking. *"I'm getting to be too old for this!"* In one continuous motion, he dodged a blast and spun to meet his adversary, catching him under the chin with a fatal blow.

A deep purple glow pulsed hypnotically around the five domes of the command center with four smaller structures surrounding a larger sphere in the center. Troops from both sides were pushing the front lines back and forth across the plaza, neither holding ground for long. Skiffs dueled with small saucers, diving and soaring into the first streaks of sunlight in the morning sky.

Simian anticipated reinforcements for Dark Forces arriving momentarily and raised the *messenger* on his wrist to his mouth, "We have to strike the central dome now!"

A dozen *seers* flew above the fighters on the ground and formed a ring, firing down on the five structures. Maze and Lala led the first advance, while Simian plunging through the blistering torrent, his sword pealing a long tear in the top of the central dome to reveal a dark interior filled with purple *orbs* floating within a circle of giant screens. Cannon fire erupted through the wound in the outer skin of the dome, magenta tracers exploding in every direction. The blasts knocked Simian out of the sky and he fell onto the roof of one of the smaller structures, a wounded bird sliding down to the ground.

He reached through a hole in his robes and felt the warm flow of blood. The world around him exploded with a huge orange flash and a deep concussion knocked the air out of his lungs. The old Jamaican's knees buckled and he fell on the pavers, rolled on his side, and passed out.

Chapter Fourteen

Adrian slashed through a caldron of black-caped warriors and flew through the smoke above the melee, his sword leveled at the dark robed figure standing calmly on the terrace near the peak of the pyramid. A small saucer rose behind the pink stone monument and took aim on the approaching *seer.*

Young Adrian felt his anger and determination wane in a moment of panic but, in the next instant, his resolve was restored by a strange calm that wrapped around his body like a warm blanket. Everything slowed and he could see each face in the armies slaughtering each other on the plaza, the movement of the saucer, the amused expression on Marcus' face, and he knew that a long moment would lapse before the charges escaped the muzzles of the guns that were directed at him.

Ponte's decision to hold him back, while so many others went off to fight, leaving him to the menial tasks of the preparations for Destiny's voyage, had wounded him like a hot knife plunging into his soul. It was the Professor's less than subtle reminder that he, of all the *seers*, could not lose focus.

He allowed his senses to open completely, for the first time in days, and was overwhelmed by the intensity of the dark energies in the planes and the cries of those who were fighting and dying across the planet. In that instant before four purple flames erupted from the cannons on the black saucer, he realized that dear and familiar auras and voices were missing from the chorus that produced the sound of life.

The fireballs pulsed as they traced through billowing smoke and Adrian felt that he could almost reach out to grab one as it sizzled past. The guns fired again and the young *seer* dropped a few feet to watch them whiz overhead. Marcus was no longer smiling but held his sword out, ready to fire a blast at the blur closing on him through another volley of shimmering purple blisters.

A trio of charges flashed from the tip of the sword and Adrian spun into a corkscrew as they passed, landing just at the edge of the terrace at the top of the pyramid.

Marcus screamed, "There are too many of us in too many places. You'll never win!"

Adrian ducked, as his enemy lunged to strike the first blow. Sparks showered down the side of the pyramid, as their swords clashed, trailing their deadly duel around the precipice in the deep red halo of the rising sun, each retreating before regaining the advantage. Marcus was much stronger and more nimble than Adrian might have expected, after their previous confrontation and, even with his perception of motion slowed, he knew that he would have to earn this victory, if he was fortunate enough to survive.

The sights and sounds of the battle vanished into a distant din and he focused on the dark, blazing, fearless eyes that seemed to anticipate each thrust and parry. The two *seers* floated into the air and tumbled in odd circles, sparks dripping down on the cap of the pyramid into the tiny chamber that once sheltered The Book of Natural Balance.

Marcus twirled and caught Adrian across the shoulder. The young warrior could smell his own flesh burning and feel the blood oozing from the gash, as he stumbled near the center of the terrace, his sword skittering across flat stones. He reached to catch it but Marcus landed between the weapon and its master. "Now isn't this an interesting turn of events?"

Adrian crawled backwards until his body was pressed against the stone door to the alcove.

"Weren't you the one…? Why, yes, you were the one who threatened to kill me the last time we met. I didn't think that your attitude was particularly hospitable, especially when I tried to offer a chance for peace between our peoples. I think that qualifies as aggressive behavior. I would have expected better manners from the most renowned *seer* on the planet!" smiled the dark *seer*, inching closer and closer, his sword held out so it might land just under Adrian's chin. "I believe that we have a score to settle but I thought you might want to know that I've been informed that the fighting in South America is at a stalemate, Morgan's Knot is about to be attacked, and, even more interesting, Beta has captured your beautiful friend Alius. I believe they'll be meeting with Zepallo within the hour!"

The sky exploded with thousands of hummingbirds fluttering inside bubbles that glowed in the first blazing glint of the sun at dawn, the sound of their wings and the chorus of the chirps creating a pulsating white noise that blocked out the sounds of the battle on the plaza. Adrian felt Orana's strength, dedication, and her spirit flow through his body and slipped his fingers under the edge of the heavy stone door to pry it open. Marcus lunged but Adrian flipped over backwards and willed the door shut. He slipped into the vectors, appeared a moment later on the edge of the terrace, and grabbed his sword. Marcus was still hammering at the stone with the handle of his weapon, each blow producing a shower of purple sparks cascading around his body.

The young *seer* walked slowly across the pale pink stones and tapped him on the shoulder. Marcus spun around to find Adrian's sword resting on his Adam's apple. "Now what were you saying about Alius?"

The dark *seer* stared straight into Adrian's eyes, "I said that Beta had captured your little friend and would be taking her to Zepallo!"

"Unless you tell me where they've taken her, I see no reason to spare your life," replied Adrian but his mind was suddenly filled with Orana's voice. "Stop wasting time on this little twit, there are more important things that you need to accomplish. You've been so wrapped up in your own little dramas that you've missed the whole point! It isn't about winning the battles, it's winning the war!"

The young *seer* hesitated and Marcus stole the moment to swing his sword at Adrian's head. He ducked, caught the dark *seer's* leg, and flipped him on his back. He pointed his sword at this chest.

Orana screamed, "Stop it! You are needed elsewhere now!"

Adrian stared at the stone door, which opened slowly. He looked down at Marcus, "Get up!"

Marcus stood and Adrian pushed him inside the tiny sanctuary. "The battle will be over by the time you figure out how to get out of here. You can't escape into the dark vectors from inside this tomb. It's in a vortex of positive vectors. I'm sure some of my friends will be happy to take you prisoner after they've finished off your troops! Perhaps we'll trade you for Alius, when the Dark Forces have been defeated."

As the heavy stone door swung shut, Marcus yelled, "Now it's time for you to fulfill my prophecy. You will stand against the Dark Lord!"

The battle continued on the plaza, although he sensed there were now more colored robes than black. He pulled the glasses from his pocket and put them on. Touching the arm, he said, "Dadeus! Can you hear me?"

"Yes, who is this?"

"It's Adrian. Raffe's been wounded and the Dark Forces are going to invade Morgan's Knot. I have to go."

"I understand," replied the old Keeper. His voice was quivering.

"Can you hold them?"

"Mary's troops have been decimated and they've morphed into a guerrilla force in the forest. We've destroyed most of the saucers but our cannon are finished. If you can leave Destiny, we might have a chance."

"Fine," said Adrian. "I hate to run out on you."

"Adrian, you have no other choice. If the Dark Forces capture Morgan's Knot, the game is up!"

"Thanks. Oh, by the way, there's a prisoner in the cap of the pyramid. Marcus is a powerful *seer* and probably heir to the throne. So be careful."

"I'll see that we have several *seers* in attendance! By the way, I've just learned that Raffe is in the infirmary. He's alive."

"Good. Have you heard anything from Ponte?"

"No, all communications were lost several hours ago."

"I'll let you know what happens," said Adrian as he dropped the glasses into his pocket and lifted into the vectors. He could feel Alius' fear and panic but he knew that his duty called him to Morgan's Knot.

He listened for Orana's voice but the vectors were filled with the sounds of war. The once clear colors were dim, a haze of dark energy grated and groaned, and the paths twisted and vibrated as never before.

He felt as if he was swimming upstream against a strong current but his destination was not growing closer.

Orana's words echoed around inside his mind, "You've missed the whole point!" In a flash, he saw the aqua color of the ocean and heard Coke's voice, "Water is the key to all life on the planet."

He wanted to ask, *"But how does that help us?"* but there was no one in the vectors to answer the question.

Adrian landed on the path outside the observatory. There was no movement on the island, the torrential rains continued unabated, and he sensed that the invasion was imminent. He ran up the steps and heaved the heavy door open, charged through the parlor, into the elevator and down to the workshops.

The Golden Crystal was spinning madly and the lights were pulsing. He barged through the door to the Professor's workshop and Ponte, Nanchez, and Sammy all turned to stare. The shoulder and sleeve of his robes were soaked in blood and his face was smeared with soot. He stammered, "They're going to invade the island."

Nanchez chuckled, "Our friends and neighbors are ready for them!"

Ponte rushed to help the young *seer*, who stumbled to a seat on a stool. "What's happening?"

The Professor leaned in front of Adrian, his little glasses were so close that he could see the reflection of his own eyes. "Tell me, how goes it on the Island of the Children?"

"It's a stalemate. Raffe's been wounded. Mary's forces were overwhelmed and the two forces were fighting to the last man in the plaza when I left. I did capture Marcus but he said that Alius had been taken captive!"

"That's what we've heard too," said Ponte quietly. "Fortunately, she and her friends managed to blow up the command center, which stopped the advances of the Dark Forces, at least for the moment. We've been trying to monitor the progress in South America but no one has been able to communicate with Simian. Travis sent a message that they managed to knock out the transportation center and they've taken control of almost half of the north-south corridors.

The unfortunate part of all of this is that the Positive and Negative energies are almost perfectly matched and neither side has the capacity to overcome the other."

"When we opened the vectors and started pouring energy into the Southern Hemisphere, the Dark Forces knew, instantly, that they never had control of the systems on Morgan's Knot, which is why we've been expecting an invasion," added Sammy.

"If we can't defend the island, then they will, indeed, control all of the powers. It's as simple as that," said Nanchez.

"There has to be another way," sighed Adrian, as he stared at his friends. "We have to counter-attack or create a diversion."

"I'm not sure that we have the power or enough fighters to do much more than defend the island. I've set up a shield that will slow them down and everyone on the island's been preparing defensive positions. It's just a matter of time."

The aqua color flashed through Adrian's mind, his lesson in the depths of the ocean accompanied by Coke's words, "Water is the key to all life on the planet…" He reached up and touched to golden crystal that hung on the slender golden chain around his neck. Orana's voice screamed, "You've missed the point! It isn't about winning the battle, it's winning the war that's important!"

Adrian smiled slowly, "I know how to do this…"

Coke pushed open the door to the workshop to allow Ester to wheel in another little wooden cart covered with dishes that offered the scents of real food. "Ah, Adrian! You look horrible," said the slender old woman as she rushed to him. "Let me have a look at that wound. We'll be needing Doctor Stevens."

Adrian hugged her back, "There isn't time for that right now. We have a war to win."

Ponte let a curious little smile replace the frustrated scowl that creased his brow. They had all benefited more than once from Adrian's insights and he expected another one in the next moment or two, "What is it that you're thinking, lad?"

"Are Masters Chi and Jung still here?"

"Yes, they're in the observatory."

"Call them," said Adrian quietly. "Is Sir Isaac in England?"

"Yes, the Dark Forces haven't found his laboratory yet. Energy from his Positive Crystal is still on the network."

"Good! We'll be sending Sammy and the two Masters to help him construct some portals. I think that we'll be needing a half dozen just like the ones they created to move the beams to the interface."

Everyone in the room stood silently staring at the young *seer,* until Nanchez finally sputtered, "What are you going to use the portals for?"

Adrian looked from one face to another and purposely waited until Masters Chi and Jung appeared at the door, "What would happen if you were to create a portal that opened in their command centers on one side and deep in the ocean on the other?"

~

Zepallo stared at the screens lining the enormous cavern beneath the mountains in North Korea. The expeditionary forces fought to a draw in South America and communication with Gamma had been lost. An energy shield prevented an overview of the battle on the Island of the Children and hours had passed since they last heard from Marcus. The Command Center in Southern Africa was overrun and destroyed and the advances of their armies had slowed. The technicians created circuits to siphon off waves of positive energy that the Forces of Light were pouring into the Southern Hemisphere but, until the Keepers on Morgan's Knot were taken, the positive and negative vectors would continue neutralizing each other. Cadeau spoke for many of their brightest and most capable technicians, when he suggested the whole system might implode, destroying everything on the planet.

The experiment at the North Pole funneled only partial power to a central point where it could be focused. This was the first time that the power from all of the Crystals, positive and negative, had been channeled and no one could possibly know the outcome.

He turned to the center screen, which displayed the movements of the troops across the planet. A dozen minisubs were on course for Morgan's Knot, scheduled to rendezvous with an invasion force in less than six hours. Repeated surges through the systems on the island, which were tied through the Dark Crystal, had no effect on the quantity of power being forced through the positive vectors. Despite their best efforts, every Positive Crystal on the planet was exporting full power into the circuits.

The most positive event had been the capture of Adrian's little friend, Alius. He instructed Beta to take her to the chalet in the mountains of Switzerland and looked forward to seeing her again. It was secluded, private enough to deny her access to the command centers. Her knowledge of the structure of the Forces of Light might prove invaluable and he was absolutely sure that Adrian would appear. He looked forward to their meeting, the young master had triumphed in previous confrontations but he would not be so fortunate this time. This would be a duel to vanquish the only threat to the purity and purpose of his lineage.

The Dark Lord turned to Regis, who bowed. "I'll be going to the chalet for the next two hours to question our most valuable hostage. Keep me informed of the progress of our campaign. On my return, I will direct the attack on Morgan's Knot."

"As you wish, Sire."

Zepallo stepped off the edge of the floating command pod and landed at the entrance to the maze of tunnels and locks protecting the workers in the chamber from the energies of the Dark Crystal. He reached up and removed the black crystal from the chain around his neck. His injuries required months of recovery and The Doctor had denied him access to the powers. He could feel the intensity increase as each lock closed behind him with a whoosh and a click. The currents flowed from his fingertips to his core, replenishing his strength in tiny increments. When, finally, he reached the cavern that held the Black Crystal, a wail of ecstasy reverberated through the entire complex. He opened his arms and inhaled the energies of the only power that he worshipped, this black goddess transformed him from mere mortal to the most powerful *seer*, the most dominant leader, on the planet. He would not be denied.

~

Masters Chi and Jung escorted Sammy to the secluded laboratory in the plains of England, after a short discussion over the last secure lines in the network, between Sir Isaac and those crammed into the tiny workshop beneath the observatory.

Ester insisted that Adrian needed more than just one bowl of her rather bland stew, so he was almost relieved when Dr. Stevens arrived to tend to his wound.

The Doctor tut-tutted as he examined the gash in the young *seer's* shoulder, gripping Arian's jaw to stare into his eyes, "I thought we agreed that we weren't going to go on meeting like this?"

"Tragic accident. I must have slipped."

"If you'd slipped the other way, it would have been your head!"

"How about a lucky accident?"

"I'll take that," laughed Dr. Stevens. "Do you have time to heal or are you going off to fight again?"

"They've taken Alius…"

"I see. Alright, I'll clean it out with my cleansing waters and we'll patch you up for the moment. That's the best I can do," he said, cutting away the burnt remnants of sleeve of his blue robes. "This is probably going to hurt."

An hour later, Adrian could move the fingers of his left hand and the pain in his shoulder became almost bearable. Unfortunately, he could not raise his arm above his chest. Ester appeared with new robes that were only slightly too large, "These are the best I can do for the time being."

"I really appreciate it," replied Adrian with a hug. "Do we have any idea when the invasion might start?"

Ponte turned to him, "If we knew that everyone could relax until they arrive!"

Nanchez peered at a *messenger* at the far end of the workbench, "Actually, we might have a hint. Our scopes are showing a small armada of minisubs moving from all directions towards the island. I'd say that they'll arrive in…four to five hours."

"Do you know where my parents are?"

"Yes, they're up at a battle station at the House of the Four Seasons, where they can cover a good stretch of the eastern coast."

"I'd like to see them. Then I'll try to find Alius. I've got a pair of Dadeus' glasses and I'll check in to see what's happening. Call me if the invasion begins before I get back."

Ester hugged him and Ponte patted him on the back, "There isn't anyone to accompany you. Are you sure that you're up to facing Zepallo and who knows how many others?"

The young *seer* hesitated for a moment and mumbled, "I won't be alone…and Alius came for me, when I was locked in that crystal."

Ponte sighed, "I know but I wish I could offer a better solution. Just know that we want both of you to return safely. You don't have to win the war on your own."

"I know," blushed Adrian.

Coke put an arm around his good shoulder, "I hope you know how proud I am to be a part of all of this and yet I feel so helpless. Be careful."

Adrian smiled, bowed his head and moved into the vectors. A moment later, he was standing on the path near the vegetable patch. Red tomatoes, tall corn, squash, beans, and lettuces overflowed the south end of the garden. It had been months since he last had a moment to marvel, to smell the salt air blowing in off the ocean, and to feel the fragile peace of this place.

A light flickered in the barn, so he walked through the torrent of rain across the yard and in through the workshop. Where the trolley and the wagon once rested, three crystal cannon were nestled on articulating turrets. His mother raced over to hug him and noticed that he winced, "Are you wounded?"

"It's only a little gash on my shoulder. Dr. Stevens stitched it up a little while ago."

John asked, "How's it going out there?"

"It's a war. South America and Africa are at a stalemate. Our friends on the Island of the Children are hanging on but just barely. There's an invasion planned for Morgan's Knot in four or five hours,

Raffe's injured, no one's heard from Simian in hours, and, somehow, Beta managed to capture Alius."

Morgan walked up behind him and carefully draped a long arm across his shoulders, just as she had during their return voyage from the Island of the Children, "Then you have to go get her."

Adrian winced and hugged her with his good arm, "I was worried about how you'd react."

"It's the right thing to do, especially for you."

"I'll be back before the Dark Forces arrive. I promise. In the meantime, we've come up with a plan that might win this war once and for all, but, if that doesn't work, then we'll have to defend the observatory. We can't let them take control of the powers."

Sara whispered, "You know this scares me…?"

"And you know that I have no other choice. I love you…"

He kissed her on the cheek, bowed his head, and returned to the vectors.

~

Flaring flames leapt from the circular fireplace at the center of the meeting room in the chalet, dulling the chill. Snow fell horizontally through an angry sky, buffeting the windows on the north, swirling over the roof into drifts on the south terrace.

Beta sat cross-legged several feet above the hearth, warming his hands before the fire. "It won't be long now," he laughed. "My Lord will be here shortly and I know he's anxious to speak with you."

Alius floated in mid-air twenty feet above the stone floor, her arms outstretched as if she were a marionette suspended by the strings of a wicked puppeteer. A large black diamond pendant swung gently back and forth from a chain around her neck. Beta placed it there before they moved into the dark vectors from the burning complex just north of Cape Town. Its spell rendered her incapable of controlling her own body.

Raffe warned her about the effects of their black diamonds after being held captive in the cavern beneath New York City. "I couldn't speak or move unless I was commanded by Zepallo. I felt like a human robot but my mind continued to function in absolute desperation and I knew that you and Adrian would find a way to rescue me. I struggled to find the strength or focus to get rid of that crystal, so I could help."

Alius could think and she knew that Adrian would come for her, in spite of the way she treated him on the beach, and that frightened her because everyone else was fighting battles around the globe. He was brave enough and foolish enough to come alone. She concentrated...first on chocolate, so he would know that her message was authentic, then on the snow-covered mountains, although she wasn't sure where they were…and finally she repeated, over and over, *"Adrian, it's a trap…Adrian, it's a trap."*

She watched Beta stoking the fire. There was a sinister smile on his lips as he glanced up at her occasionally, "It won't be long now. My Master should be arriving momentarily."

Alius thought, *"If he's your Master, then you're his slave…but you're worse than that because you're his fiendish incarnation."*

"I understand that you began your career as a *seer* on the Dark Side. It's unfortunate you had a change of heart. Perhaps you might reconsider that decision?" He glanced up, "No? Too bad, we would make a lovely couple, don't you think?"

The air in the room stirred with a whoosh and a ball of purple electricity materialized beneath her. Zepallo extended his arms and smiled at Beta, "You've done well, my son."

"I'm afraid our armies are merely holding the Forces of Light in a stalemate. The command center is a shambles, so I wouldn't count that as a success."

"We have a legion ready to invade Morgan's Knot in a little over three hours. Once we take control of the Powers, the resistance will vanish. Our young guest might provide us with valuable information. Perhaps she can help expedite our plans."

He turned and pointed to Alius, "Come down from there!"

The blond *seer* floated down to hover in front of the Dark Lord. She could not avoid the intensity of his blistering blue eyes. The power was terrifying and, if she could move her body or form words with her mouth, she would not hesitate to defy him, but her stifled screams echoed around inside her head.

"Tell me about the Golden Crystal on Morgan's Knot!"

Her mouth fell open and, in spite of her determination, uncontrollable words tumbled out, "It's large and it's gold."

"I know that!" screamed Zepallo. "We know it's under the observatory. How well is it defended?"

"I don't know. I left before they began preparing the defenses."

"What did they do the last time?"

Alius tried to resist but her thoughts were being pulled from her mind, "We had plenty of *seers* to hold off your fighters and Professor Ponte constructed a shield around the tower."

"Is the dear Professor still in charge of all of the Keepers?"

"Yes."

"Who is second in command?"

"Nanchez."

"Are there others on the island?" hissed the Dark Lord.

"Of course, there are!" smiled Alius in a fleeting fit of defiance.

"How many?"

"I have no idea."

"Well, this serves no purpose! What about Adrian?"

"What about Adrian?"

"Where is he?"

"The last report I heard was that he was on his way to the Island of the Children to fend off your invasion."

"That was hours ago. Where is he now?" Zepallo moved close to Alius' face and peered into her soul.

A sharp pain plunged through her eyes and detonated at the back of her skull. She tried to think of anything but Adrian but it was almost as if Zepallo pulled the words past her lips, "He's probably on his way here."

The Dark Master smiled at Beta, "That's why I'm so proud of you! Miss Alius is probably one of the most powerful woman *seers* in the world but, as you see, even the strongest will can be overwhelmed by the things that you have learned. Domination doesn't always have to result from the use of brute force. There are more subtle ways to achieve our goals."

Beta blushed and bowed his head, "We are not well defended here."

"Oh, but I think this intimate little party will be much more enjoyable if its just the four of us." He lifted the index finger of his right hand and guided Alius back to her place, suspended near the ceiling, "Let's leave you there for the moment for safe keeping."

Chapter Fifteen

Adrian moved into the plane of the Tropics and slowed his speed, for he had no idea of where they might have taken Alius. He needed time to concentrate. He closed his eyes and opened his senses to the vibrations. The planes were filled with the clash of powers, the screams of the dying, and the grating of the dark energies.

He could see purple and golden surges plowing back and forth across the planet, clashing waves of fighters, and the terrified expression on his mother's face, as he slipped into the vectors. Suddenly, his mouth was filled with the taste of chocolate and the air grew cold. Far in the distance, he sensed Alius' voice…it was a whisper, a call, repeated again and again, *"Adrian, it's a trap."* The sound was coming from the east.

The memory of her walking away from him, without so much as a real good-bye, tore at his heart. They had disagreed over the past few years but, since their battle on the mountain, they were closer than brother and sister and always joined their strengths in confrontations with Zepallo and his warriors. It could not end this way. She had to believe that he loved her, exactly as he always had…from their first real conversation on the lawn outside the observatory.

He felt guilty about his relationship with Morgan. She always knew the answers, the right thing to do in any situation. It seemed as if she could see inside his heart and he always felt like a little kid in her presence. She was beautiful and he loved the way she kissed. He wondered how Alius kissed. That was all too confusing, so he concentrated on the sound of her voice and followed it across the cold violent waters of the Atlantic, over the coast of France, and headed for the Alps, the closet mountains in the direction of Alius' call.

Gathering his robes close to his body against fearsome winds and blinding snow, he followed the chant into a blizzard crashing through the mountains. In the distance, he heard the whisper of Orana's voice, "You've learned to listen and you are just beginning to learn to see. Seeing along the vectors is only a small part of the talent but that is why we are called *seers.* In time, you will learn to see beyond the moment, into the future, as well as the past, through the planes and the various levels of reality. That vision is a heavy burden that you must carry with you like a sack of coal across your shoulders and, once you begin the journey, you can never turn back."

"I've come this far, there can be no retreat," thought Adrian as he closed on a magnificent chalet carved into the rocky peak of a tall mountain. He circled around the enclave several times. Alius energy was strong and he noticed a few guards, hunkered down against the cold in guard towers around the edge of the cliff. At the center stood a large, graceful lodge with light glowing in the windows and smoke streaming horizontally from the chimney. Faint traces of heat glowed through the walls and he realized that he could see three human shapes. Alius was hanging near the ceiling and her glow was very warm. The other two, clumps of frigid glacial blue, were standing near a fireplace at the center of a round room. Their auras were deep magenta and the Dark Lord's power radiating from inside the building sent a shock wave up the young *seer's* spine, detonating at the base of his skull.

Slipping out of the aqua plane, he materialized just beneath the peak of the roof to find Zepallo and Beta staring up at him, "Ah, you've finally arrived. We've been waiting for you!"

The Dark Lord pointed towards the ceiling with the index finger of his right hand and a bolt shot through the air, striking Alius in the stomach. Her body folded over and she screamed in agony.

Adrian shuddered at the sound of his enemy's evil cackle and started to move to her defense, when a second pulse struck him in the thigh, spinning him wildly around the circular chimney. He tucked into a ball, accelerating his speed and descending towards Zepallo.

Beta swept into the air, his sword drawn and waited for Adrian to come around the chimney but the young *seer* reversed course flying past the young master, raking his shoulders with the tip of his blade.

Zepallo folded his arms and watched the confrontation, as his clone plunged to the floor, picked himself up, and flew back to the fight. The youngsters tumbled and rolled through the room, swords clashing, raining showers of sparks across the ancient stones. Beta drove Adrian up the arch of the ceiling and fired a blast from a few feet away but the young *seer* slipped into the vectors, returned behind his rival, and caught him with a mighty blow as he turned.

The clone was dead before his body hit the floor and Zepallo's tortured wail rattled the glass and shook the timbers of the building to the foundation. Adrian glanced at Alius, suspended helplessly, with fear in her eyes.

The Dark Lord rose up on the opposite side of the chimney in a rage. A deep purple aura pulsed and swirled around his body. He extended his right hand and fired repeated charges at Adrian, as they circled the stone column. "Come out where I can see you. Don't you think it's about time that we had this out, once and for all?"

Adrian moved between Zepallo and Alius and hovered beneath the curved ceiling. The Dark *seer* raised his index finger and pointed it at Adrian's heart but hesitated for a moment and touched his hand to his ear. He stared incredulously at the young *seer*, "What have you done?"

Adrian smiled and lunged at his enemy, his sword firing blast after blast, as he closed on his target. Zepallo extended his sword to meet the attack but the young *seer* swooped to his right and caught his elder with a blow to his bicep. Zepallo swung around in astonished agony, his sword extended, catching Adrian's right leg, as he zipped past. A second run brought an explosion of sparks as they thrust and parried, each protecting their wounds and vying for a moment of opportunity.

Alius felt as if she were suspended in a glass bubble, unable to move or speak, an observer watching the two most powerful *seers* on the planet charging each other, rolling and tumbling around the room, in a struggle that would end in death. Zepallo pulled away and fired a blast from his right hand that caught Adrian across the chest. His body flew against the curve of a beam, slithered down the stone wall, and crumpled face down on the floor.

She started chanting inside her mind, "Adrian, just know I love you!" over and over, as the Dark Lord slowly descended to stand over him, clutching his arm, blood dripping down his hand.

Zepallo looked up at Alius, "I'm receiving reports that five of our command centers are flooding. I seem to remember something similar happening in the Caucuses not too long ago. It's time to put an end to this once and for all!" He leaned over, extended his index finger to the middle of Adrian's back, and whispered, "He still doesn't know…"

The young *seer* was dazed and just barely conscious but Orana's voice screamed inside his head, "This isn't about you! It's about the survival of The Balance and The Powers!" The room filled with the sound of thousands of hummingbird wings fluttering in unison and he felt her strength surge through his body. "Stop playing possum and finish this!"

Adrian flipped over, catching Zepallo's legs and knocking him to the floor just as his right hand touched the fabric of the young *seer's robes.* The blast zipped past his face, as he extended his sword and caught the dark *seer* beneath the chin. His face contorted, as a horrifying squeal gurgled from his throat. His eyes raged with a strange combination of emotions…surprise, anger, determination…but not desperation, not fear…then, in a final moment, he stared at the bloodied young *seer* with an air of contempt, a knowledge of something more than death. It was as if he was saying, "We're not finished with this business…"

The dark energies surging through his body erupted through blazing eyes and fragmented into a thousand blue-gray sparks swirling around the circumference of the round room, ascending with each successive pass until they exploded through the timbered ceiling.

Purple flames burst from the Dark Lord's robes, hissing and cracking as they rose to meet snowflakes falling through what remained of the roof. Within moments, his corpse was consumed and disappeared in a rank iridescent inferno.

Freed from the bonds of her trance, Alius drifted down through a tangled collapse of splintered beams and crumpled stones, attempting to catch Adrian as he screamed and crumpled to the floor, blood gushing from his forehead, the gash in his chest, and jagged tears in his thighs.

Chapter Sixteen

Morgan and Alius sat with their arms intertwined, sobbing quietly in a warm patch of morning sun streaming through the window in Adrian's bedroom. Alius was still exhausted, after summoning the last of her depleted powers to drag Adrian's limp body back through the vectors. Almost two weeks had passed and he had not stirred. Dr. Stevens visited every few hours, tending to his wounds with his healing waters and antibiotics, monitoring his vital signs for any fluctuation. Dr. Stevens could not predict whether he would wake from the coma or when, but there was little that anyone could do except wait.

The Doctor was exhausted with tending the wounded, who arrived aboard Grace from the battle in Africa. Hope arrived a day later and packed the domes with hundreds of fighters who needed medical attention. Sara and Elsie organized the residents of the island to mind the injured, so that no patient was ever left without a guardian, who sat by their bedsides ready to provide whatever might be needed.

George and John led a legion of workmen preparing graves in the old graveyard beyond the Old School on the ridge. Those *seers* and Keepers who survived the war were arriving in expectation of a massive funeral to be held the following morning. Destiny was still moored above the small lagoon on the Island of the Children, where similar ceremonies were planned.

Sir Isaac, Sammy, and Masters Jung and Chi were heralded as heroes for constructing the portals that flooded five command centers barely minutes before the minisubs were to reach Morgan's Knot. Ponte and Nanchez noted that the power surging through the dark vectors dissipated in less than an hour. The Dark Forces retreated from the battles and vanished into the vectors, leaving a wake of destruction as the only evidence of their conquests. All systems in the positive vectors returned to running in normal mode.

Desperate rumors buzzed through the Forces of Light, until Master Chi created a clearinghouse for information on the status of the world and those who had died, gone missing, or been injured. It also became a hub where people could volunteer to help on Morgan's Knot or go out to those places that suffered during the battles to begin reconstruction. Keepers rushed to the most vital points in the power grid in the southern hemisphere the day after the war ended and most of the systems had been patched or repaired and integrated into the circuits within the first week.

Morgan turned to Alius, "I'm sorry that my caring for Adrian caused you so much pain."

Alius rested her head on the taller girl's shoulder, "We both love him and, to tell you the truth, we're all too young to understand these feelings yet."

"Does this mean that we're at that 'awkward' age?"

Alius giggled, staring at a battered Adrian, swaddled in bandages across his chest, around his shoulder, both legs, and his head, where he crumpled to the stone floor during the battle in the villa. Her fear subsided but the feeling of helplessness, of being controlled by Beta and Zepallo still haunted her. She squeezed Morgan's hand.

Gabrielle and Dadeus were communicating through the observatory until the systems in the domes were restored to their original configurations. The latest missive reported that Raffe survived but was still confined to bed. The losses on the Island of the Children had been substantial and they were still finding bodies in the jungle. The dome beneath the Pacific was as crammed with wounded as the new domes off the coast of Morgan's Knot. It would be many years before the Forces of Light could recover.

Marcus escaped into the vectors, when inexperienced *seers* were sent to retrieve him from the vault at the top of the pyramid. No one knew what happened to Gamma, no body was found in South America, nor did they find any trace of Simian, who seemed to have disappeared completely.

The two girls stood and leaned over the bed as Adrian suddenly began to cough and sputter. His fingers twitched and his legs stirred and Sara and Elsie rushed to the bedside.

The young *seer's* lips moved. He was trying to say something. Alius put her ear close to his mouth and heard him whisper, "Chocolate."

The Cast of Characters

Adrian – son of John and Sara – long and lanky, blond hair and intense blue eyes

John – Adrian's father – a large man with dark hair and dark eyes, sailor and ship designer

Sara – Adrian's mother – blond, blue eyes, housewife, grew up on Morgan's Knot, daughter of the former *seer,* Paul

George – Adrian's uncle – tall, strong, rough hands, salt and pepper hair

Elsie – Adrian's aunt and Sara's sister – small, round, impish, mother to everyone

Molly and Megan – George & Elsie's twin daughters – curly blond hair blue eyes, a year younger than Adrian

Morgan Keelty – sister of Josh – tall, long curly brown hair, green eyes

Joshua Keelty – Morgan's brother – dark eyes, jet-black hair

Ian Sheridan – Kelly's brother and Adrian's second cousin – tall, slender

Kelly Sheridan – Ian's younger sister – incredible smile, brown eyes, blond curls

Spot and Dusty – dolphins

Professor Ponte – Keeper of the Powers on Morgan's Knot, astronomer, teacher, and Adrian's teacher

Ester – Ponte's wife - highly intelligent and Ponte's equal, slender, big glasses, thin lips, small teeth

Tic – talking black and white tomcat, Adrian's guide in the animal world

Brandy – Keelty's Irish setter and Adrian's companion and protector

Travis – harbormaster and captain of the Hope

Jasmine – Travis' fishing trawler

Dr. Stevens – doctor on the island

Dr. Carringsworth - Headmaster of the upper school

Mrs. Hammon - political science teacher

Daphne & Dante – deer

Damien – their foal

Beggar – small bear

Ashton and Ashford – Beggar's cubs

Magnus – golden eagle

Harriet & Harry – hawks

The Book of Wisdoms – The Golden Book on Morgan's Knot

The Book of Knowledge – The Silver Book used by the *Others* to master the Dark Powers

Jamaica

Simian – wise old Jamaican *seer*, Sammy's uncle

Sammy – Simian's nephew – young Keeper in training

Lorraine – Simian's wife

The *Others*

Alius – daughter of Jofre – the *Other's seer* - petite, blond, blue eyes, tough, independent, and beautiful

Jofre – father of Alius and Master of the *Others* – a huge domineering man with white eyes

Mandor – Supervisor of Production and Security – dark eyes, long straight white hair

Nanchez – Keeper of the Dark Powers – a grumpy giant of a man with white hair, dark eyes

The Island of the Children

Raffe – young, athletic, and naïve *seer*

Gabrielle – leader of the Underworld – Mary's husband, long white hair and beard

Mary – Gabrielle's wife, *seer*

Dadeus – Keeper of the Powers for the underworld

Book of Natural Balance – The Golden Book on the Island of the Children

Soule and Amy – diving instructors

Additional Characters

Sky – tiny Thai *seer* – from the Temple of Spiritual Harmony, Thailand

Master Chi – M*aster seer* - Temple of Ancient Truths – Himalayas

Master Jung – slender old Keeper – Temple of Ancient Truths

Mantis – Sky's mentor

Sir Isaacs – English Keeper

Shambala – African *seer*

Mambazi – little girl in Shambala's village

Danali – Keeper in Shambala's village on Lake Victoria

Lala & Maze – *seers* from the southern tip of South America

President Bartlett – former President of the United States and Chancellor of the School of *Seers* and Keepers

Natalie – Bartlett's secretary

Lord Robbins – Canadian ambassador to the United Nations and a Whisperer for Legio Obscurum

Sir Jonathon – John's Scottish father and Adrian's grandfather – submariner and spymaster

Colburn Tierney – Sir Jonathon's attorney

Martina Tierney – Coke's wife

Captain Maniford Ruhl – captain of the Destiny

Cappy – school bus driver and captain of Grace

The Plane of the Animals

Orana – the oldest *seer* on the planet and Adrian's mentor

Unis – female unicorn

Gerald – the lion

Legio Obscurum

Zepallo – The Dark Lord – Unchallenged sovereign over the Council of Ollapez

Cadeau - Senior Security Technician – Korean complex

Regis – Senior Regent for Command and Control – Korean complex

The Doctor - a brilliant and determined renegade scientist with a shock of white hair over a pallid complexion, dark deep-set eyes, German accent

Alpha, Beta, and Gamma – Zepallo's clones

Whisperers – surrogate moles buried in positions of power in the seats of governments, the pinnacles of military commands, corporations and industries, and every major religion.

Alexandria

Lyra – young student seer

Raman – Lyra's father and wealthy trader

Thesius – philosopher and keeper of the secrets

Shiera – seer and Lyra's guide in her lessons

Ganimum and Agus – scholars at the Library of Alexandria

Preview

An Island in the Darkness

Morgan's Knot – A Serial Fantasy
Episode IX

By

Eric T. Stiller, Jr.

Adrian's wounds, suffered during the battle at the chalet in the Alps, mended over the past months, although he never wore regular clothes and favored his right leg. His blue robes concealed testaments to the pain he endured, except for the gash on his forehead and a ragged scar behind his ear, hidden beneath waves of long blond hair, but nothing could heal the searing gloom raging through his raw and tender core. A sadness in his blue eyes betrayed the torment, for the boy bore the wounds of an old man, aged by years of war and struggle, and life denied him time to render the terrors into wisdoms and the nightmares into prayers.

The young *seer* stood before the Chancellor's desk, in his office in the third dome of the complex beneath the cold waters of the North Atlantic. The former President was a friend and a guide who shared an absolute dedication to the war against the Dark Forces and the establishment of this center for learning but, in this moment, their current roles were determined by circumstance. Adrian was a student and Chancellor Bartlett was the Headmaster of the International School of Seers and Keepers as well as the traditional school for the children of the island, which was split between the upper school in the first dome and the lower in the strange old buildings on the ridge.

An overstuffed manila file lay open on the desk, although the sheer volume of information was rather pointless because Bartlett knew everything there was to know about the young *seer*. He was fascinated by the boy in the blue robes from the moment Adrian and Alius materialized on the lawn outside the Oval Office and spoke with eloquence and intelligence regarding the threats that Sir Jonathon warned him about several years previously. There was a certain delightful irony in the fact that the old spymaster found the core of the Forces of Light in his own grandson.

Bartlett had witnessed his bravery, was awed by his commitment, and agreed with the Elders that this young man was 'the one' who possessed the capacity to lead them to a final triumph over the Dark Forces, which, incidentally, seemed in complete disarray after the battles in South America and Africa, the deaths of Beta and Zepallo, the disappearance of Gamma and Marcus, and the flooding of five command centers.

There was general agreement that the Forces of Light succeeded in battle but the war would continue in some new form with a new and less predictable leader. The Keepers left no doubt that other command centers were fully functional and it was simply a matter of when, not if, the Dark Forces would rebuild to strike again.

The problem at hand was that young Adrian was not so young anymore. Upon graduation, every student of the regular school on the island was expected to attend a university on the mainland, where they would earn at least a Bachelor's degree in a subject that might benefit the rest of the population of the island. Some went on to become doctors or engineers, communication specialists or masters of agricultural sciences. A few became writers, artists, or musicians and there were those who chose to remain in the real world for one reason or another. Adrian's mother, Sara, stayed to allow John to fulfill his ambitions in the Navy and as a ship designer. Those skills were being put to good use on Morgan's Knot.

As a student and teacher in both schools, a leader within the Forces of Light, and a young man who was coming of age, Adrian had choices to make about his future.

"As you know, every student of the regular school has gone on to college," smiled Chancellor Bartlett. "You, on the other hand, attend both schools as a student and teach other *seers* and children in your own courses. The point is that you will have to make some decisions about what you wish to do to continue your education."

Adrian stared at the floor. He could not imagine leaving the island, abandoning his duty, to attend normal classes at some university on the mainland. How would he ever keep his life as a *seer* a secret from other students? Somehow, he could not see himself going out for sports or joining a fraternity.

"I'm not really sure what I want to do. I feel a responsibility to the island, to everyone who depends on me."

"I understand but, if you are truly to become the leader that everyone hopes, then you must continue to grow, to learn everything you can about the world around us, about how and why people interact with each other as allies or in conflict, and to gain the skills to bring disparate groups together." He paused, "You have demonstrated incredible insight, unquestioned bravery, and the ability to lead and motivate our forces by your example but you are not complete. These abilities only hint at your potential. If you are to carry Orana's mantle, then you must have the tools and the knowledge to make wise and educated decisions that will affect all mankind. I think you already know that."

Adrian nodded, "I've known since I first learned about the responsibility that accompanies the title of *seer*. Tic the cat warned me a long time ago. That's when I started worrying about whether I was worthy, I guess I still do."

"I know exactly how you feel," said the former President, as he stood and walked around the desk to put an arm around Adrian's shoulders. "No one understands the weight a leader carries with him through every minute of every day. There's no one else to turn to when you face your worst fears or your most formidable enemies. You must stand alone and you have no choice but to believe in yourself and your decisions."

The young *seer* looked into the Chancellor's knowing eyes, "Then you understand why I feel that I'd be abandoning everything that I 've worked for over the past five years."

"View this opportunity as a leave of absence. You're available if you're needed and you'll return to your post when you have completed your course of instruction. At this point, it's time for you to start considering your options. You have plenty of time to make a decision, you don't graduate until next year. Ponte has supplied us with a list of universities on both sides of the Atlantic that have made special arrangements for our students over the years. I suggest you learn as much as you can about those that might offer areas that interest you. Almost everyone on the island attended these schools. Talk with them about their experiences. I, obviously, would be happy to tell you about my time at Harvard."

Adrian took the folder and walked to the door. Turning, he said, "Thank you for your time."

Bartlett started laughing and crossed his arms over his chest, as he leaned against the desk, "Son, this is an opportunity that most young people look forward to…a chance to be on your own, without parents or family. Some do well, others fall prey to temptations. I believe that you will succeed and that you'll enjoy the experience. This education is about learning to think."

The young *seer* tried to smile, "I'll consider the list."

"Is there something else?"

Adrian hesitated, "I have to report to our friends in the plane of the animals and I'm afraid that we haven't accomplished enough."

"The Crystal Foundation has made great strides in leading the change in industry. President Shannon, at my suggestion, has created a Department of Nature, which is staffed by representatives from the animal kingdom, and every other agency within the United States government is working in coordination with their perspectives. The same is true of the United Nations."

"Production of greenhouse gases in the United States has dropped by nearly twenty percent in less than a year and almost every other country on the planet is joining the Earth First campaign that Mrs.

Tierney started after the war. We've made progress and, although we're just beginning, that should be enough to show our good faith."

"I won't know until I get there," said Adrian quietly. "After all that they've done for us, I would hate to disappoint them."

The President smiled, "The Industrial Revolution has been rolling along for more than two hundred years, gobbling up natural resources and spewing out pollution. It takes time to change old habits and even longer to quell the expectations of consumers who demand the products and the conveniences of modern life."

"I don't want to make excuses. I guess I wish that people would understand, that they would take responsibility for themselves."

"Your speech to the United Nations started the process and the media campaign has reinforced your message. It might take a generation before we see dramatic changes in our world but I'll guarantee you one thing…we will never go back."

A small smile lifted the corners of the young *seer's* lips, "I appreciate your confidence and your advice."

The Chancellor pressed his index finger to his lips, "You're at a uniquely difficult age. Most young men are concerned about athletics or their next date. You have to suffer through these changes with the weight of the world on your shoulders…literally. Just don't forget that you're allowed to have fun."

"It would be nice if they gave you an instruction manual."

The former President laughed, "I've had that same thought about a lot of things that happen in life. Certainly, there are references for just about everything that either of us might be curious about but, you're right, no one hands you a little booklet with all the answers at precisely the right moment. Perhaps after we figure out how to save the world, we should go into publishing."

Adrian's sullen mood lifted a little as he closed the door behind him.

~

He was proud of his part in the defeat of the Dark Forces but the months of recovery provided the opportunity to spend hours alone…thinking. Fear was not the issue, although he was constantly reminded of the scars that he had seen on his three-hundred-year-old self which were appearing on his own body at a much more rapid pace than he imagined at the time of their first meeting in the white plane. That person was vibrant, fearless, and confident of the future. He wondered how he might transform himself from a wounded child into that wise and powerful warrior, what battles lay between here and there, and what wisdom might he glean from his travels along that path to calm his doubts and fears.

Adrian felt confident about his abilities as a *seer* but there were moments in combat when everything disappeared from his mind, when he had no idea about the next step. In his early battles with Zepallo, he could see into his rival's very core and the young *seer* knew that he would not be defeated. That confidence was gone, replaced by a terror of making a mistake that might affect the population of the entire planet.

In the world of Morgan's Knot, he was not so sure about who he was as a person. His celebrity still annoyed him and the deference shown by the citizens of the island and the *seers* and Keepers who passed through the school made him feel that he was a freak object to be studied and observed or, worse, revered. Although his friends made every effort to visit during those months, the more time he spent alone, the more he craved the isolation.

Morgan and Alius were diligent caretakers, sometimes alone but often together and, in his delirium, he could not fathom their relationship. It seemed that they had made some sort of pact to share him during his convalescence rather than compete for his affections. He found it all confusing but, in a way, their bond relieved him of having to choose between them. Each occupied a vital and vibrant place in his heart and he could not imagine life without either, yet, in his depression, he could not express his true feelings to anyone.

Orana had appeared only once, since the war, as the first hummingbird, a harbinger of summer. She flitted through the open window and landed on the post at the foot of his bed, chirping merrily. Her aura spread like a glistening halo that filled the room with golden kindness. "I'm glad to see that you are recovering. I was worried there for a minute."

"I wasn't sure that I could survive, let alone defeat him."

"I know. I'm sorry you were injured but I already knew that you would win. If you'll remember your lessons, then I have to believe that you knew in your heart that this was not your last battle."

Adrian was quiet for a moment, "There are times when I seem to forget everything…"

"The point is that you summoned that inner strength and saw your path clearly."

"I would be dead if you had not screamed at me…"

"I was not there…you were alone."

The young *seer* stared at the tiny bird for a long moment before he whispered, "I'm not sure that I'm worthy of the position you left for me."

"I did not make a mistake. I believe that and so must you. Someday you'll master the art of seeing into the future, then you'll finally understand your destiny. I can't give you a forecast or see into some crystal ball to tell you everything that will happen but I know that you'll find your way, that you will lead our people, and, for brief periods, you'll bring peace to the world. I also know that, someday, you'll be ready to accept yourself for who you really are."

"There's a pain that still tears at the inside of my body."

"In the death of your enemy, a little piece of you dies too. In your case, you were far more than just rivals. You knew that from the beginning."

"We could see into each other's thoughts, into each other's soul…"

"And not only did you find terrible visions there, you found something more."

"There was a connection…"

"A bond…?"

"Yes," whispered Adrian.

"There will come a time when all of this will make sense but this is not the moment."

The young *seer* pondered the thought in frustration. "We won the battles. We did not win the war."

"No…you are correct. They will rise again and you'll be called on to meet them in combat. That fight will take many forms. Be wise enough to see the weakest points in yourself and the world of the Light because they will attack only when they believe they can claim a victory."

"Sometimes I feel that I don't have the strength…the will to see it through."

"As I've told you so many times, once you begin this journey you can never go back."

Adrian felt ashamed…small…vulnerable…

"You're only a boy, a boy who's been asked to do things far beyond your age or your maturity. You've shown cunning, insight, and sheer bullheaded bravery, and you have succeeded. That's all that matters. Treasure your triumphs and build on your strengths, you'll become the person, the *seer*, we both know you can and will be. I believe in you, now it's time for you to believe in yourself."

Adrian stared at her, "I know you're right…"

"I'm always right or didn't I explain that to you?" giggled the beautiful bird, with Orana's merriment. Her eyes twinkled and her aura touched him like a warm caress.

The young *seer* laughed, pressing his hand against the wound on his chest to ease the pain.

"You have time to heal, to renew your balance, and to see the path ahead. Use it wisely."

With that, the hummingbird was consuming by golden glow that exploded in a shower of sparks and she was gone.

He wanted to ask about Simian, who disappeared during the battle in South America without a trace. If only Ponte had allowed him to join the crew of The Hope, Simian might still be alive. Adrian could not attend the ceremony at the cemetery on the ridge but, months later, he had gone to sit by a memorial stone that was placed on an outcropping of rock that pointed to sunrise in the east. Perhaps someday the old Jamaican would return but, in the meantime, the young *seer* could feel him at a great distance and he felt in his heart that his mentor had moved into the plane of energies, the same space that Orana occupied. He hoped they were together.

Shambala's attack on the airfield in Africa changed the course of the battle, while Lala and Maze destroyed the command center in Buenos Aires with the help of thousands of warriors, citizens, and animals. The last of the Dark Forces on the Island of the Children vanished into the vectors shortly after Zepallo died, leaving a transport saucer and two fighters behind.

Casualties on both sides were substantial, the dead and wounded overwhelmed the capacities of the islands. Hope and Grace discharged hundreds of injured fighters who were housed in the domes and tended by the few doctors and medical Keepers and the citizens of Morgan's Knot, who had been spared an invasion.

When he meditated, the sounds of the vibrations were vibrant and warm. The grating of the dark energies faded into the background. Certainly, there were still conflicts in isolated areas around the globe but the invasions allowed the citizens of the world to understand the enormity of the threat. Adrian hoped they would realize that, by contrast, every other excuse for war and killing seemed insignificant in the shadow of the power of the Dark Forces.

He searched through the dark vectors but found no trace of Marcus or Gamma in the planes, although he sensed their energies far removed from the normal channels. One or the other would surely claim Zepallo's throne and each bore terrifying traits…Gamma continuing the Dark Lord's messianic march toward world domination or conniving Marcus who would find more subtle methods to carve up the planet.

The most frightening discovery, in his meditative travels, was Zepallo's shadow. It was different than the powerful spirit he confronted so many times. This was more a feeling, a sense that the Dark Lord was out there watching, waiting patiently in the darkness to pursue his prey like a sleek black cat in the twilight of the jungle.

In this time, Adrian conjured the child cowering beneath the ancient oak in the forest behind their house on the bay, crying because his world was about to change and there was nothing he could do to alter the events that were carrying him along. Little did he know that the feeling of being lost and alone would follow him through these years, a stalker he could not escape.

The adventure continues in

An Island in the Darkness

Morgan's Knot - A Serial Fantasy
Episode IX

The survivors of the war attempt to claim the title of Dark Lord of the throne of Legio Obscurum through a series of spectacular attacks that draw out a wounded and depressed Adrian to face the final clone in a *seer's* duel, with the future of mankind in the balance.

Eric T. Stiller is an author, an award-winning commercial photographer, an educator and advocate, and a Master Gardener.

<u>His novels</u>

<u>The Morgan's Knot Serial Fantasy</u>

Morgan's Knot
Island of the Children
Ice Island
Islands of Concrete and Steel
Islands of the Mind
Islands of the Sky
Islands of Dark Miracles
Islands of Wisdom

(for mature audiences)
Dealer
Nellis Gray
SunnyBreeze
Mac Murphy

Visit: www.rickstiller.com for more of his books, photographs, and music and www.morgansknot.com for the latest on the Morgan's Knot series.

If you enjoyed this story, please give it a five-star review on my Amazon sales page and like my 'Eric T. Stiller - Author page on Facebook.

www.ingramcontent.com/pod-product-compliance
Lightning Source LLC
LaVergne TN
LVHW091053080826
845145LV00002B/730

* 9 7 8 1 7 3 2 6 5 0 5 3 4 *